LIVESTOUR

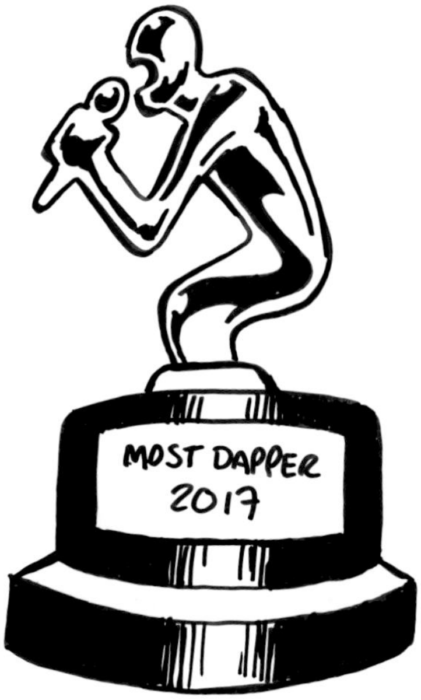
MOST DAPPER
2017

FOR STUART –
MAY ALL OF YOUR CLONES
TREAT YOU WITH THE
RESPECT YOU DESERVE.

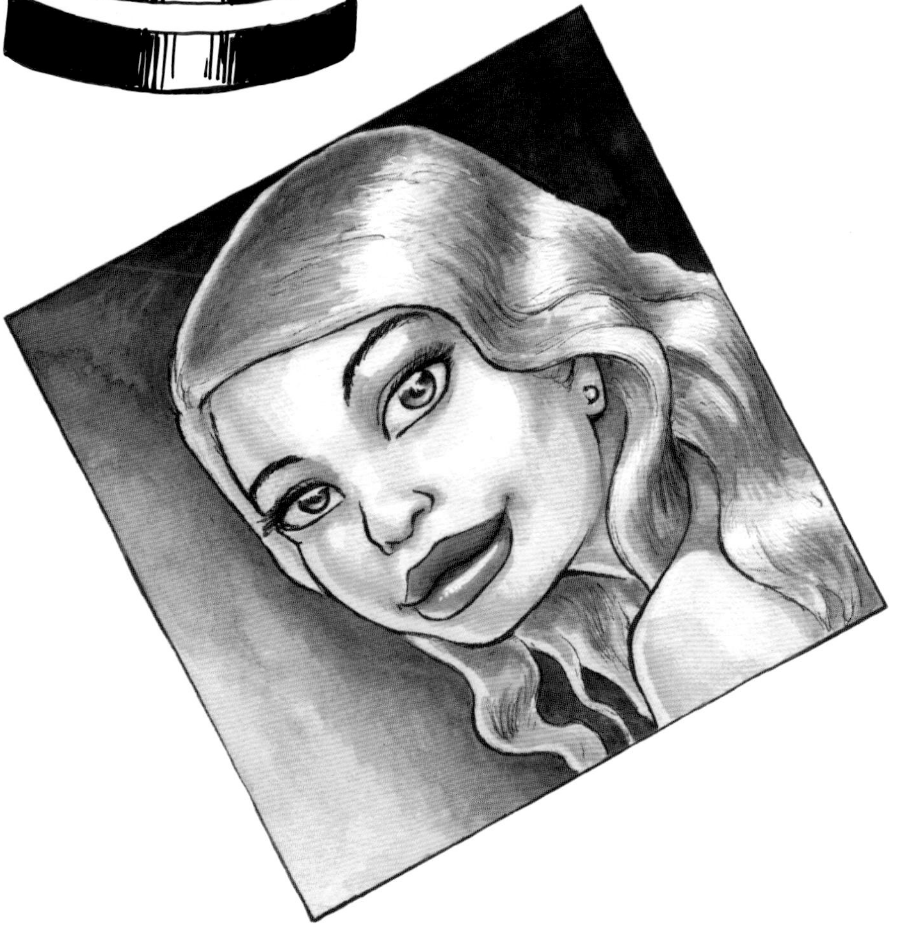

Acknowledgements

Special thanks to Dan Franklin, Corinne Pearlman, Graeme Calvert, Karrie Fransman, Nicola Streeten, Simone Lia, Tom McRae, Matt Foster, Sam Copeland and Neil Bradford for their help, advice and guidance.

Thanks to all my friends and family for their encouragement and for not minding that I barely saw them because I was busy making a big comic book; and thanks to my extended UK comics family for being a constant source of wonder, expletives and delight.

Most of all thanks to Xavier, whose unwavering love and support and tolerance of my absenteeism have carried me through my ridiculous career. I could never have done this without him.

This book is for Xavier,
my Number One Guy

BRITTEN & BRÜLIGHTLY
HANNAH BERRY

ADAMTI
Hannah B

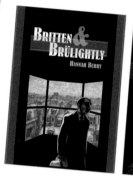

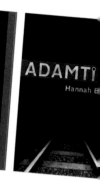

Other graphic novels by Hannah Ber

LOTTERY FUNDED

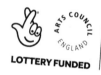

Supported using public funding by
ARTS COUNCIL ENGLAND

1 3 5 7 9 10 8 6 4 2

Jonathan Cape, an imprint of Vinatge Publishing,
20 Vauxhall Bridge Road,
London SW1V 2SA

Jonathan Cape is part of the Penguin Random House group of companies whose addresses can be found at *global.penguinrandomhouse.com*

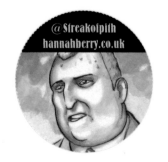

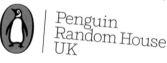

Penguin Random House UK

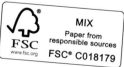

www.vintage-books.co.uk

A CIP catalogue record for this book is available from the British Library.

ISBN 9780224097659

Printed and bound in China by C&C Offset Printing Co., Ltd

TT Moons Thin Demo font by Jovanny Lemonad

FSC www.fsc.org MIX Paper from responsible sources FSC® C018179

@Streakofpith
hannahberry.co.uk

LIVESTOCK

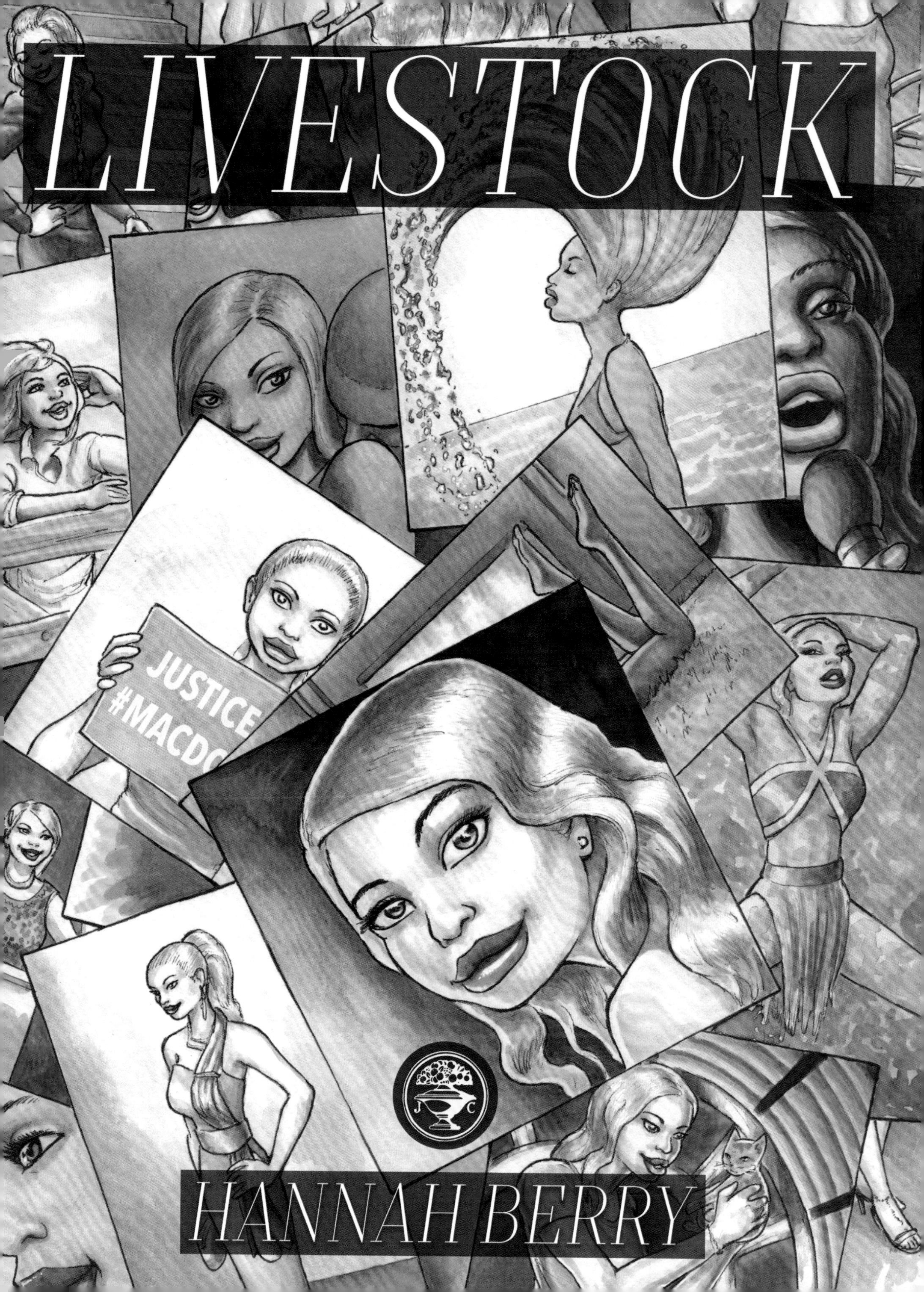
JUSTICE
#MACDO

HANNAH BERRY

WHAT'S TRENDING

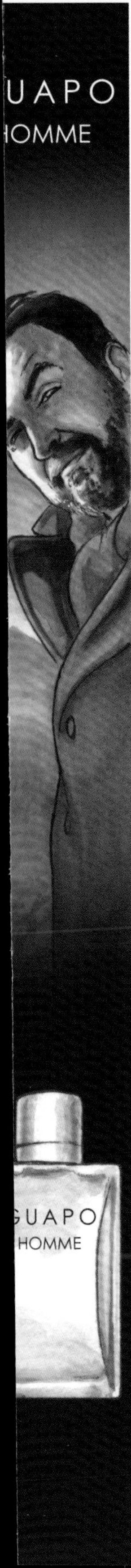

UAPO
HOMME
UAPO
HOMME

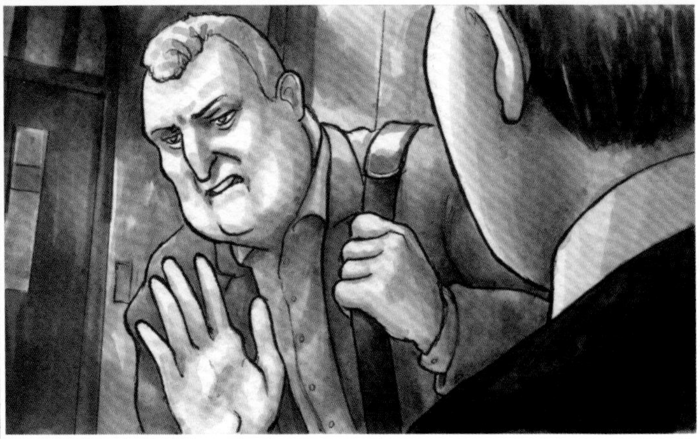

'FRANKENSTEIN' FREARS DUCKS DIFFICULT CLONE QUERIES

Disgraced minister Duncan Frears confronted following revelation that Scientific Jurisdictions Act has allowed secret production of human clones for last 5 years

165 comments

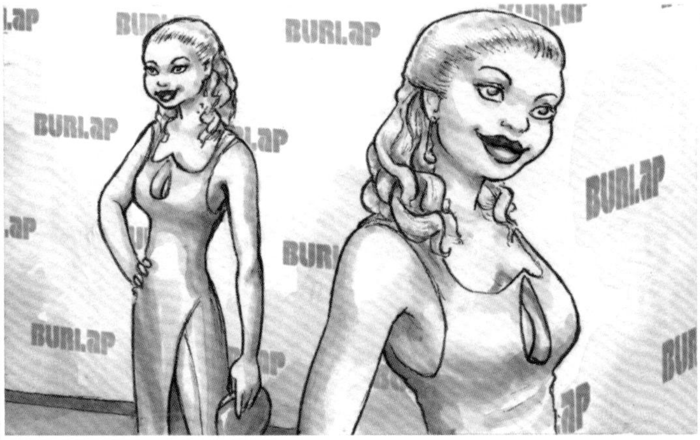

BURLAP
BURLAP
BURLAP
BURLAP

OH CLEMENTINE DARLING!

Young singer wows onlookers with stunning dress and sexy curves at high-end charity fashion extravaganza

98 comments

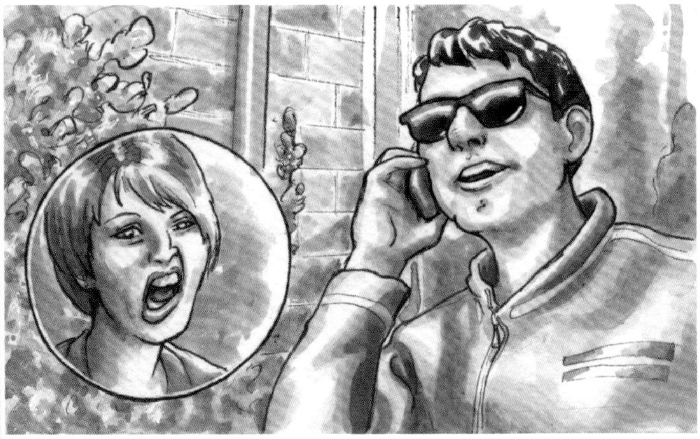

HONEY BOILER

Nightmare ex-girlfriend Honey Hopkins 'won't stop calling and sending messages' begging *Hearts & Minds* actor Nick to come

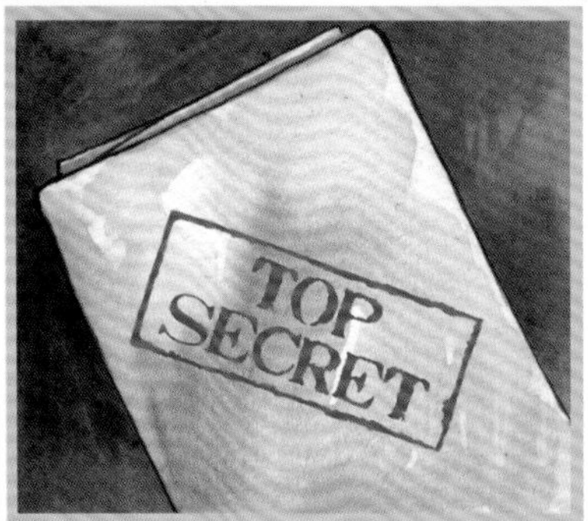

TOP SECRET

EMAIL-GATE DETAILS FINALLY REVEALED: read the secret 'Frankenstein Bill' concerns that only came to light after government aide Rose Burton's tragic traffic accident

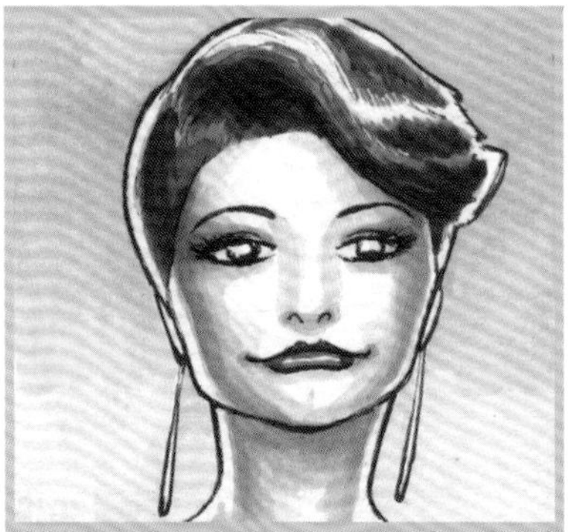

CORAL'S NEW LOOK: singer restyles ahead of book launch

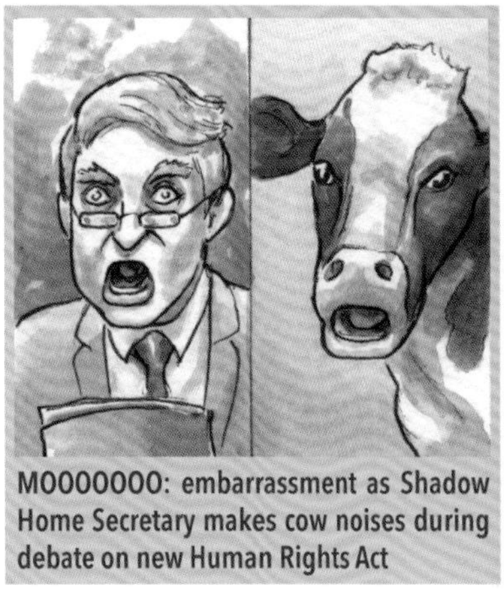

MOOOOOOO: embarrassment as Shadow Home Secretary makes cow noises during debate on new Human Rights Act

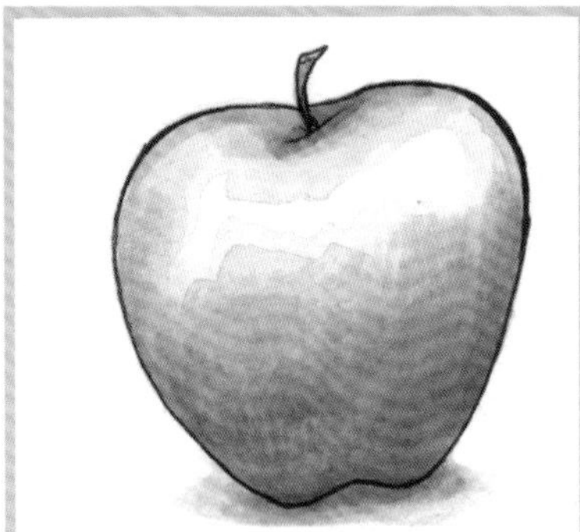

QUIZ: What kind of apple are you?

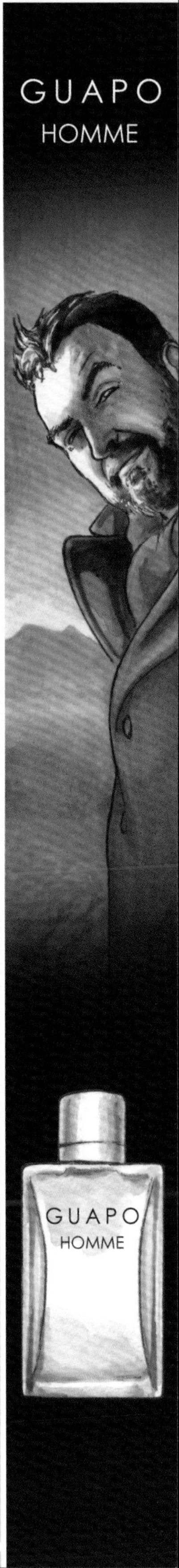

GUAPO
HOMME
GUAPO
HOMME

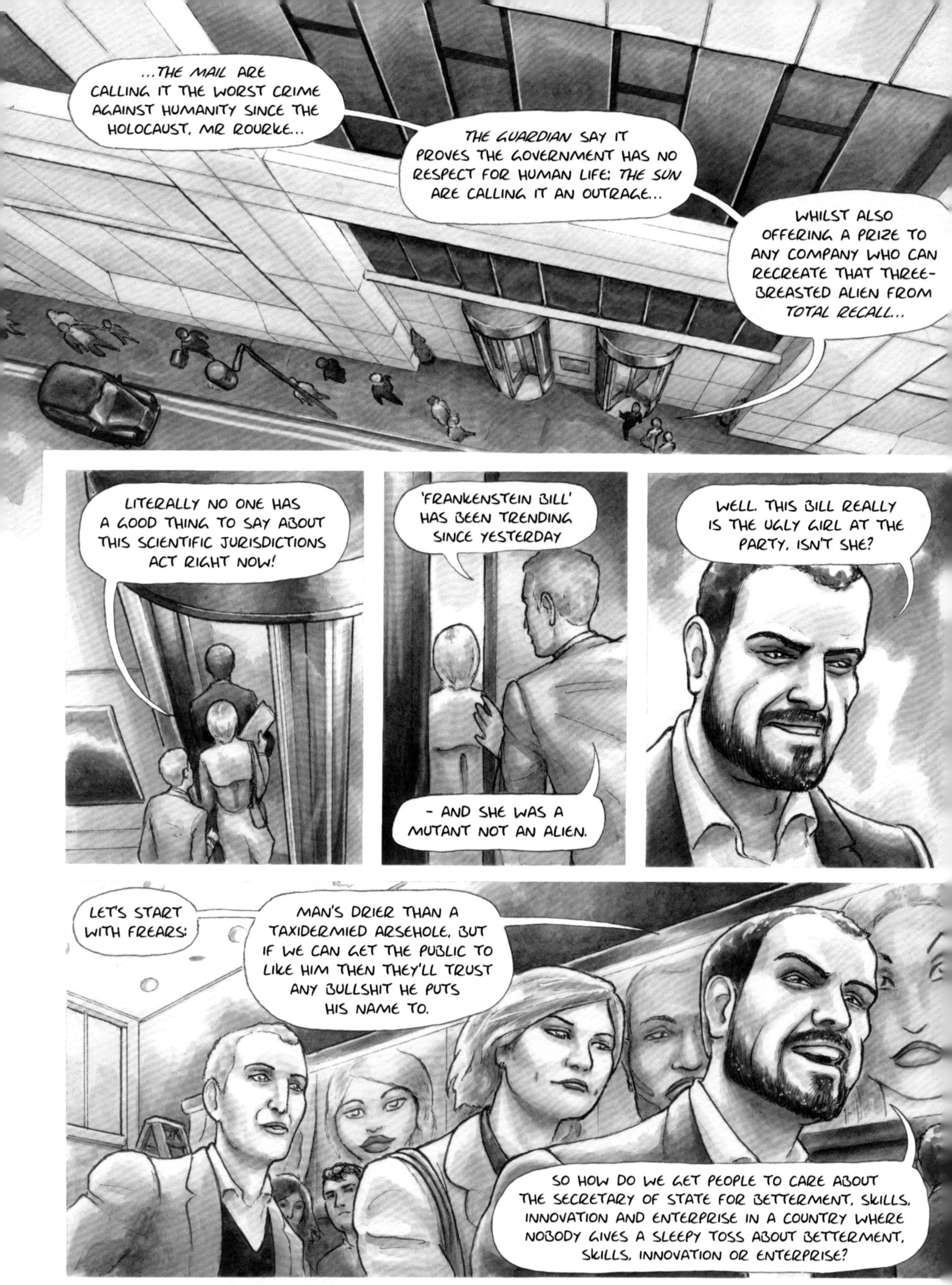
...THE MAIL ARE CALLING IT THE WORST CRIME AGAINST HUMANITY SINCE THE HOLOCAUST, MR ROURKE...
THE GUARDIAN SAY IT PROVES THE GOVERNMENT HAS NO RESPECT FOR HUMAN LIFE; THE SUN ARE CALLING IT AN OUTRAGE...
WHILST ALSO OFFERING A PRIZE TO ANY COMPANY WHO CAN RECREATE THAT THREE-BREASTED ALIEN FROM TOTAL RECALL...
LITERALLY NO ONE HAS A GOOD THING TO SAY ABOUT THIS SCIENTIFIC JURISDICTIONS ACT RIGHT NOW!
'FRANKENSTEIN BILL' HAS BEEN TRENDING SINCE YESTERDAY
- AND SHE WAS A MUTANT NOT AN ALIEN.
WELL. THIS BILL REALLY IS THE UGLY GIRL AT THE PARTY, ISN'T SHE?
LET'S START WITH FREARS:
MAN'S DRIER THAN A TAXIDERMIED ARSEHOLE, BUT IF WE CAN GET THE PUBLIC TO LIKE HIM THEN THEY'LL TRUST ANY BULLSHIT HE PUTS HIS NAME TO.
SO HOW DO WE GET PEOPLE TO CARE ABOUT THE SECRETARY OF STATE FOR BETTERMENT, SKILLS, INNOVATION AND ENTERPRISE IN A COUNTRY WHERE NOBODY GIVES A SLEEPY TOSS ABOUT BETTERMENT, SKILLS, INNOVATION OR ENTERPRISE?

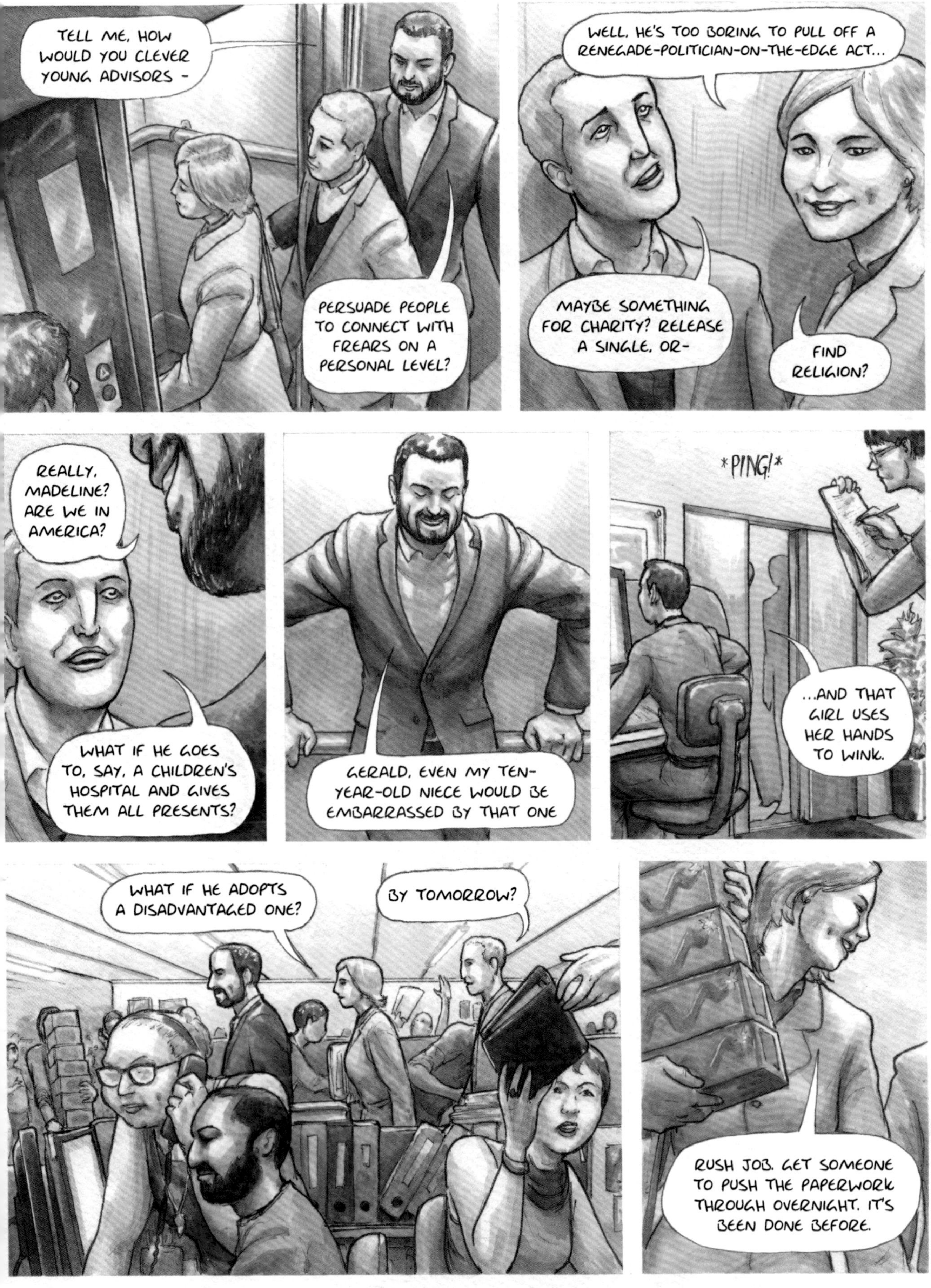
TELL ME, HOW WOULD YOU CLEVER YOUNG ADVISORS -
PERSUADE PEOPLE TO CONNECT WITH FREARS ON A PERSONAL LEVEL?
WELL, HE'S TOO BORING TO PULL OFF A RENEGADE-POLITICIAN-ON-THE-EDGE ACT...
MAYBE SOMETHING FOR CHARITY? RELEASE A SINGLE, OR-
FIND RELIGION?
REALLY, MADELINE? ARE WE IN AMERICA?
WHAT IF HE GOES TO, SAY, A CHILDREN'S HOSPITAL AND GIVES THEM ALL PRESENTS?
GERALD, EVEN MY TEN-YEAR-OLD NIECE WOULD BE EMBARRASSED BY THAT ONE
PING!
...AND THAT GIRL USES HER HANDS TO WINK.
WHAT IF HE ADOPTS A DISADVANTAGED ONE?
BY TOMORROW?
RUSH JOB. GET SOMEONE TO PUSH THE PAPERWORK THROUGH OVERNIGHT. IT'S BEEN DONE BEFORE.

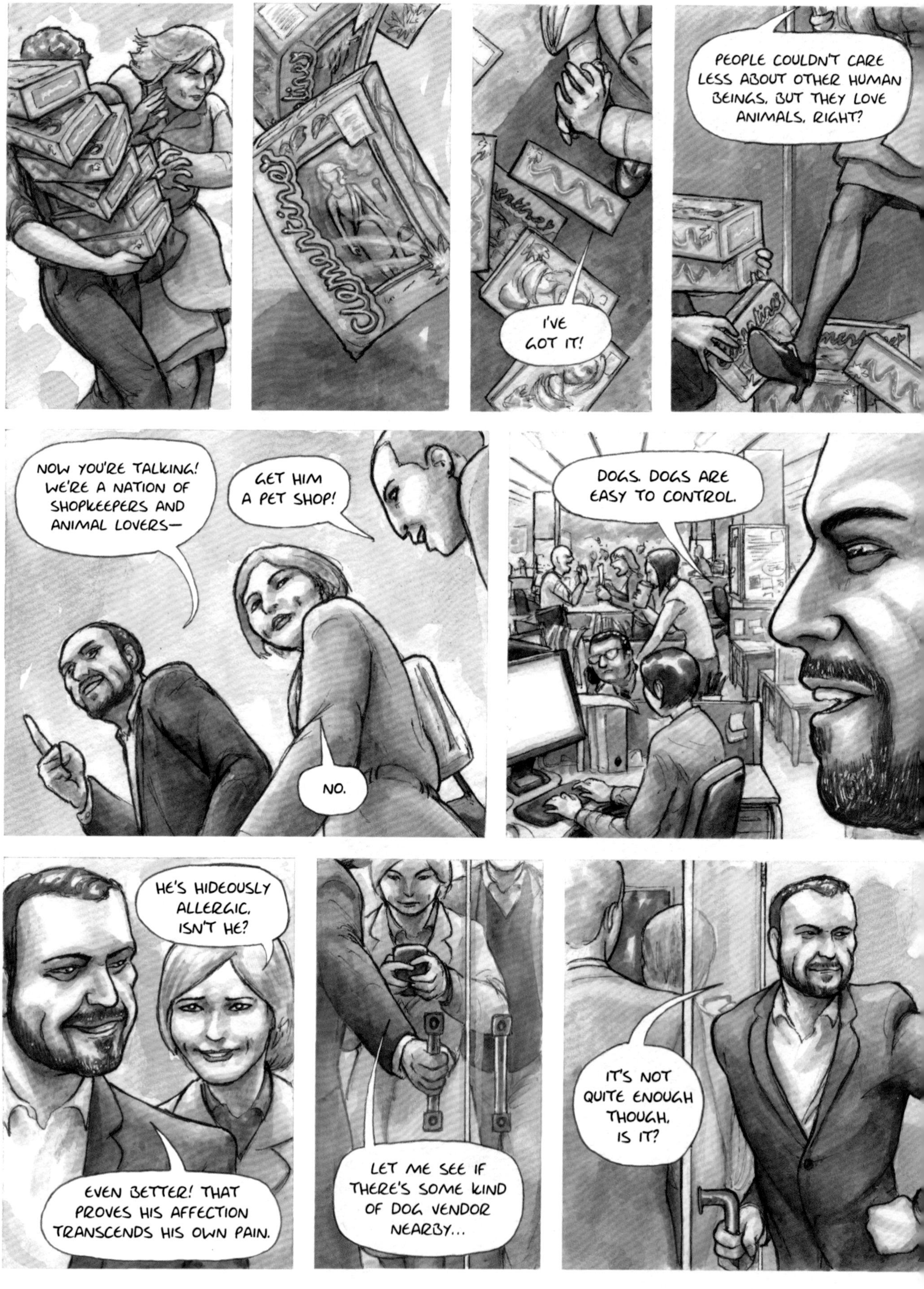
I'VE GOT IT!
PEOPLE COULDN'T CARE LESS ABOUT OTHER HUMAN BEINGS, BUT THEY LOVE ANIMALS, RIGHT?
NOW YOU'RE TALKING! WE'RE A NATION OF SHOPKEEPERS AND ANIMAL LOVERS—
GET HIM A PET SHOP!
NO.
DOGS. DOGS ARE EASY TO CONTROL.
HE'S HIDEOUSLY ALLERGIC, ISN'T HE?
EVEN BETTER! THAT PROVES HIS AFFECTION TRANSCENDS HIS OWN PAIN.
LET ME SEE IF THERE'S SOME KIND OF DOG VENDOR NEARBY...
IT'S NOT QUITE ENOUGH THOUGH, IS IT?

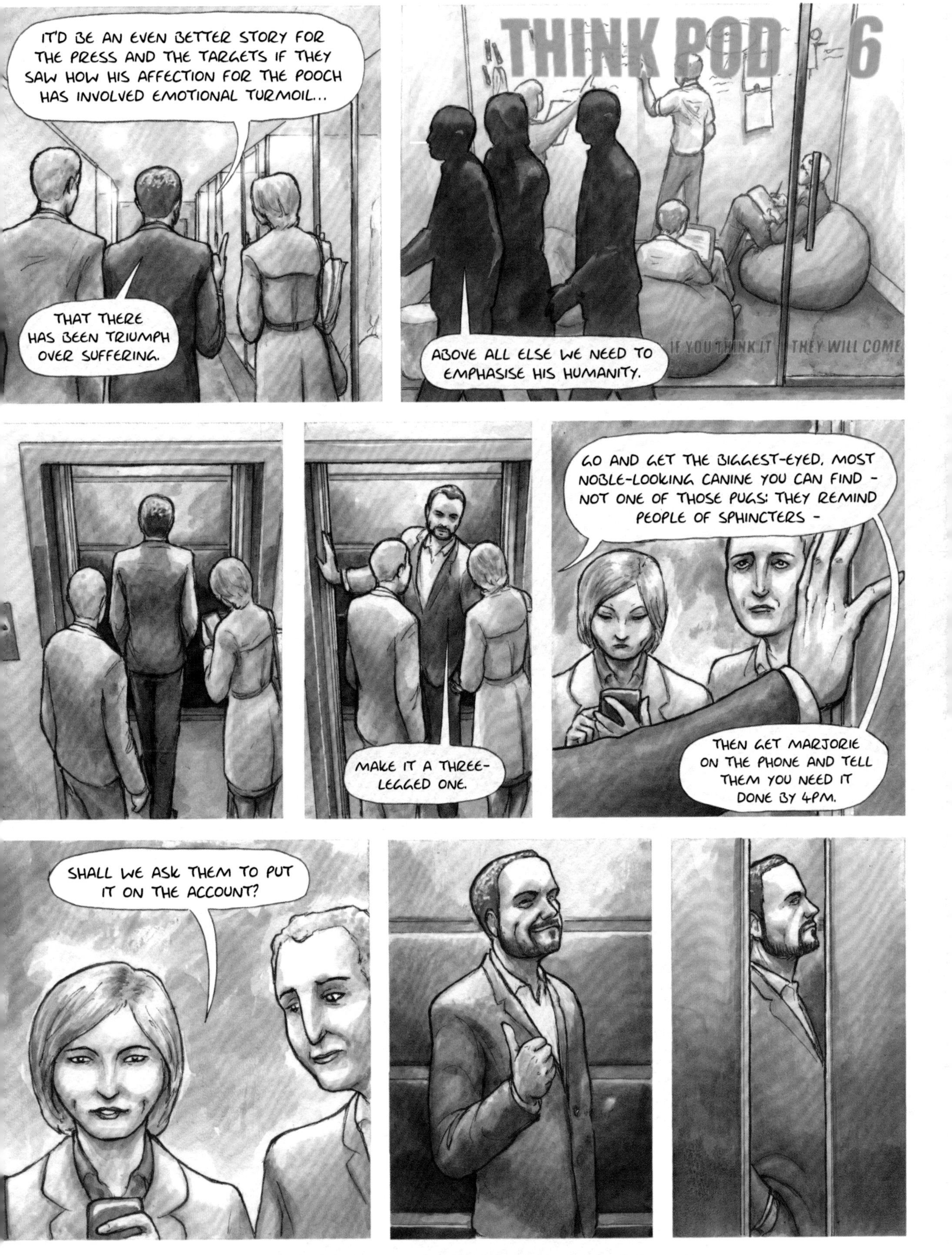
IT'D BE AN EVEN BETTER STORY FOR THE PRESS AND THE TARGETS IF THEY SAW HOW HIS AFFECTION FOR THE POOCH HAS INVOLVED EMOTIONAL TURMOIL...
THAT THERE HAS BEEN TRIUMPH OVER SUFFERING.
THINK POD 6
ABOVE ALL ELSE WE NEED TO EMPHASISE HIS HUMANITY.
IF YOU THINK IT THEY WILL COME
MAKE IT A THREE-LEGGED ONE.
GO AND GET THE BIGGEST-EYED, MOST NOBLE-LOOKING CANINE YOU CAN FIND - NOT ONE OF THOSE PUGS: THEY REMIND PEOPLE OF SPHINCTERS -
THEN GET MARJORIE ON THE PHONE AND TELL THEM YOU NEED IT DONE BY 4PM.
SHALL WE ASK THEM TO PUT IT ON THE ACCOUNT?

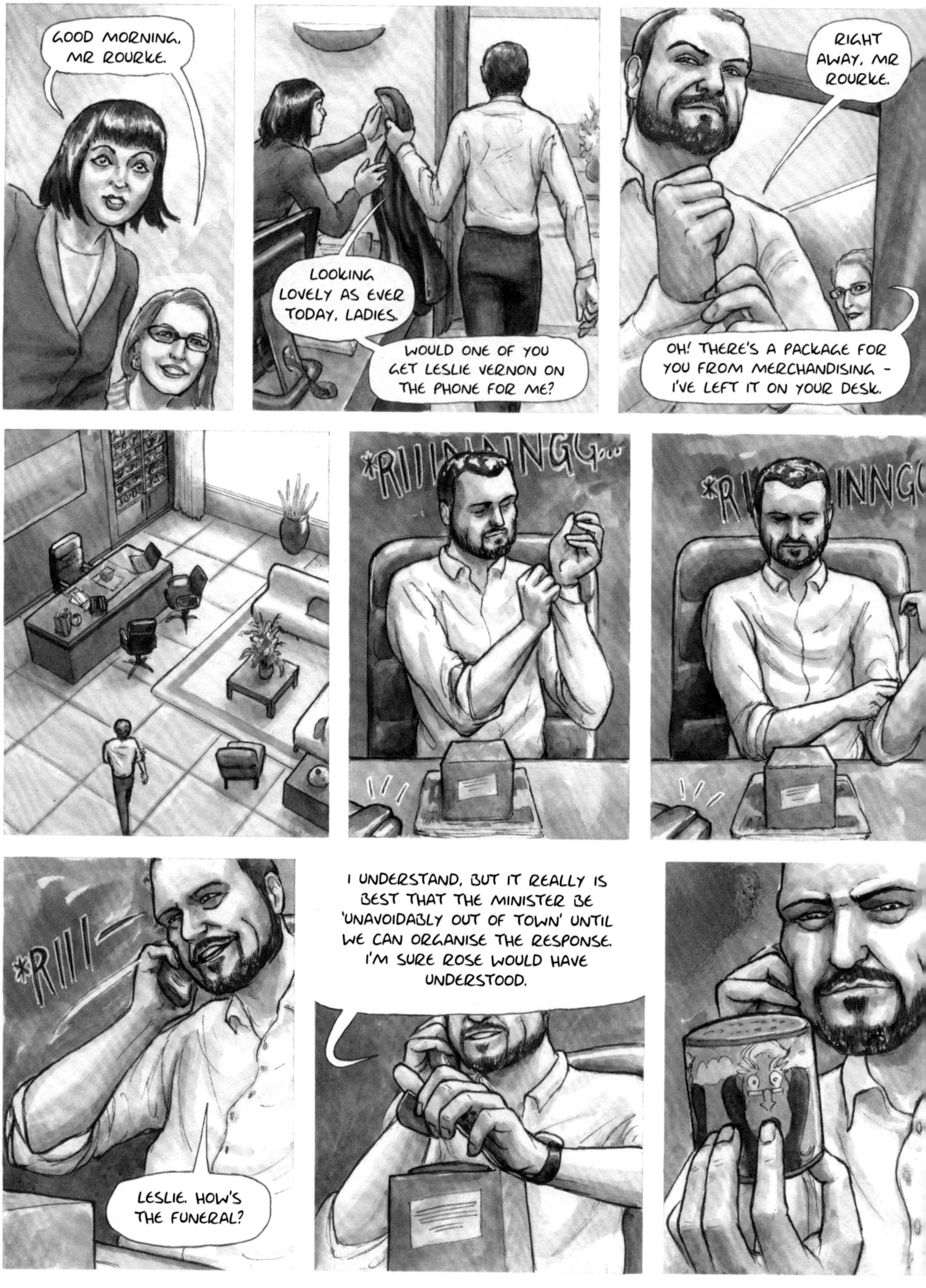
GOOD MORNING, MR ROURKE.
LOOKING LOVELY AS EVER TODAY, LADIES.
WOULD ONE OF YOU GET LESLIE VERNON ON THE PHONE FOR ME?
RIGHT AWAY, MR ROURKE.
OH! THERE'S A PACKAGE FOR YOU FROM MERCHANDISING - I'VE LEFT IT ON YOUR DESK.
*RIIINNNGG...
*RIIINNNGG
*RIII—
LESLIE. HOW'S THE FUNERAL?
I UNDERSTAND, BUT IT REALLY IS BEST THAT THE MINISTER BE 'UNAVOIDABLY OUT OF TOWN' UNTIL WE CAN ORGANISE THE RESPONSE. I'M SURE ROSE WOULD HAVE UNDERSTOOD.

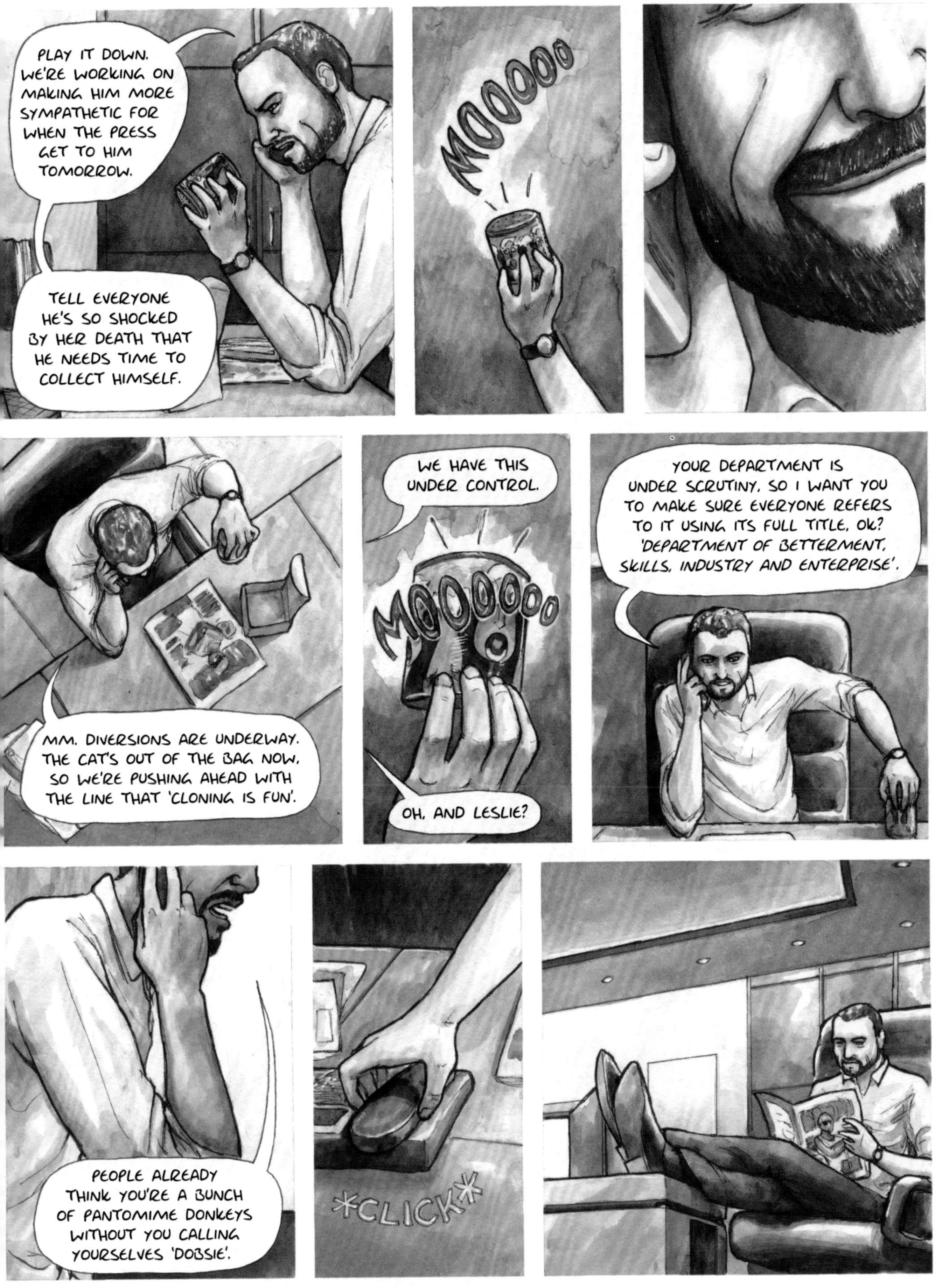
PLAY IT DOWN. WE'RE WORKING ON MAKING HIM MORE SYMPATHETIC FOR WHEN THE PRESS GET TO HIM TOMORROW.
TELL EVERYONE HE'S SO SHOCKED BY HER DEATH THAT HE NEEDS TIME TO COLLECT HIMSELF.
MOOOOO
MM. DIVERSIONS ARE UNDERWAY. THE CAT'S OUT OF THE BAG NOW, SO WE'RE PUSHING AHEAD WITH THE LINE THAT 'CLONING IS FUN'.
WE HAVE THIS UNDER CONTROL.
MOOOOOO
OH, AND LESLIE?
YOUR DEPARTMENT IS UNDER SCRUTINY, SO I WANT YOU TO MAKE SURE EVERYONE REFERS TO IT USING ITS FULL TITLE, OK? 'DEPARTMENT OF BETTERMENT, SKILLS, INDUSTRY AND ENTERPRISE'.
PEOPLE ALREADY THINK YOU'RE A BUNCH OF PANTOMIME DONKEYS WITHOUT YOU CALLING YOURSELVES 'DOBSIE'.
CLICK

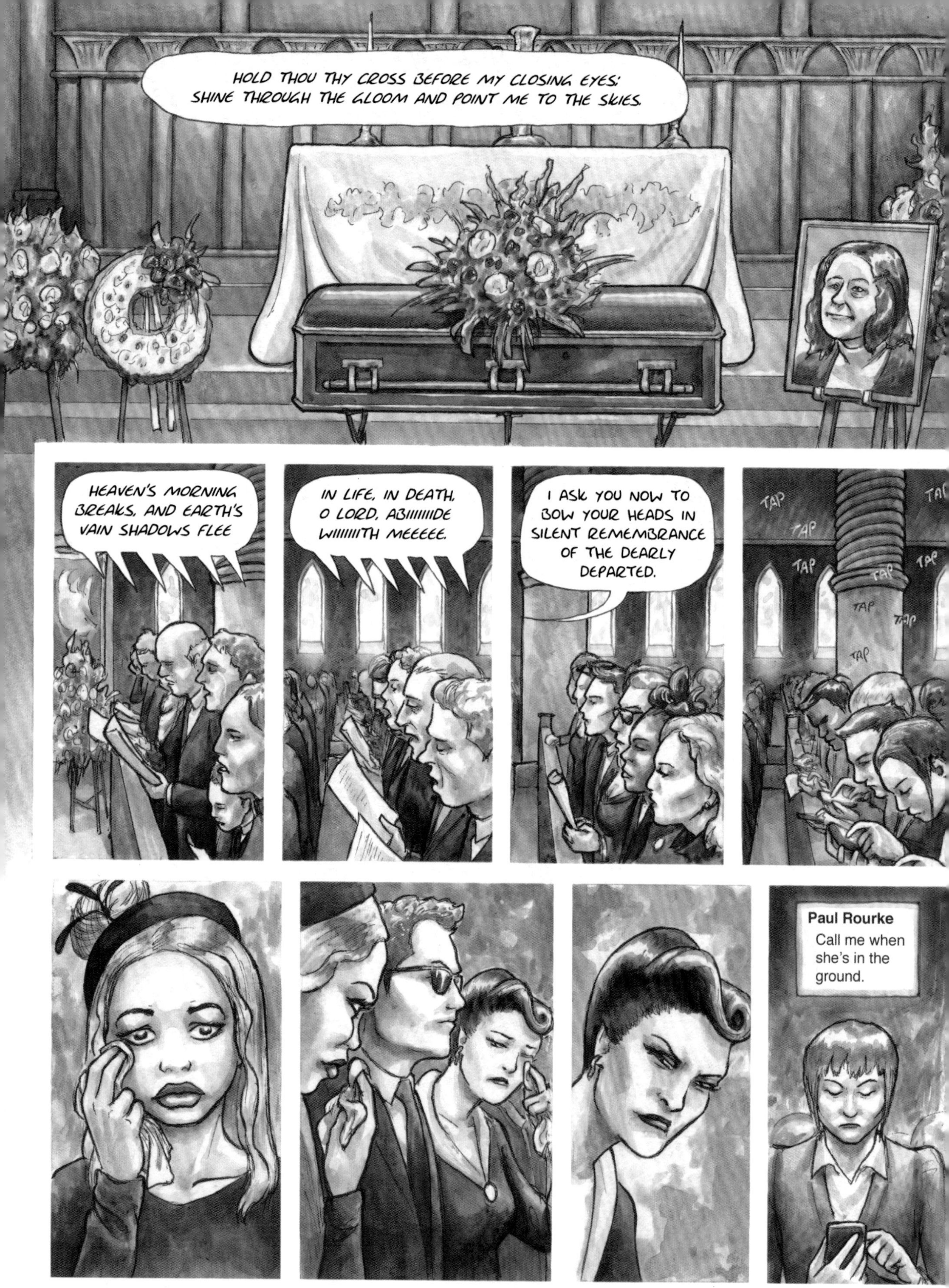
HOLD THOU THY CROSS BEFORE MY CLOSING EYES;
SHINE THROUGH THE GLOOM AND POINT ME TO THE SKIES.
HEAVEN'S MORNING BREAKS, AND EARTH'S VAIN SHADOWS FLEE
IN LIFE, IN DEATH, O LORD, ABIIIIIIDE WIIIIIITH MEEEEE.
I ASK YOU NOW TO BOW YOUR HEADS IN SILENT REMEMBRANCE OF THE DEARLY DEPARTED.
TAP TAP TAP TAP TAP TAP TAP TAP TAP
Paul Rourke
Call me when she's in the ground.

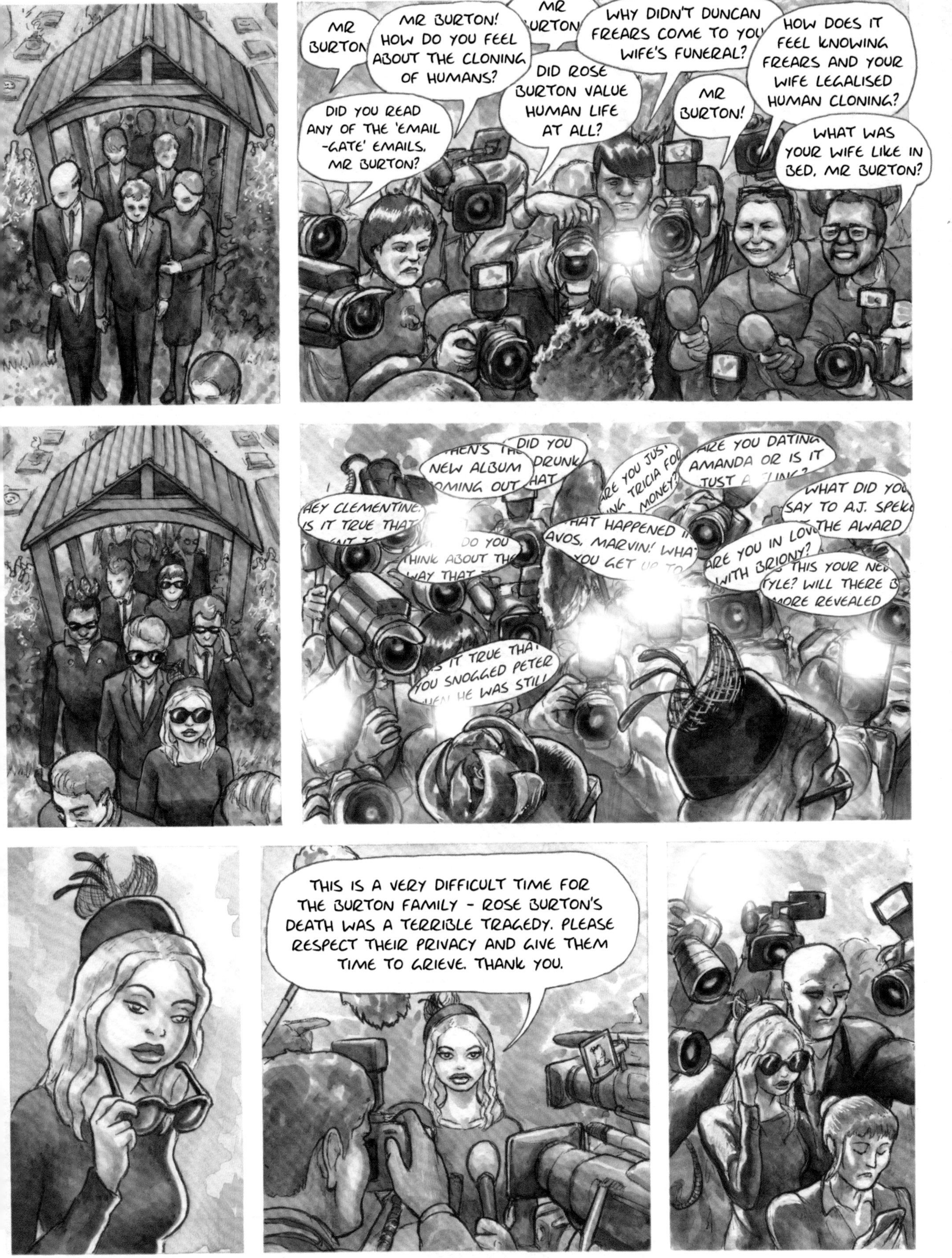
MR BURTON
MR BURTON! HOW DO YOU FEEL ABOUT THE CLONING OF HUMANS?
DID YOU READ ANY OF THE 'EMAIL -GATE' EMAILS, MR BURTON?
MR URTON
DID ROSE BURTON VALUE HUMAN LIFE AT ALL?
WHY DIDN'T DUNCAN FREARS COME TO YOU WIFE'S FUNERAL?
MR BURTON!
HOW DOES IT FEEL KNOWING FREARS AND YOUR WIFE LEGALISED HUMAN CLONING?
WHAT WAS YOUR WIFE LIKE IN BED, MR BURTON?
NEW ALBUM OMING OUT
DID YOU DRUNK HAT
AMANDA OR IS IT JUST
WHAT DID YOU SAY TO A.J. THE AWARD
IS IT TRUE THAT
DO YOU THINK ABOUT THE
AVOS, MARVIN! YOU GET
WITH BRIONY?
THIS YOUR NEW YLE? WILL THERE MORE REVEALED
IT TRUE THAT YOU SNOGGED PETER
THIS IS A VERY DIFFICULT TIME FOR THE BURTON FAMILY - ROSE BURTON'S DEATH WAS A TERRIBLE TRAGEDY. PLEASE RESPECT THEIR PRIVACY AND GIVE THEM TIME TO GRIEVE. THANK YOU.

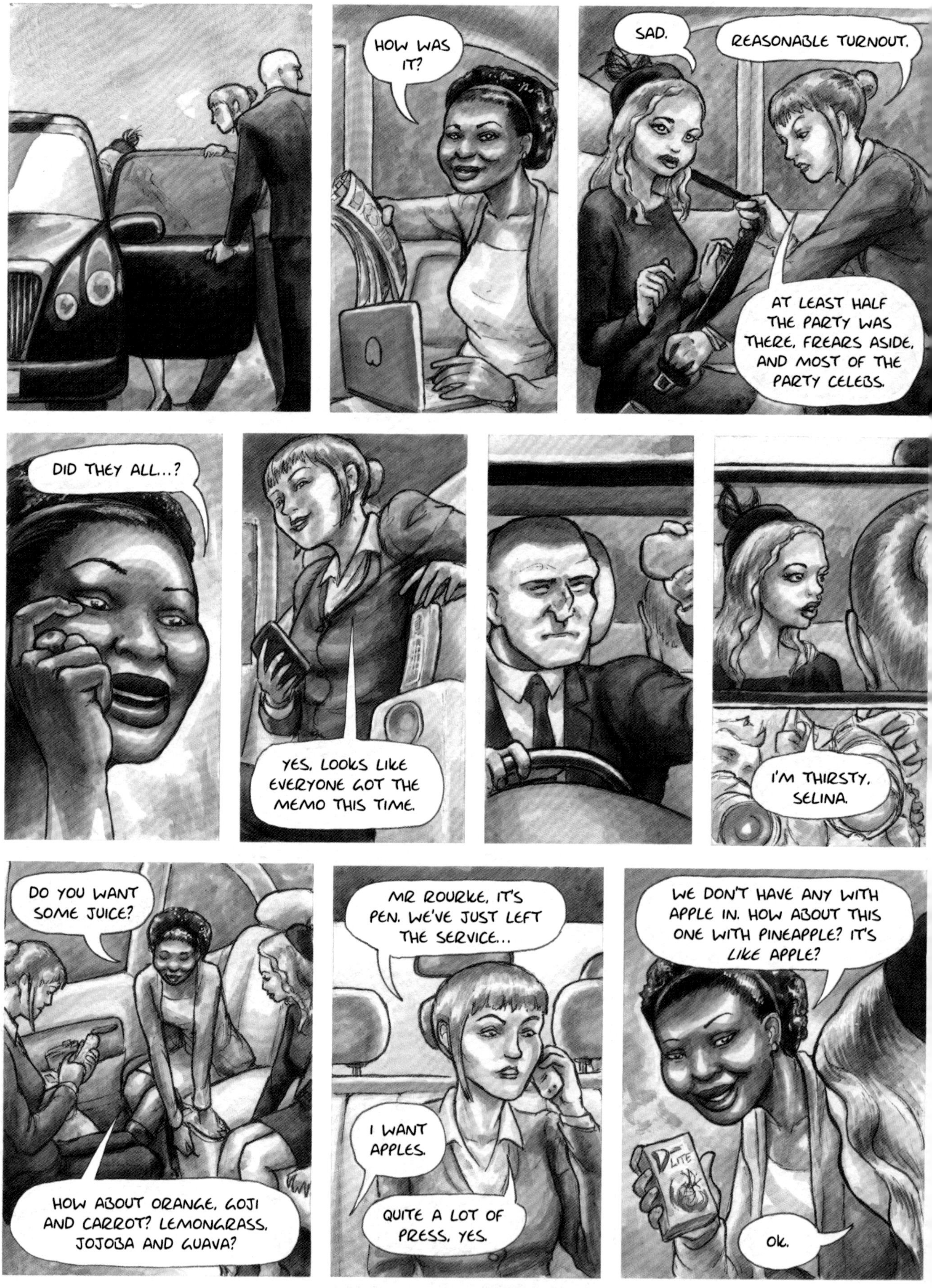
HOW WAS IT?
SAD.
REASONABLE TURNOUT.
AT LEAST HALF THE PARTY WAS THERE, FREARS ASIDE, AND MOST OF THE PARTY CELEBS.
DID THEY ALL...?
YES. LOOKS LIKE EVERYONE GOT THE MEMO THIS TIME.
I'M THIRSTY, SELINA.
DO YOU WANT SOME JUICE?
HOW ABOUT ORANGE, GOJI AND CARROT? LEMONGRASS, JOJOBA AND GUAVA?
MR ROURKE, IT'S PEN. WE'VE JUST LEFT THE SERVICE...
I WANT APPLES.
QUITE A LOT OF PRESS, YES.
WE DON'T HAVE ANY WITH APPLE IN. HOW ABOUT THIS ONE WITH PINEAPPLE? IT'S LIKE APPLE?
OK.

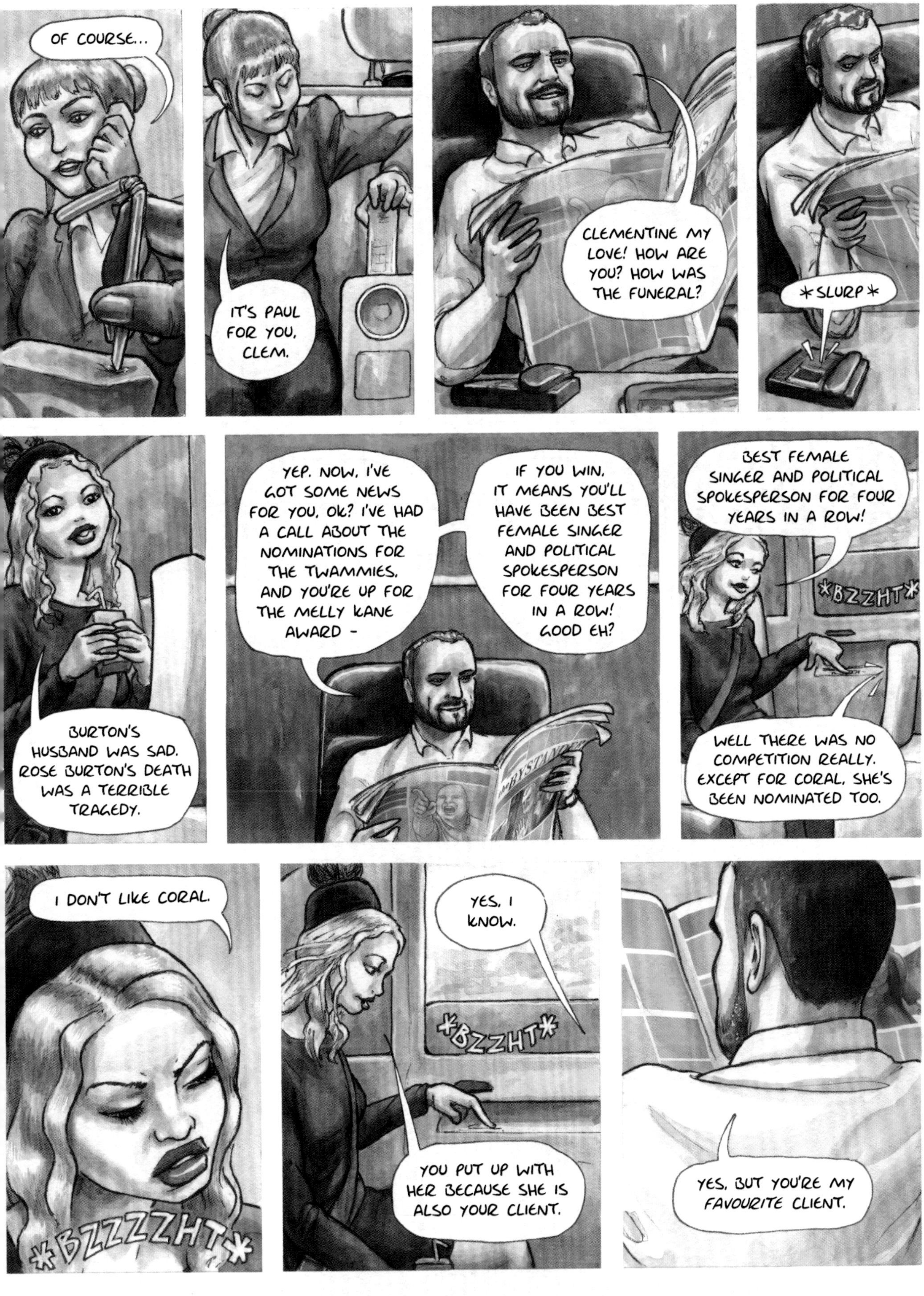
OF COURSE...
IT'S PAUL FOR YOU, CLEM.
CLEMENTINE MY LOVE! HOW ARE YOU? HOW WAS THE FUNERAL?
SLURP
BURTON'S HUSBAND WAS SAD. ROSE BURTON'S DEATH WAS A TERRIBLE TRAGEDY.
YEP. NOW, I'VE GOT SOME NEWS FOR YOU, OK? I'VE HAD A CALL ABOUT THE NOMINATIONS FOR THE TWAMMIES, AND YOU'RE UP FOR THE MELLY KANE AWARD -
IF YOU WIN, IT MEANS YOU'LL HAVE BEEN BEST FEMALE SINGER AND POLITICAL SPOKESPERSON FOR FOUR YEARS IN A ROW! GOOD EH?
BEST FEMALE SINGER AND POLITICAL SPOKESPERSON FOR FOUR YEARS IN A ROW!
BZZHT
WELL THERE WAS NO COMPETITION REALLY. EXCEPT FOR CORAL, SHE'S BEEN NOMINATED TOO.
I DON'T LIKE CORAL.
BZZZZZHT
YES, I KNOW.
BZZHT
YOU PUT UP WITH HER BECAUSE SHE IS ALSO YOUR CLIENT.
YES, BUT YOU'RE MY FAVOURITE CLIENT.

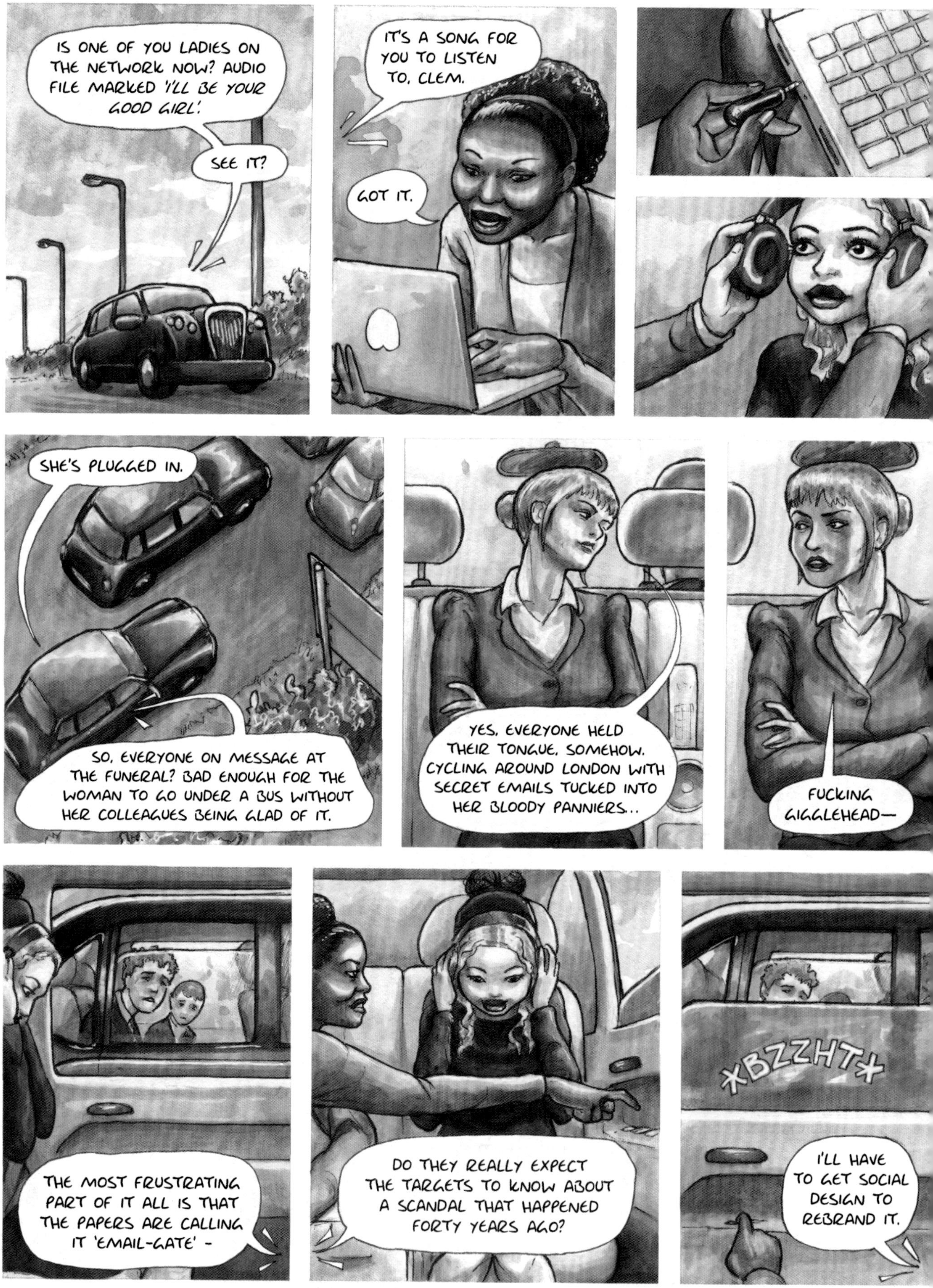
IS ONE OF YOU LADIES ON THE NETWORK NOW? AUDIO FILE MARKED 'I'LL BE YOUR GOOD GIRL'.
SEE IT?
IT'S A SONG FOR YOU TO LISTEN TO, CLEM.
GOT IT.
SHE'S PLUGGED IN.
SO, EVERYONE ON MESSAGE AT THE FUNERAL? BAD ENOUGH FOR THE WOMAN TO GO UNDER A BUS WITHOUT HER COLLEAGUES BEING GLAD OF IT.
YES, EVERYONE HELD THEIR TONGUE, SOMEHOW. CYCLING AROUND LONDON WITH SECRET EMAILS TUCKED INTO HER BLOODY PANNIERS...
FUCKING GIGGLEHEAD—
THE MOST FRUSTRATING PART OF IT ALL IS THAT THE PAPERS ARE CALLING IT 'EMAIL-GATE' -
DO THEY REALLY EXPECT THE TARGETS TO KNOW ABOUT A SCANDAL THAT HAPPENED FORTY YEARS AGO?
BZZHT
I'LL HAVE TO GET SOCIAL DESIGN TO REBRAND IT.

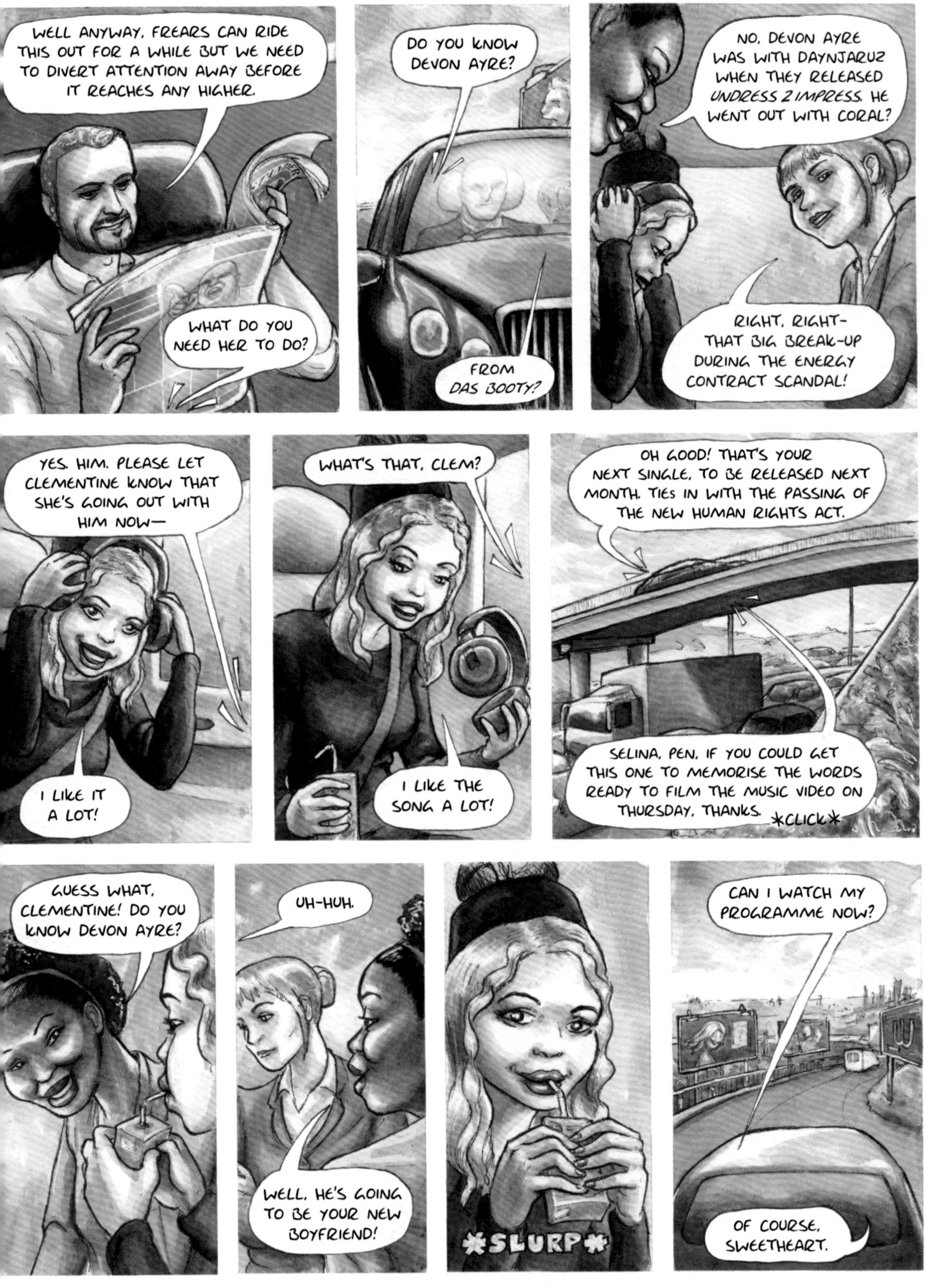
WELL ANYWAY, FREARS CAN RIDE THIS OUT FOR A WHILE BUT WE NEED TO DIVERT ATTENTION AWAY BEFORE IT REACHES ANY HIGHER.
WHAT DO YOU NEED HER TO DO?
DO YOU KNOW DEVON AYRE?
FROM DAS BOOTY?
NO, DEVON AYRE WAS WITH DAYNJARUZ WHEN THEY RELEASED UNDRESS 2 IMPRESS. HE WENT OUT WITH CORAL?
RIGHT, RIGHT- THAT BIG BREAK-UP DURING THE ENERGY CONTRACT SCANDAL!
YES. HIM. PLEASE LET CLEMENTINE KNOW THAT SHE'S GOING OUT WITH HIM NOW—
I LIKE IT A LOT!
WHAT'S THAT, CLEM?
I LIKE THE SONG A LOT!
OH GOOD! THAT'S YOUR NEXT SINGLE, TO BE RELEASED NEXT MONTH. TIES IN WITH THE PASSING OF THE NEW HUMAN RIGHTS ACT.
SELINA, PEN, IF YOU COULD GET THIS ONE TO MEMORISE THE WORDS READY TO FILM THE MUSIC VIDEO ON THURSDAY, THANKS.
CLICK
GUESS WHAT, CLEMENTINE! DO YOU KNOW DEVON AYRE?
UH-HUH.
WELL, HE'S GOING TO BE YOUR NEW BOYFRIEND!
SLURP
CAN I WATCH MY PROGRAMME NOW?
OF COURSE, SWEETHEART.

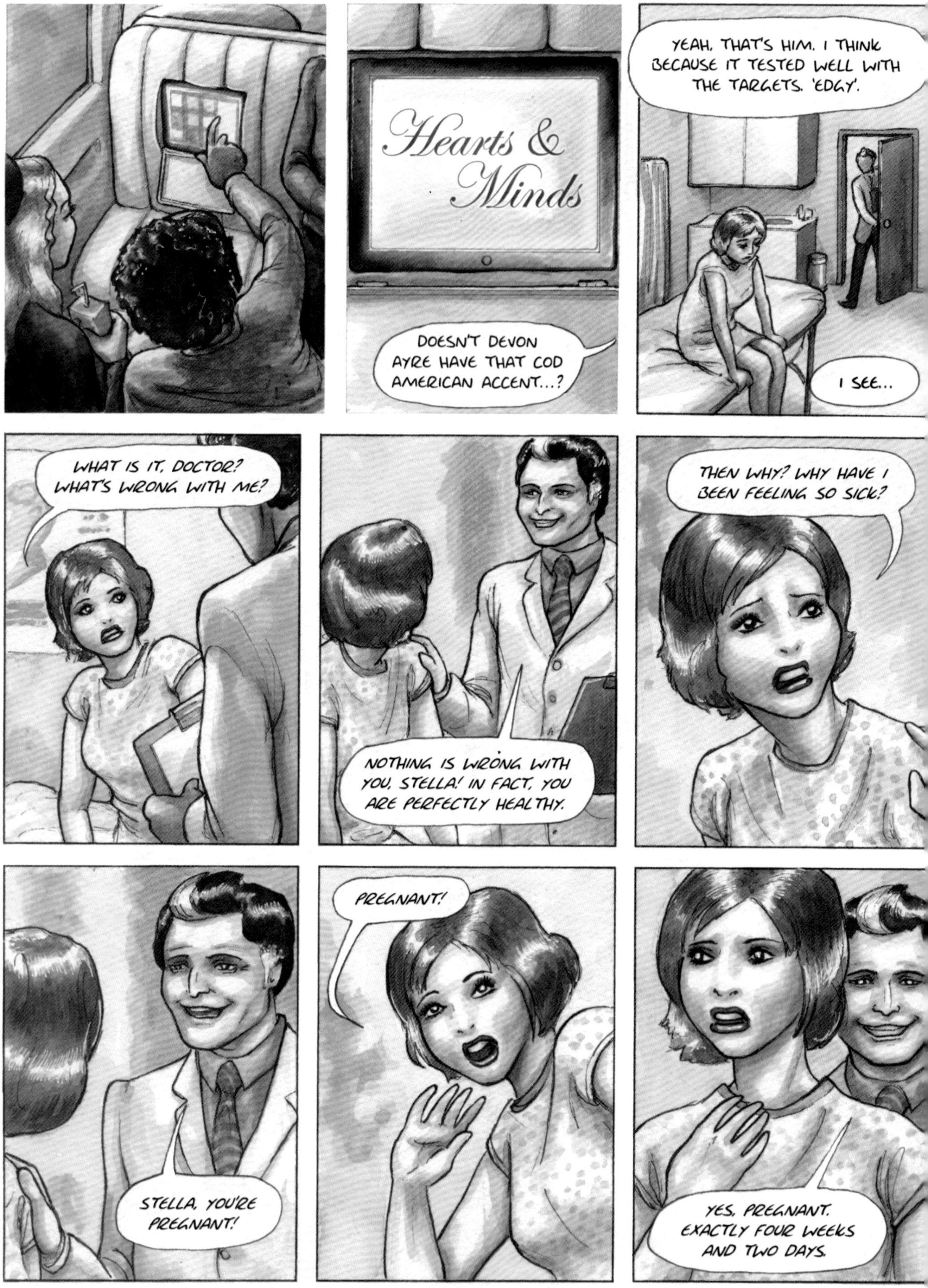
Hearts & Minds
DOESN'T DEVON AYRE HAVE THAT COD AMERICAN ACCENT...?
YEAH, THAT'S HIM. I THINK BECAUSE IT TESTED WELL WITH THE TARGETS. 'EDGY'.
I SEE...
WHAT IS IT, DOCTOR? WHAT'S WRONG WITH ME?
NOTHING IS WRONG WITH YOU, STELLA! IN FACT, YOU ARE PERFECTLY HEALTHY.
THEN WHY? WHY HAVE I BEEN FEELING SO SICK?
STELLA, YOU'RE PREGNANT!
PREGNANT!
YES, PREGNANT. EXACTLY FOUR WEEKS AND TWO DAYS.

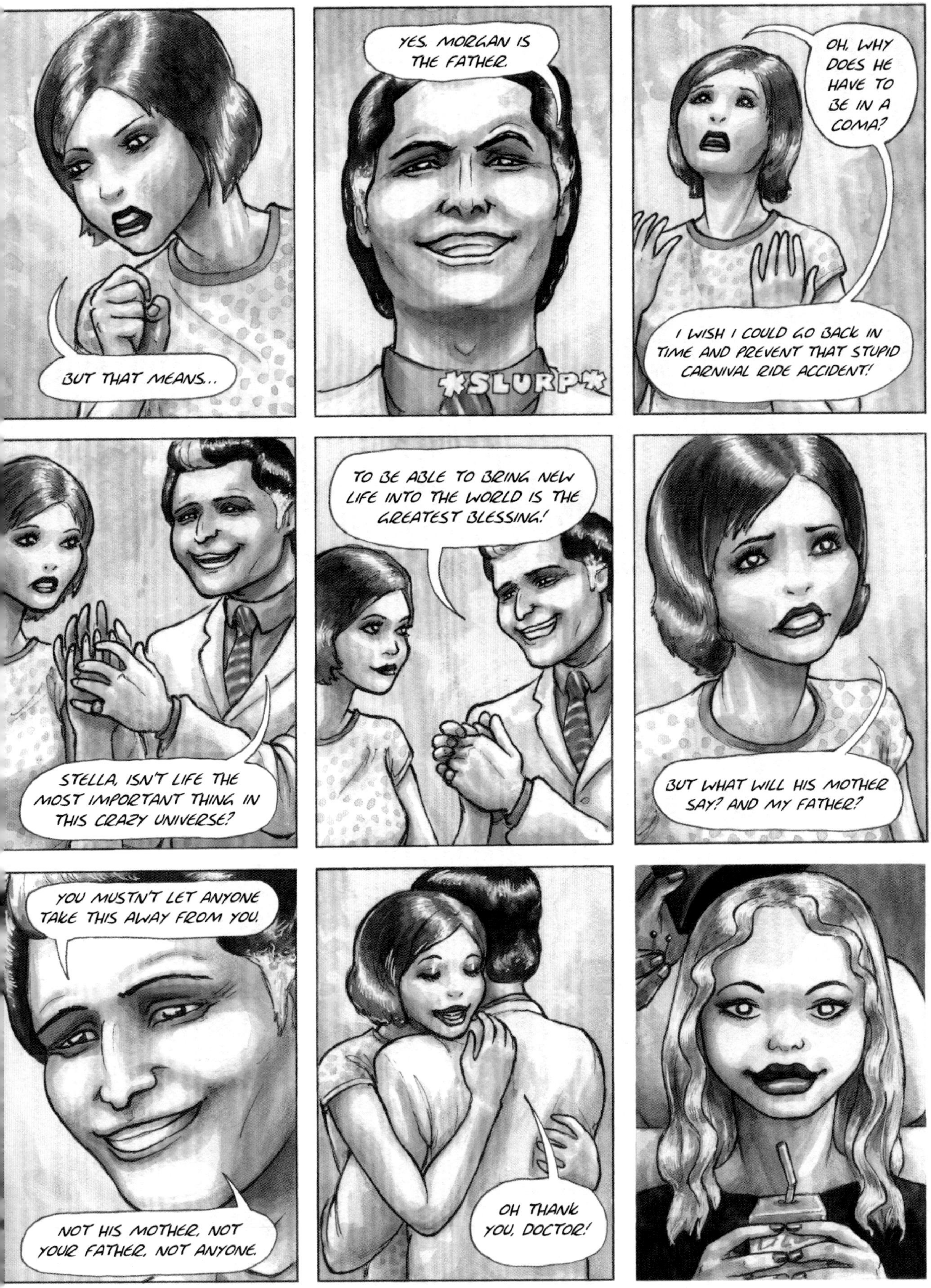
BUT THAT MEANS...
YES. MORGAN IS THE FATHER.
SLURP
OH, WHY DOES HE HAVE TO BE IN A COMA?
I WISH I COULD GO BACK IN TIME AND PREVENT THAT STUPID CARNIVAL RIDE ACCIDENT!
STELLA, ISN'T LIFE THE MOST IMPORTANT THING IN THIS CRAZY UNIVERSE?
TO BE ABLE TO BRING NEW LIFE INTO THE WORLD IS THE GREATEST BLESSING!
BUT WHAT WILL HIS MOTHER SAY? AND MY FATHER?
YOU MUSTN'T LET ANYONE TAKE THIS AWAY FROM YOU.
NOT HIS MOTHER, NOT YOUR FATHER, NOT ANYONE.
OH THANK YOU, DOCTOR!

WHAT'S TRENDING

STEVEN JOHNS
is
GRANNY AND MELISSA

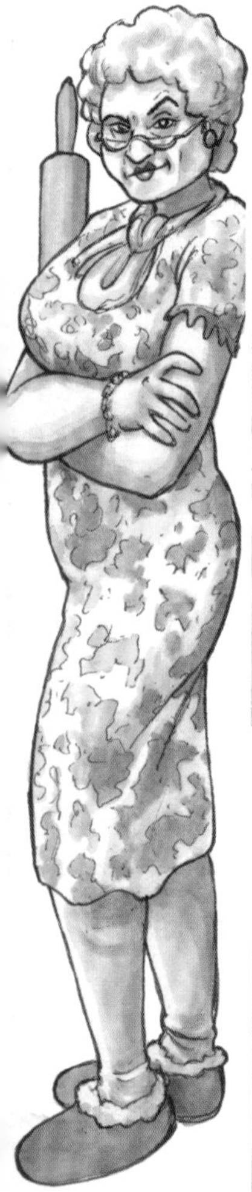

sometimes it's HARD to be a WOMAN!

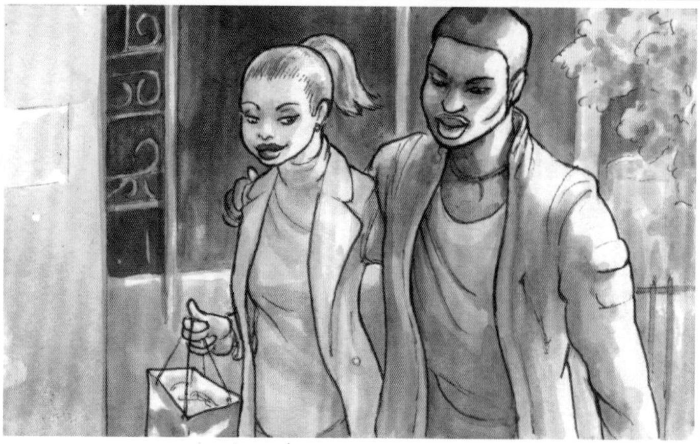

LOVE IS IN THE AYRE

Move over Az and Laura! Candid photos of this year's power couple Clementine Darling and Devon Ayre out on secret date

214 comments

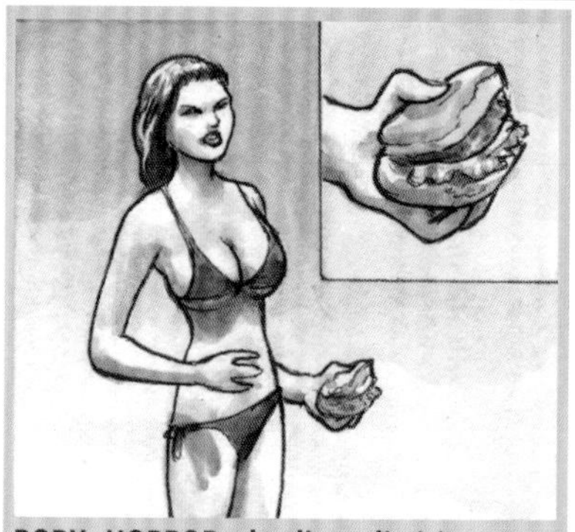

BODY HORROR: leading dietician says Claudia 'will be dead by forty-five' if she continues her disgusting diet

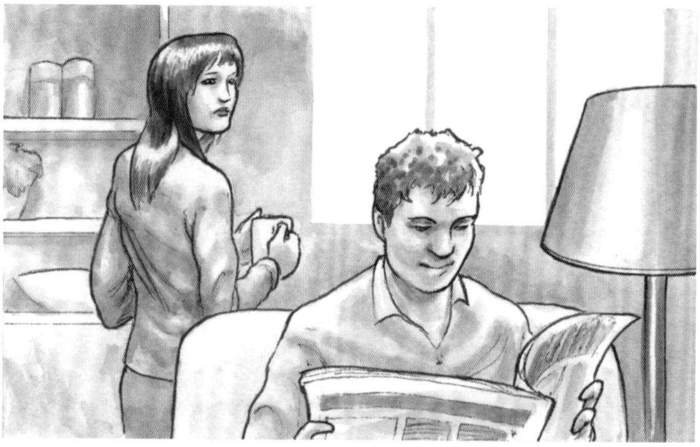

COULD YOU BE LIVING WITH A CLONE?

Experts say human clones could already be living among us - can you spot these telltale signs before it's too late?

137 comments

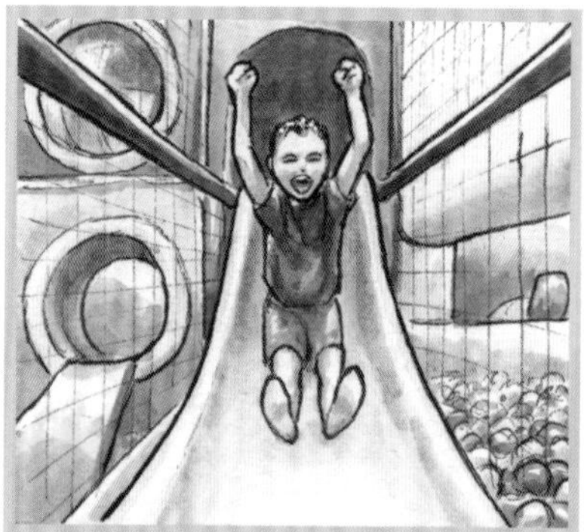

REPURPOSED FOR FUN: new proposals for old library buildings that kids will actually WANT to go to!

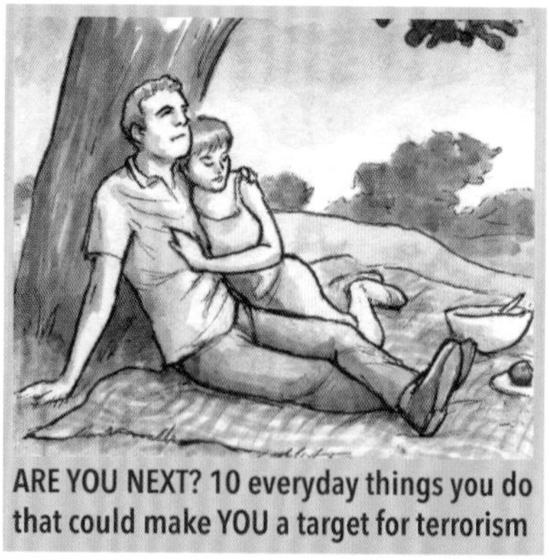

ARE YOU NEXT? 10 everyday things you do that could make YOU a target for terrorism

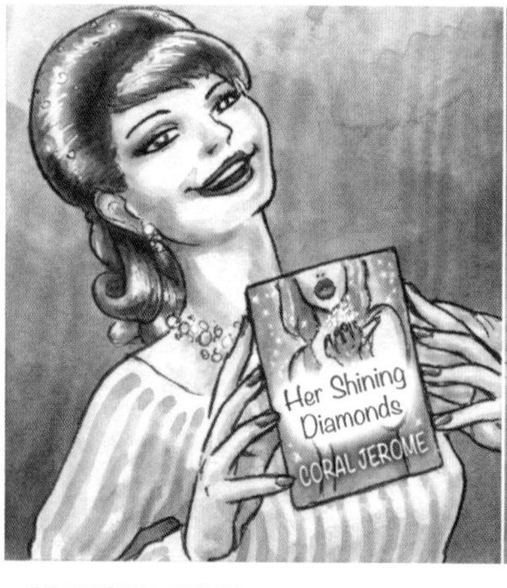
Her Shining Diamonds
CORAL JEROME

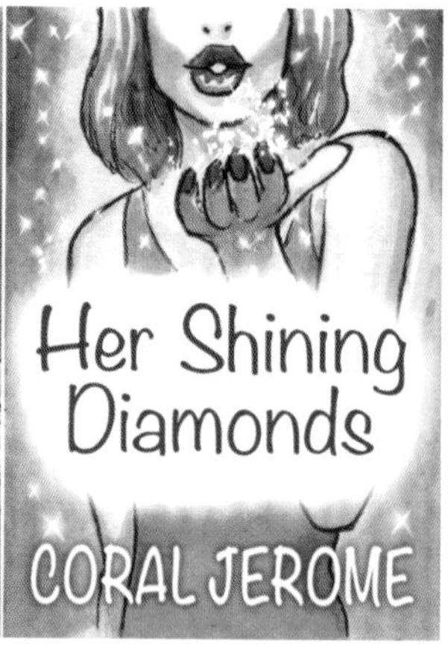
Her Shining Diamonds
CORAL JEROME

DIAMOND RUSH

Bookshops stock up ahead of release of Coral Jerome's literary debut about a woman who finds love in an unexpected place

117 comments

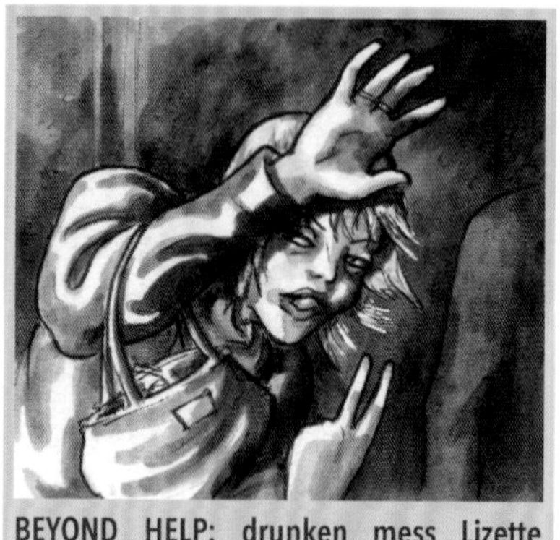

BEYOND HELP: drunken mess Lizette rumoured to be going back to rehab in desperate bid to 'get life on track'

STEVEN
is
GRA
AN
MELI

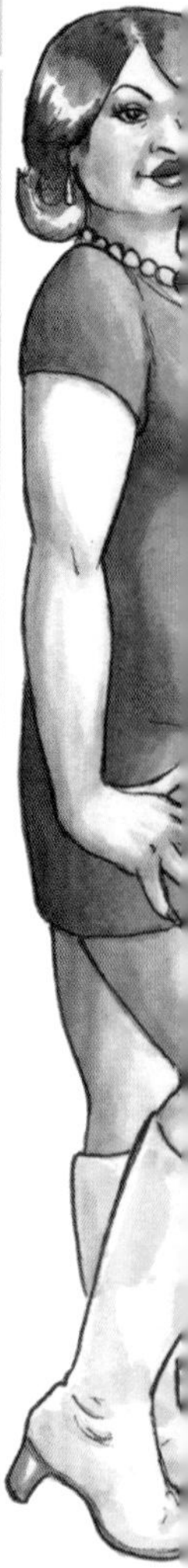

someti
it's HA
to be
WOMA

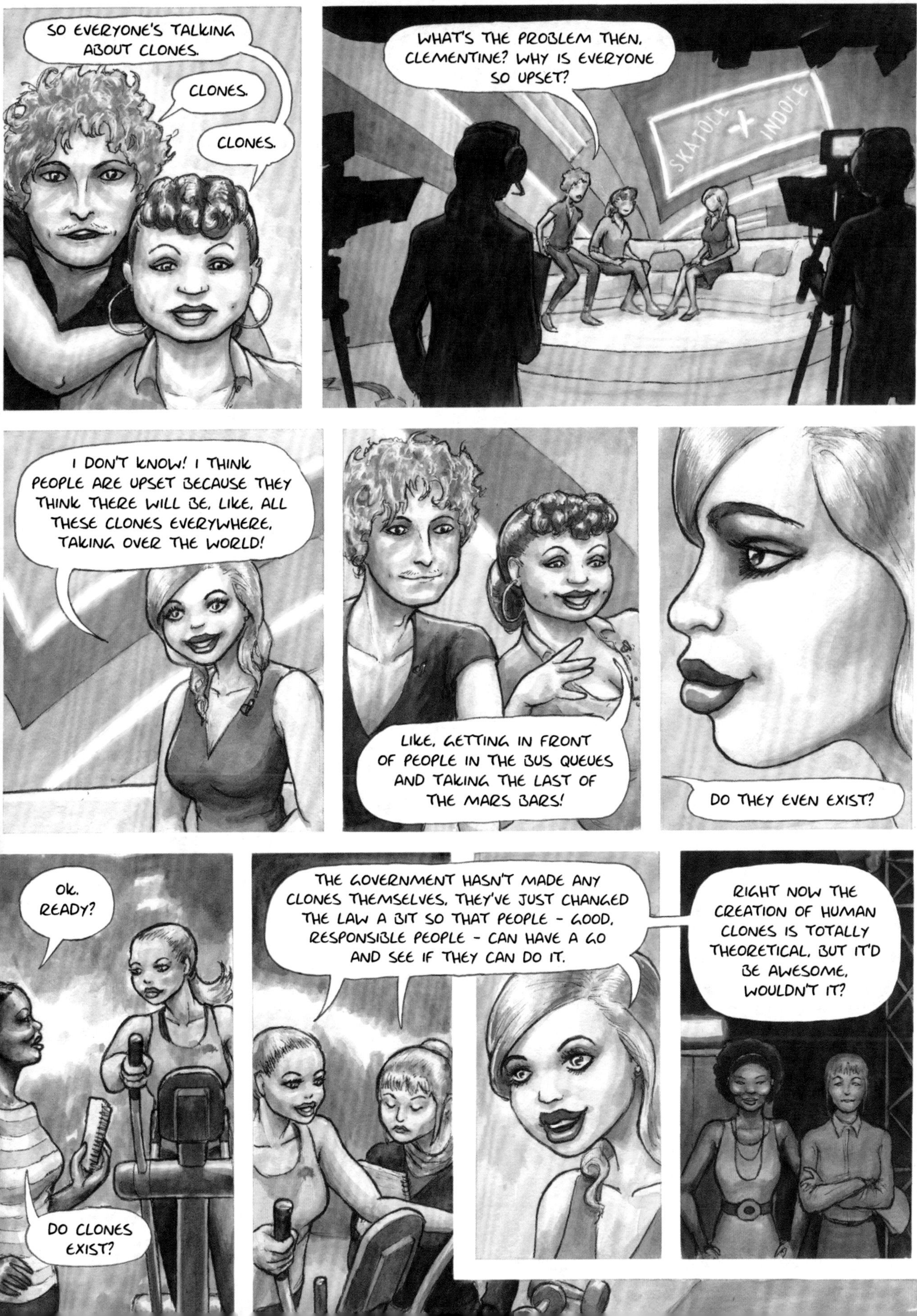
SO EVERYONE'S TALKING ABOUT CLONES.
CLONES.
CLONES.
WHAT'S THE PROBLEM THEN, CLEMENTINE? WHY IS EVERYONE SO UPSET?
SKATOLE INDOLE
I DON'T KNOW! I THINK PEOPLE ARE UPSET BECAUSE THEY THINK THERE WILL BE, LIKE, ALL THESE CLONES EVERYWHERE, TAKING OVER THE WORLD!
LIKE, GETTING IN FRONT OF PEOPLE IN THE BUS QUEUES AND TAKING THE LAST OF THE MARS BARS!
DO THEY EVEN EXIST?
OK. READY?
DO CLONES EXIST?
THE GOVERNMENT HASN'T MADE ANY CLONES THEMSELVES, THEY'VE JUST CHANGED THE LAW A BIT SO THAT PEOPLE - GOOD, RESPONSIBLE PEOPLE - CAN HAVE A GO AND SEE IF THEY CAN DO IT.
RIGHT NOW THE CREATION OF HUMAN CLONES IS TOTALLY THEORETICAL, BUT IT'D BE AWESOME, WOULDN'T IT?

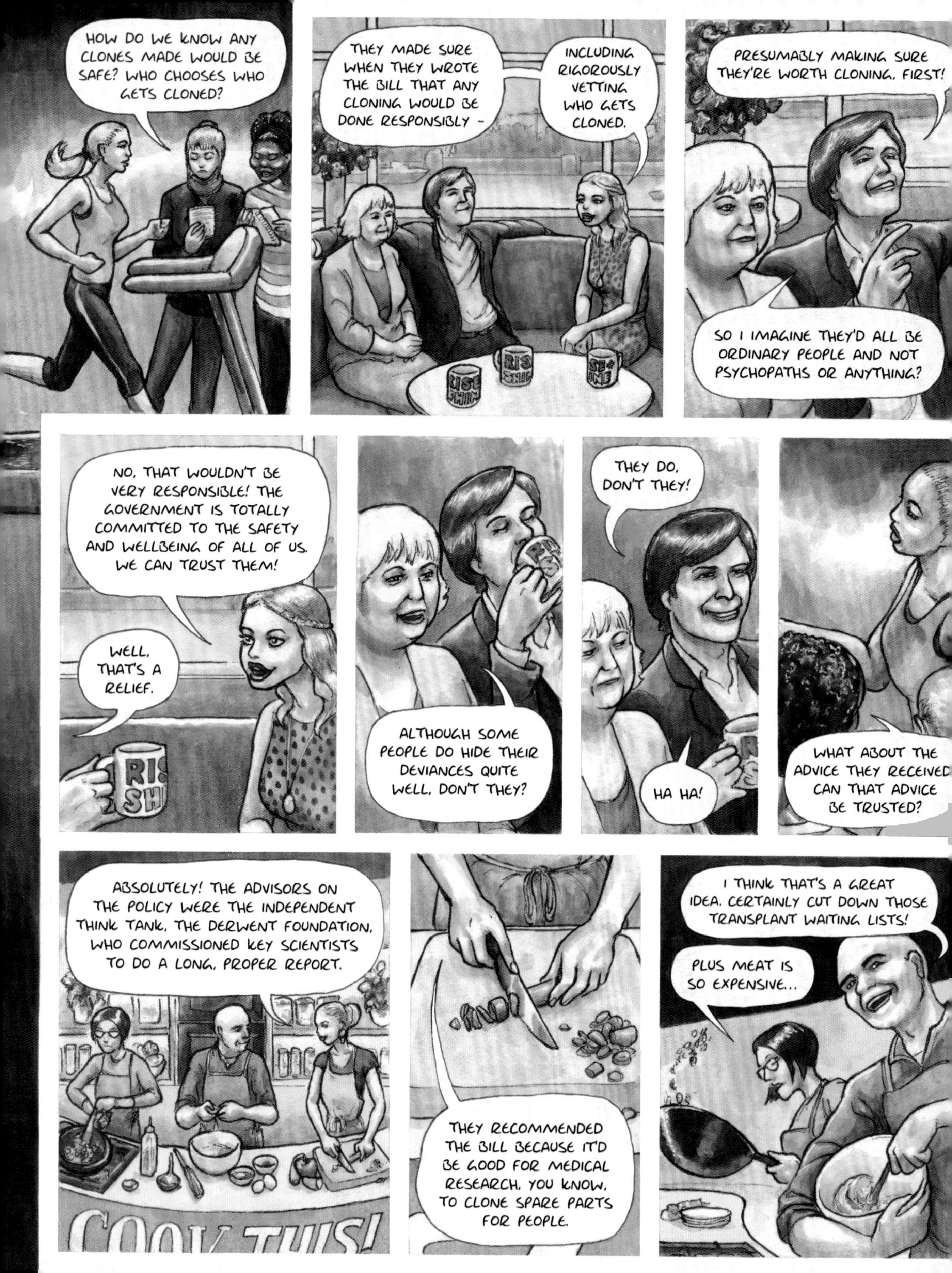
HOW DO WE KNOW ANY CLONES MADE WOULD BE SAFE? WHO CHOOSES WHO GETS CLONED?
THEY MADE SURE WHEN THEY WROTE THE BILL THAT ANY CLONING WOULD BE DONE RESPONSIBLY -
INCLUDING RIGOROUSLY VETTING WHO GETS CLONED.
PRESUMABLY MAKING SURE THEY'RE WORTH CLONING, FIRST!
SO I IMAGINE THEY'D ALL BE ORDINARY PEOPLE AND NOT PSYCHOPATHS OR ANYTHING?
NO, THAT WOULDN'T BE VERY RESPONSIBLE! THE GOVERNMENT IS TOTALLY COMMITTED TO THE SAFETY AND WELLBEING OF ALL OF US. WE CAN TRUST THEM!
WELL, THAT'S A RELIEF.
ALTHOUGH SOME PEOPLE DO HIDE THEIR DEVIANCES QUITE WELL, DON'T THEY?
THEY DO, DON'T THEY!
HA HA!
WHAT ABOUT THE ADVICE THEY RECEIVED CAN THAT ADVICE BE TRUSTED?
ABSOLUTELY! THE ADVISORS ON THE POLICY WERE THE INDEPENDENT THINK TANK, THE DERWENT FOUNDATION, WHO COMMISSIONED KEY SCIENTISTS TO DO A LONG, PROPER REPORT.
COOK THIS!
THEY RECOMMENDED THE BILL BECAUSE IT'D BE GOOD FOR MEDICAL RESEARCH, YOU KNOW, TO CLONE SPARE PARTS FOR PEOPLE.
I THINK THAT'S A GREAT IDEA. CERTAINLY CUT DOWN THOSE TRANSPLANT WAITING LISTS!
PLUS MEAT IS SO EXPENSIVE...

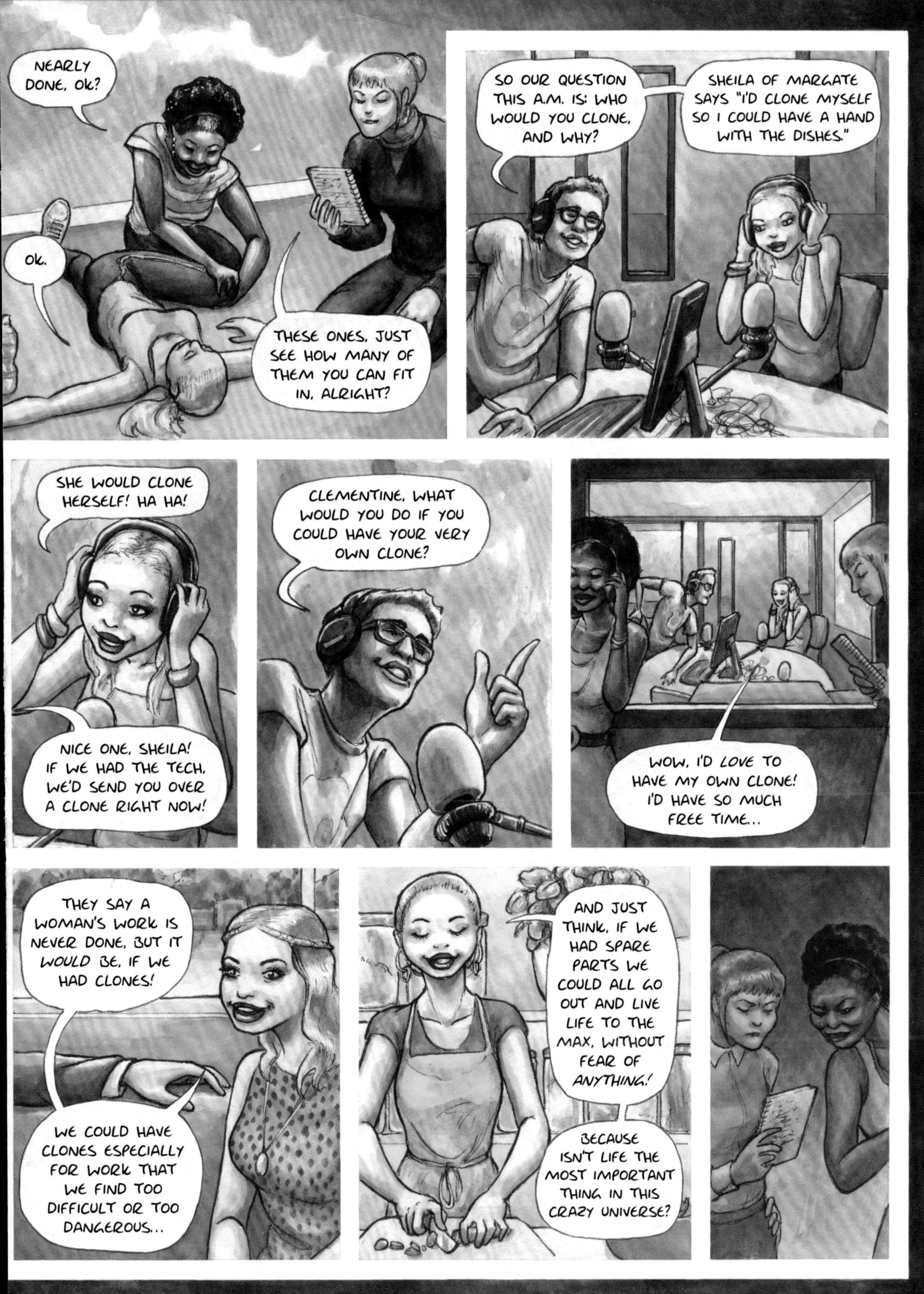
NEARLY DONE, OK?
OK.
THESE ONES. JUST SEE HOW MANY OF THEM YOU CAN FIT IN, ALRIGHT?
SO OUR QUESTION THIS A.M. IS: WHO WOULD YOU CLONE, AND WHY?
SHEILA OF MARGATE SAYS "I'D CLONE MYSELF SO I COULD HAVE A HAND WITH THE DISHES."
SHE WOULD CLONE HERSELF! HA HA!
NICE ONE, SHEILA! IF WE HAD THE TECH, WE'D SEND YOU OVER A CLONE RIGHT NOW!
CLEMENTINE, WHAT WOULD YOU DO IF YOU COULD HAVE YOUR VERY OWN CLONE?
WOW, I'D *LOVE* TO HAVE MY OWN CLONE! I'D HAVE SO MUCH FREE TIME...
THEY SAY A WOMAN'S WORK IS NEVER DONE, BUT IT *WOULD* BE, IF WE HAD CLONES!
WE COULD HAVE CLONES ESPECIALLY FOR WORK THAT WE FIND TOO DIFFICULT OR TOO DANGEROUS...
AND JUST THINK, IF WE HAD SPARE PARTS WE COULD ALL GO OUT AND LIVE LIFE TO THE MAX, WITHOUT FEAR OF *ANYTHING!*
BECAUSE ISN'T LIFE THE MOST IMPORTANT THING IN THIS CRAZY UNIVERSE?

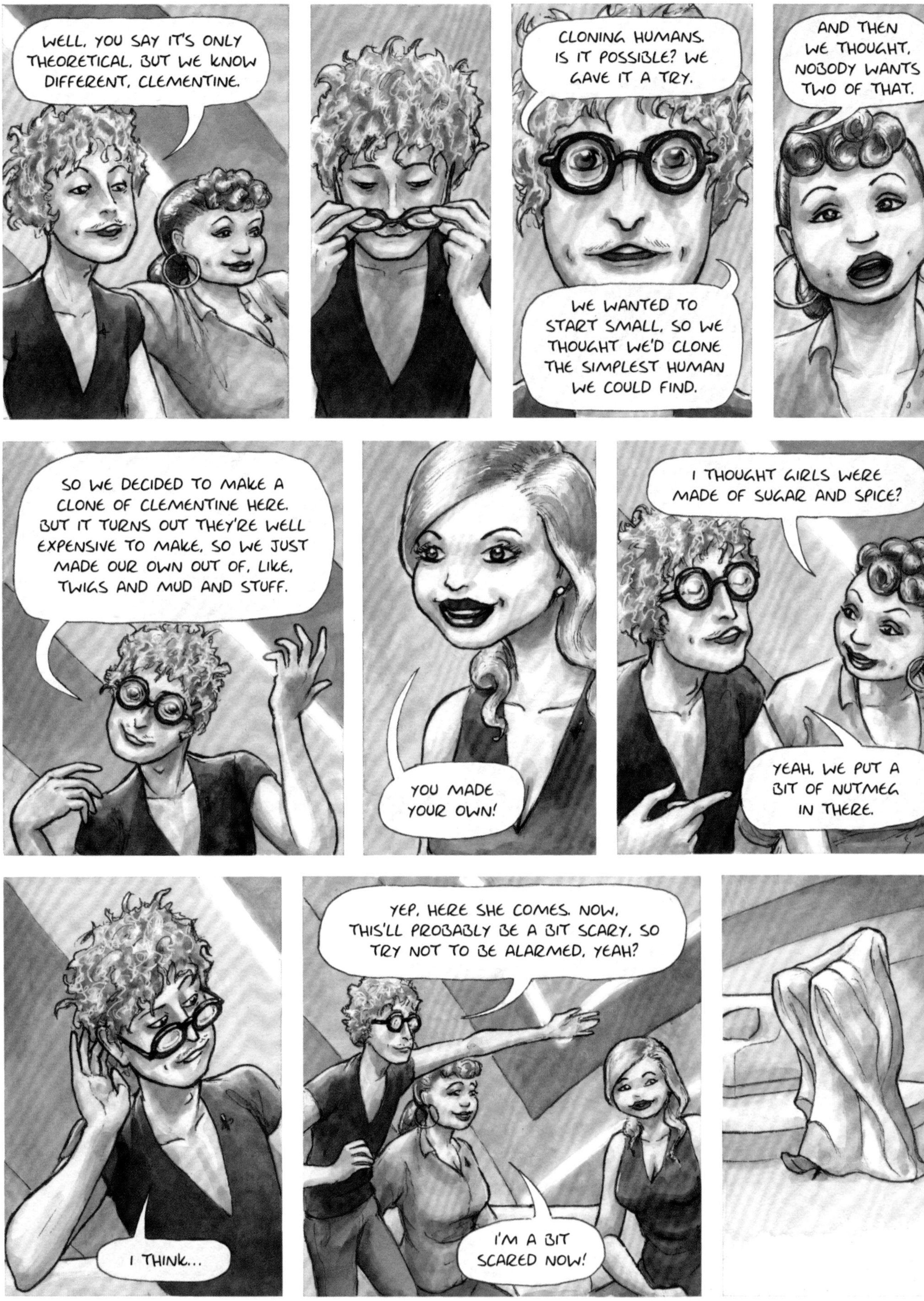
WELL, YOU SAY IT'S ONLY THEORETICAL, BUT WE KNOW DIFFERENT, CLEMENTINE.
CLONING HUMANS. IS IT POSSIBLE? WE GAVE IT A TRY.
WE WANTED TO START SMALL, SO WE THOUGHT WE'D CLONE THE SIMPLEST HUMAN WE COULD FIND.
AND THEN WE THOUGHT, NOBODY WANTS TWO OF THAT.
SO WE DECIDED TO MAKE A CLONE OF CLEMENTINE HERE. BUT IT TURNS OUT THEY'RE WELL EXPENSIVE TO MAKE, SO WE JUST MADE OUR OWN OUT OF, LIKE, TWIGS AND MUD AND STUFF.
YOU MADE YOUR OWN!
I THOUGHT GIRLS WERE MADE OF SUGAR AND SPICE?
YEAH, WE PUT A BIT OF NUTMEG IN THERE.
I THINK...
YEP, HERE SHE COMES. NOW, THIS'LL PROBABLY BE A BIT SCARY, SO TRY NOT TO BE ALARMED, YEAH?
I'M A BIT SCARED NOW!

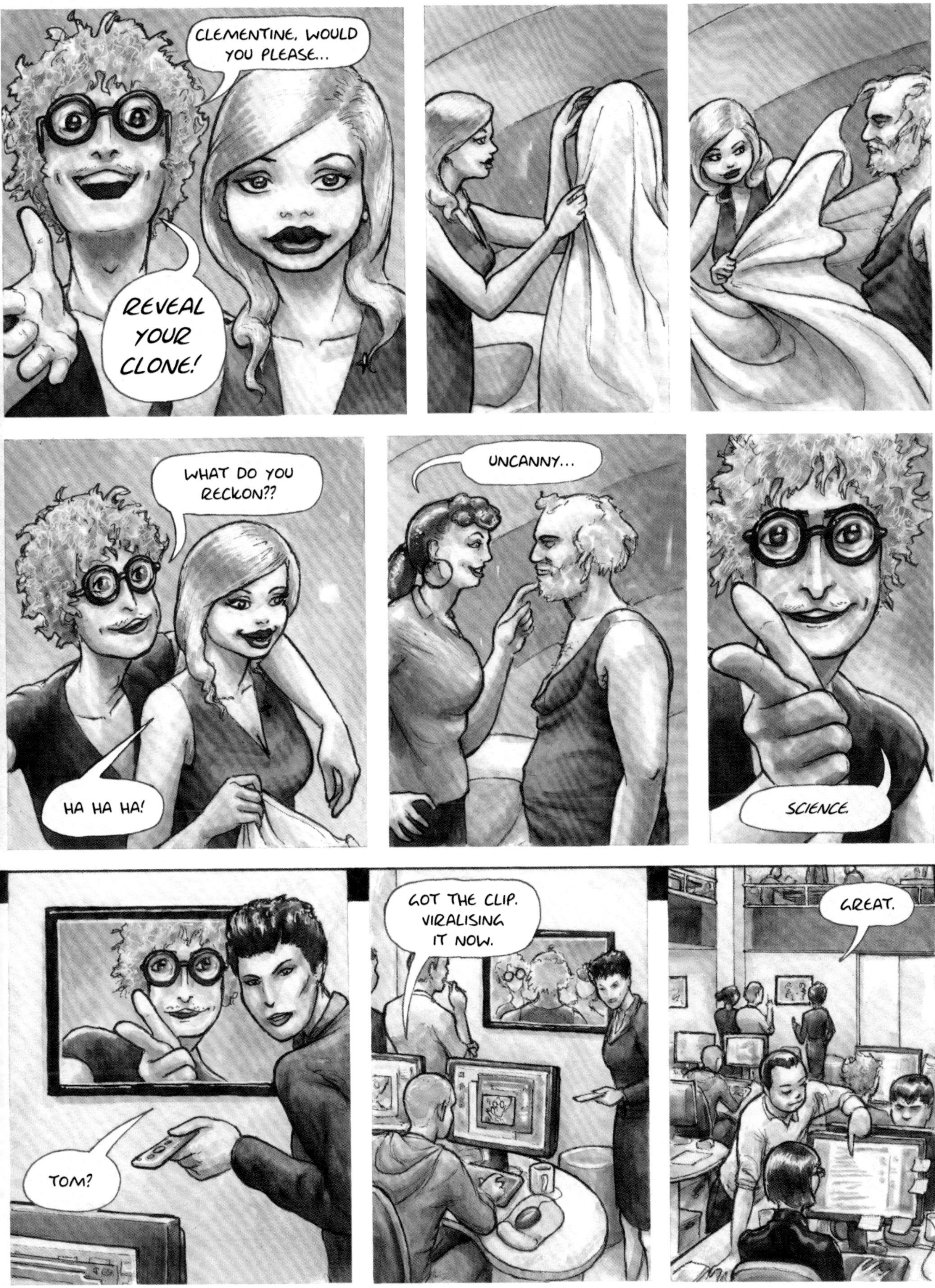
CLEMENTINE, WOULD YOU PLEASE...
REVEAL YOUR CLONE!
WHAT DO YOU RECKON??
HA HA HA!
UNCANNY...
SCIENCE.
TOM?
GOT THE CLIP. VIRALISING IT NOW.
GREAT.

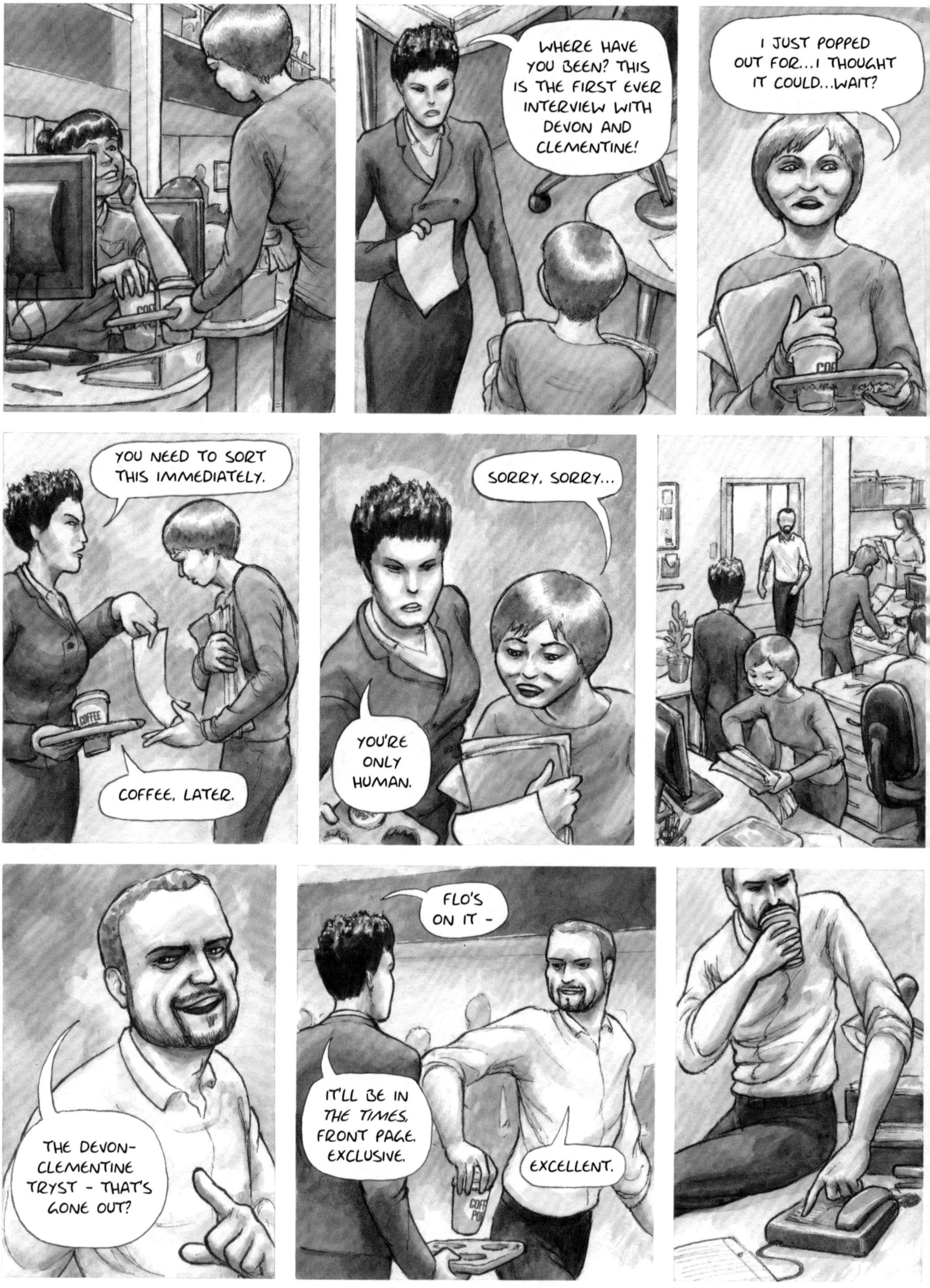
WHERE HAVE YOU BEEN? THIS IS THE FIRST EVER INTERVIEW WITH DEVON AND CLEMENTINE!
I JUST POPPED OUT FOR...I THOUGHT IT COULD...WAIT?
YOU NEED TO SORT THIS IMMEDIATELY.
COFFEE, LATER.
SORRY, SORRY...
YOU'RE ONLY HUMAN.
THE DEVON-CLEMENTINE TRYST - THAT'S GONE OUT?
FLO'S ON IT -
IT'LL BE IN THE TIMES, FRONT PAGE. EXCLUSIVE.
EXCELLENT.

AGENDAS.

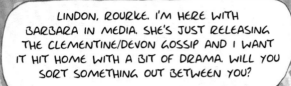

LINDON, ROURKE. I'M HERE WITH BARBARA IN MEDIA. SHE'S JUST RELEASING THE CLEMENTINE/DEVON GOSSIP AND I WANT IT HIT HOME WITH A BIT OF DRAMA. WILL YOU SORT SOMETHING OUT BETWEEN YOU?

WHAT KIND OF TIME-FRAME?

TODAY.

WE'LL GET RIGHT ON IT, MR ROURKE.

JESUS, I THINK THAT ONE'S COME UNHINGED.

THEY'RE ALL UNHINGED. LOOK AT THEM.

HEY, THE SCHEDULE HAS BEEN CHANGED FOR THIS EVENING...

WE'RE NOT DOING THE GAS AID PROMO SPOT?

NOT ANY MORE: NOW WE'RE CRASHING CORAL'S BOOK LAUNCH.

GREAT! I LOVE IT WHEN THEY START RATCHETING UP A LITTLE FEUD...

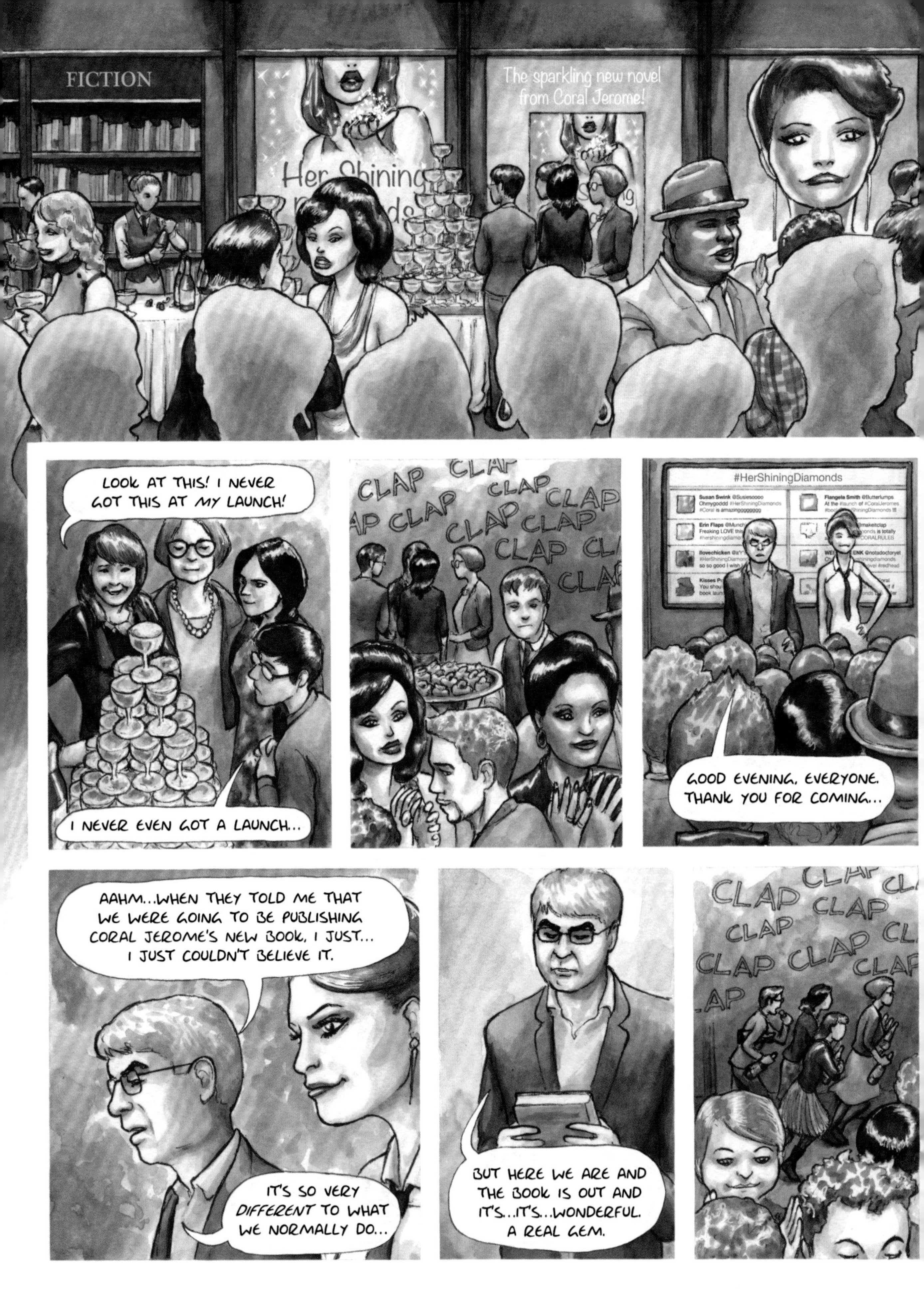
FICTION
The sparkling new novel from Coral Jerome!
LOOK AT THIS! I NEVER GOT THIS AT MY LAUNCH!
I NEVER EVEN GOT A LAUNCH...
CLAP CLAP CLAP CLAP CLAP CLAP CLAP CLAP CLAP CLAP
#HerShiningDiamonds
GOOD EVENING, EVERYONE. THANK YOU FOR COMING...
AAHM...WHEN THEY TOLD ME THAT WE WERE GOING TO BE PUBLISHING CORAL JEROME'S NEW BOOK, I JUST... I JUST COULDN'T BELIEVE IT.
IT'S SO VERY DIFFERENT TO WHAT WE NORMALLY DO...
BUT HERE WE ARE AND THE BOOK IS OUT AND IT'S...IT'S...WONDERFUL. A REAL GEM.
CLAP CLAP CLAP CLAP CLAP CLAP CLAP CLAP

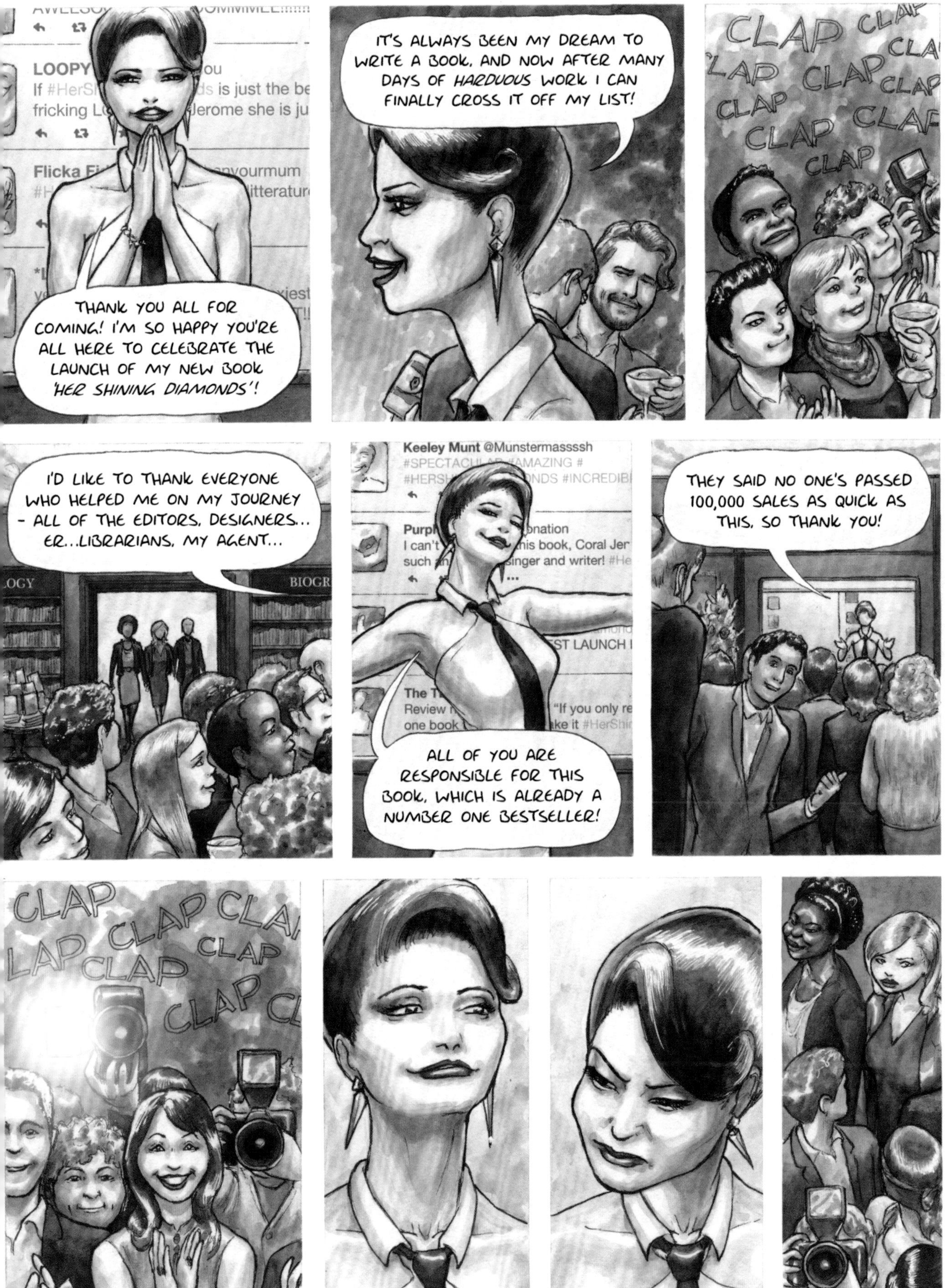
THANK YOU ALL FOR COMING! I'M SO HAPPY YOU'RE ALL HERE TO CELEBRATE THE LAUNCH OF MY NEW BOOK 'HER SHINING DIAMONDS'!
IT'S ALWAYS BEEN MY DREAM TO WRITE A BOOK, AND NOW AFTER MANY DAYS OF HARDUOUS WORK I CAN FINALLY CROSS IT OFF MY LIST!
CLAP CLAP CLAP CLAP CLAP CLAP CLAP CLAP CLAP
I'D LIKE TO THANK EVERYONE WHO HELPED ME ON MY JOURNEY - ALL OF THE EDITORS, DESIGNERS... ER...LIBRARIANS, MY AGENT...
Keeley Munt @Munstermassssh
ALL OF YOU ARE RESPONSIBLE FOR THIS BOOK, WHICH IS ALREADY A NUMBER ONE BESTSELLER!
THEY SAID NO ONE'S PASSED 100,000 SALES AS QUICK AS THIS, SO THANK YOU!
CLAP CLAP CLAP CLAP CLAP

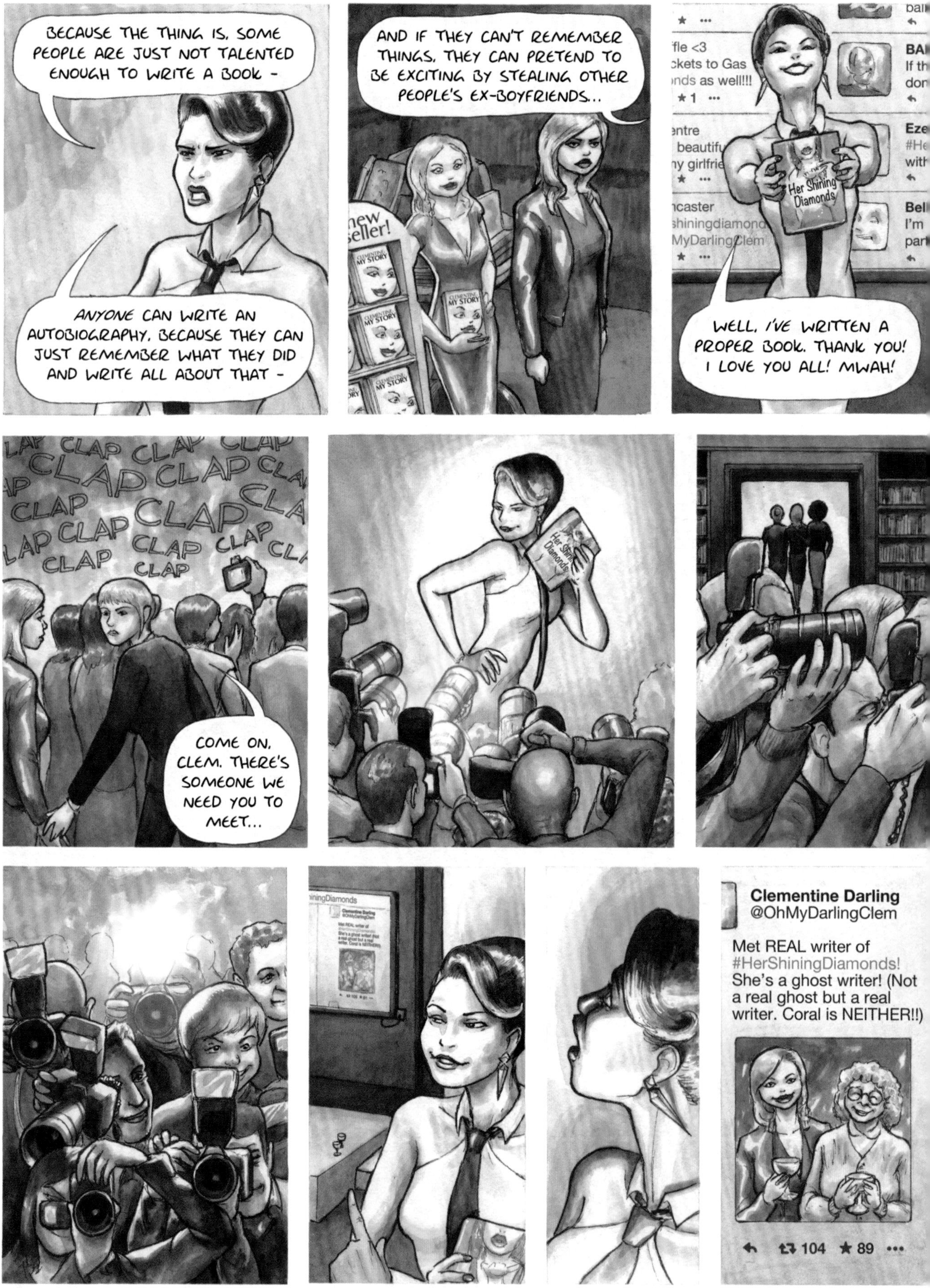

BECAUSE THE THING IS, SOME PEOPLE ARE JUST NOT TALENTED ENOUGH TO WRITE A BOOK -
ANYONE CAN WRITE AN AUTOBIOGRAPHY, BECAUSE THEY CAN JUST REMEMBER WHAT THEY DID AND WRITE ALL ABOUT THAT -
AND IF THEY CAN'T REMEMBER THINGS, THEY CAN PRETEND TO BE EXCITING BY STEALING OTHER PEOPLE'S EX-BOYFRIENDS...
new seller!
CLEMENTINE MY STORY
Her Shining Diamonds
WELL, I'VE WRITTEN A PROPER BOOK. THANK YOU! I LOVE YOU ALL! MWAH!
CLAP CLAP CLAP CLAP CLAP CLAP CLAP CLAP CLAP CLAP CLAP CLAP CLAP CLAP CLAP
COME ON, CLEM. THERE'S SOMEONE WE NEED YOU TO MEET...
Her Shining Diamonds
Clementine Darling
@OhMyDarlingClem
Met REAL writer of #HerShiningDiamonds! She's a ghost writer! (Not a real ghost but a real writer. Coral is NEITHER!!)
104
89

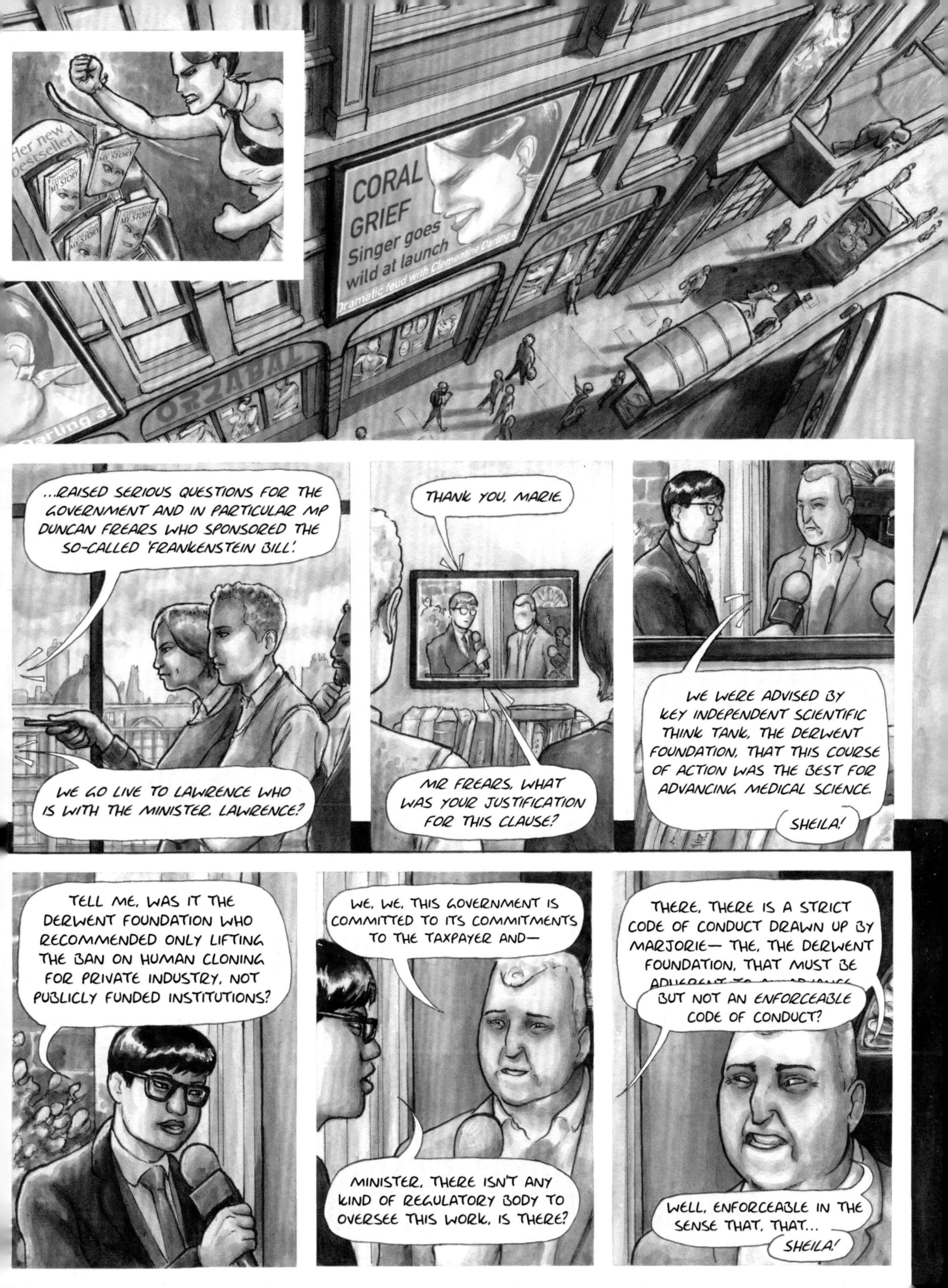
Her new bestseller!
CLEMENTINE MY STORY
CORAL GRIEF
Singer goes wild at launch
ORZABAL
...RAISED SERIOUS QUESTIONS FOR THE GOVERNMENT AND IN PARTICULAR MP DUNCAN FREARS WHO SPONSORED THE SO-CALLED 'FRANKENSTEIN BILL'.
WE GO LIVE TO LAWRENCE WHO IS WITH THE MINISTER. LAWRENCE?
THANK YOU, MARIE.
MR FREARS, WHAT WAS YOUR JUSTIFICATION FOR THIS CLAUSE?
WE WERE ADVISED BY KEY INDEPENDENT SCIENTIFIC THINK TANK, THE DERWENT FOUNDATION, THAT THIS COURSE OF ACTION WAS THE BEST FOR ADVANCING MEDICAL SCIENCE.
SHEILA!
TELL ME, WAS IT THE DERWENT FOUNDATION WHO RECOMMENDED ONLY LIFTING THE BAN ON HUMAN CLONING FOR PRIVATE INDUSTRY, NOT PUBLICLY FUNDED INSTITUTIONS?
WE, WE, THIS GOVERNMENT IS COMMITTED TO ITS COMMITMENTS TO THE TAXPAYER AND—
MINISTER, THERE ISN'T ANY KIND OF REGULATORY BODY TO OVERSEE THIS WORK, IS THERE?
THERE, THERE IS A STRICT CODE OF CONDUCT DRAWN UP BY MARJORIE— THE, THE DERWENT FOUNDATION, THAT MUST BE
BUT NOT AN ENFORCEABLE CODE OF CONDUCT?
WELL, ENFORCEABLE IN THE SENSE THAT, THAT...
SHEILA!

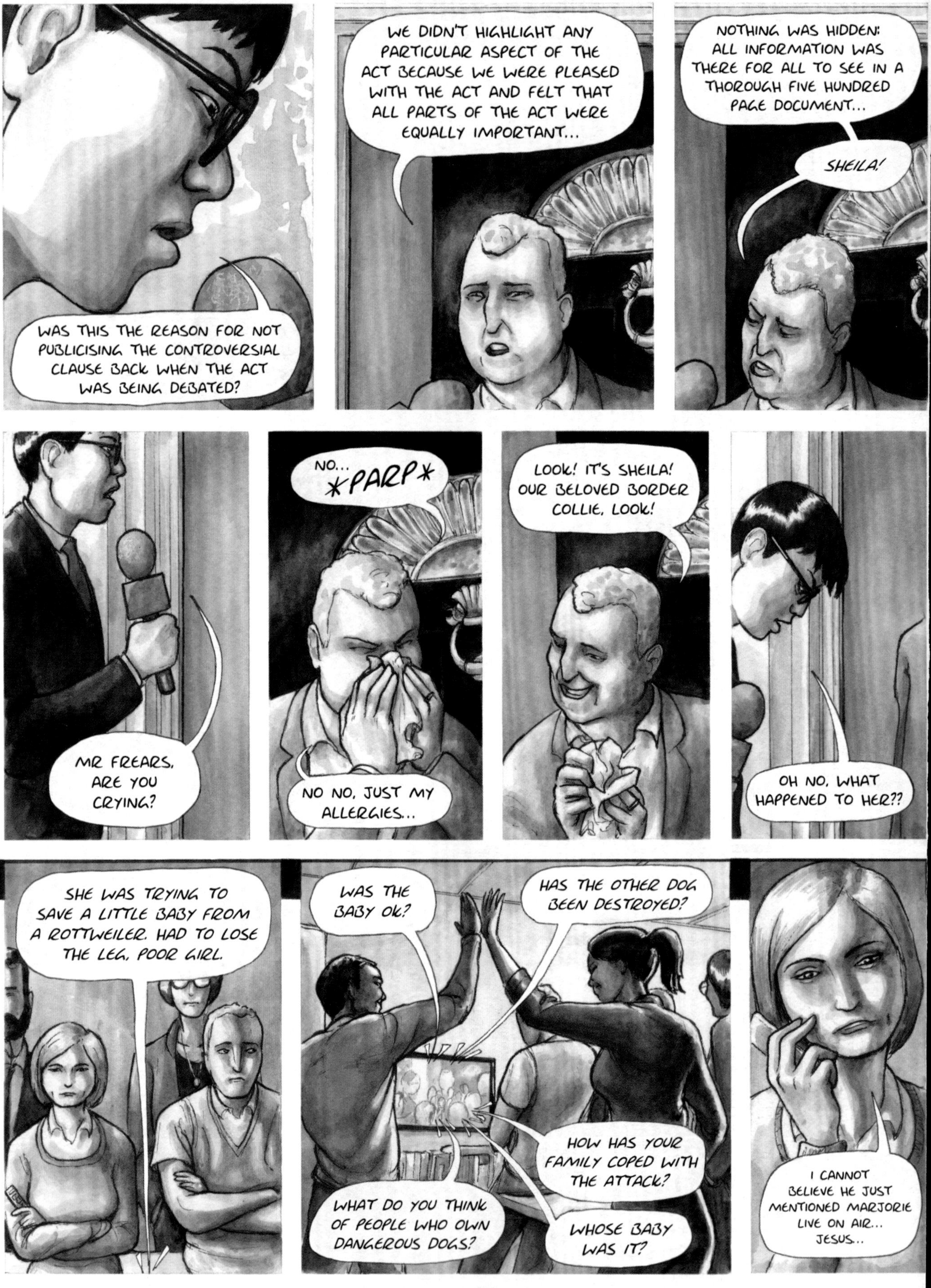
WAS THIS THE REASON FOR NOT PUBLICISING THE CONTROVERSIAL CLAUSE BACK WHEN THE ACT WAS BEING DEBATED?
WE DIDN'T HIGHLIGHT ANY PARTICULAR ASPECT OF THE ACT BECAUSE WE WERE PLEASED WITH THE ACT AND FELT THAT ALL PARTS OF THE ACT WERE EQUALLY IMPORTANT...
NOTHING WAS HIDDEN: ALL INFORMATION WAS THERE FOR ALL TO SEE IN A THOROUGH FIVE HUNDRED PAGE DOCUMENT...
SHEILA!
MR FREARS, ARE YOU CRYING?
NO... *PARP*
NO NO, JUST MY ALLERGIES...
LOOK! IT'S SHEILA! OUR BELOVED BORDER COLLIE, LOOK!
OH NO, WHAT HAPPENED TO HER??
SHE WAS TRYING TO SAVE A LITTLE BABY FROM A ROTTWEILER. HAD TO LOSE THE LEG, POOR GIRL.
WAS THE BABY OK?
HAS THE OTHER DOG BEEN DESTROYED?
HOW HAS YOUR FAMILY COPED WITH THE ATTACK?
WHAT DO YOU THINK OF PEOPLE WHO OWN DANGEROUS DOGS?
WHOSE BABY WAS IT?
I CANNOT BELIEVE HE JUST MENTIONED MARJORIE LIVE ON AIR... JESUS...

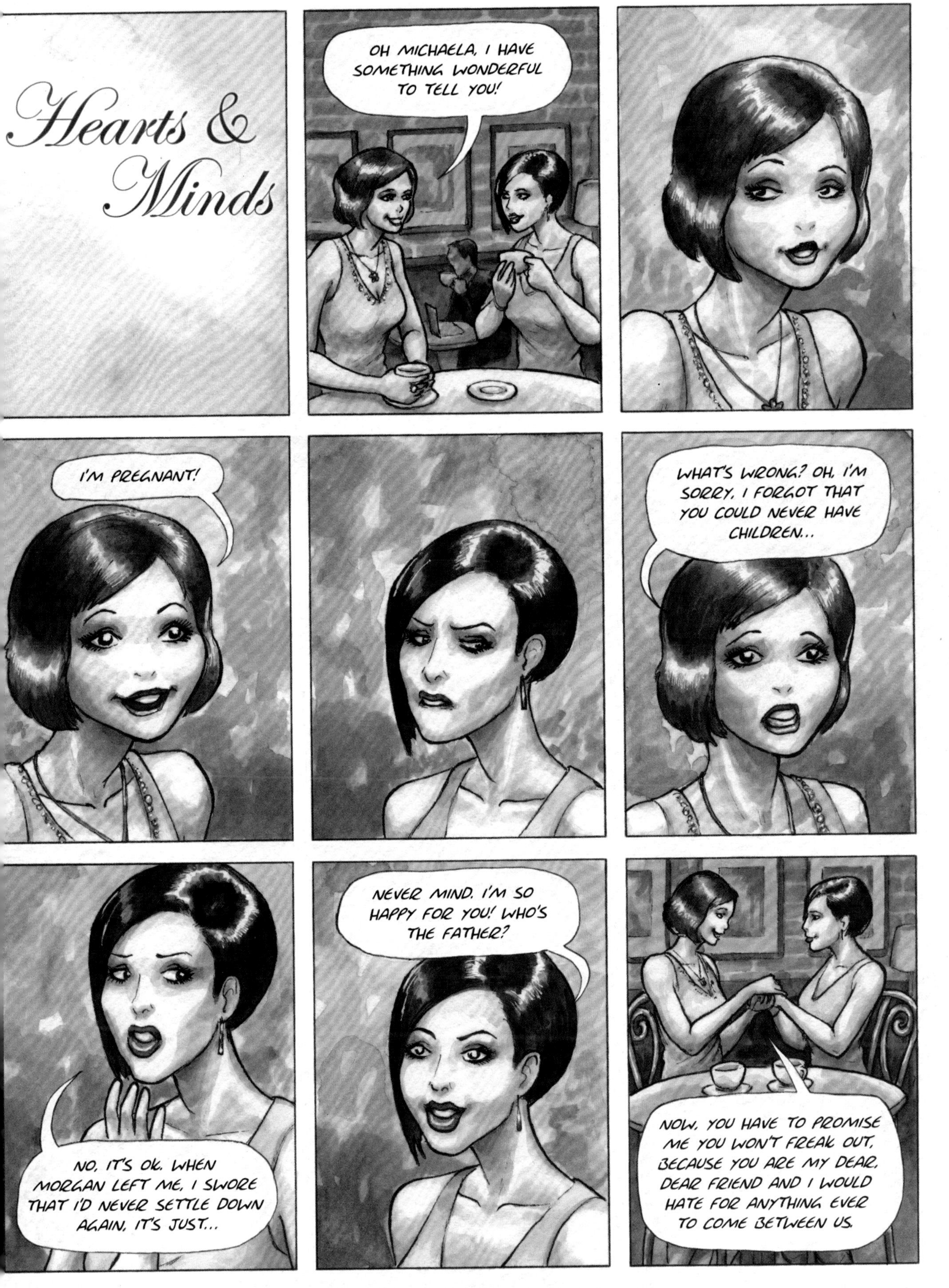
Hearts & Minds
OH MICHAELA, I HAVE SOMETHING WONDERFUL TO TELL YOU!
I'M PREGNANT!
WHAT'S WRONG? OH, I'M SORRY, I FORGOT THAT YOU COULD NEVER HAVE CHILDREN...
NO, IT'S OK. WHEN MORGAN LEFT ME, I SWORE THAT I'D NEVER SETTLE DOWN AGAIN, IT'S JUST...
NEVER MIND. I'M SO HAPPY FOR YOU! WHO'S THE FATHER?
NOW, YOU HAVE TO PROMISE ME YOU WON'T FREAK OUT, BECAUSE YOU ARE MY DEAR, DEAR FRIEND AND I WOULD HATE FOR ANYTHING EVER TO COME BETWEEN US.

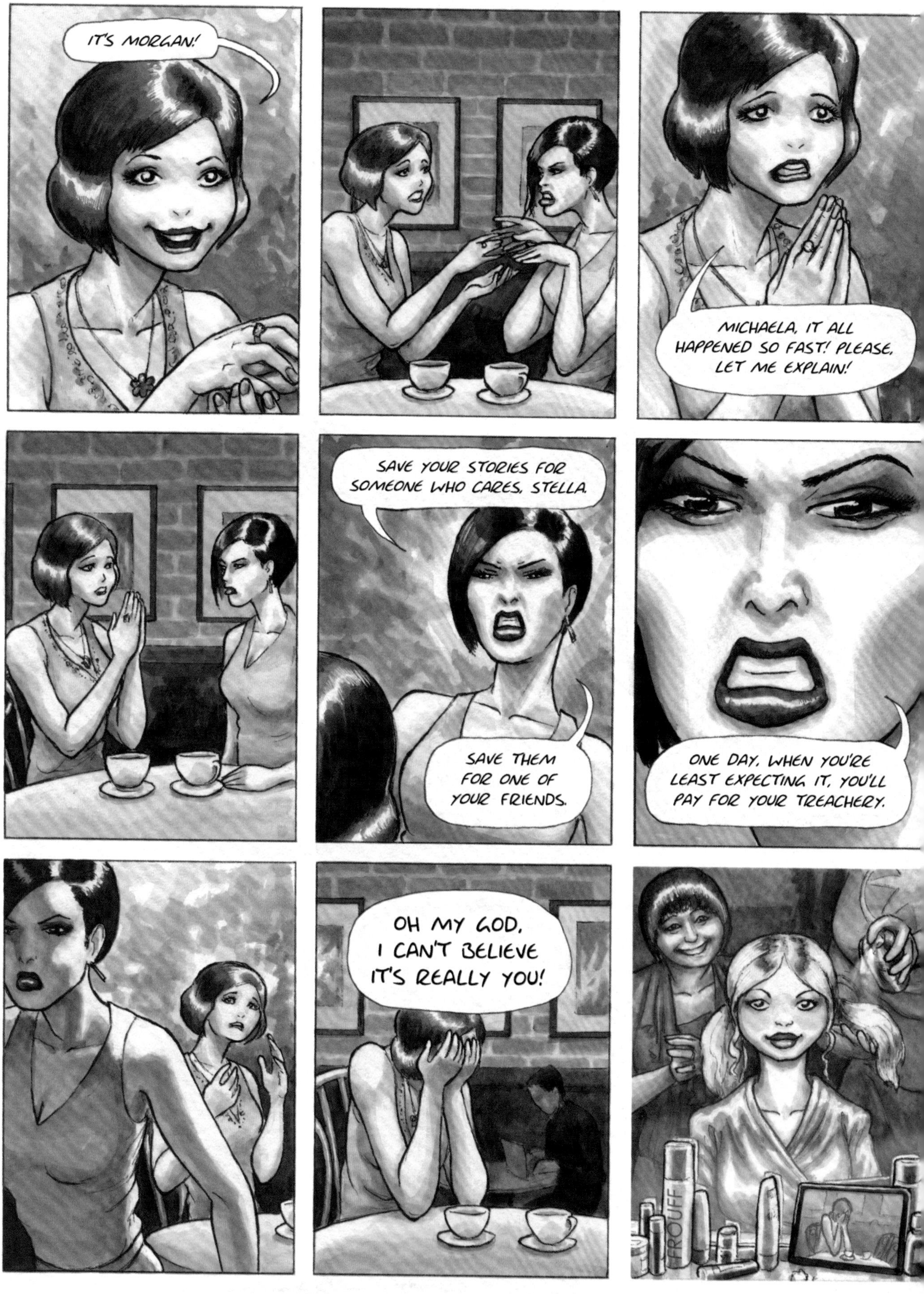
IT'S MORGAN!
MICHAELA, IT ALL HAPPENED SO FAST! PLEASE, LET ME EXPLAIN!
SAVE YOUR STORIES FOR SOMEONE WHO CARES, STELLA.
SAVE THEM FOR ONE OF YOUR FRIENDS.
ONE DAY, WHEN YOU'RE LEAST EXPECTING IT, YOU'LL PAY FOR YOUR TREACHERY.
OH MY GOD, I CAN'T BELIEVE IT'S REALLY YOU!
FROUFF

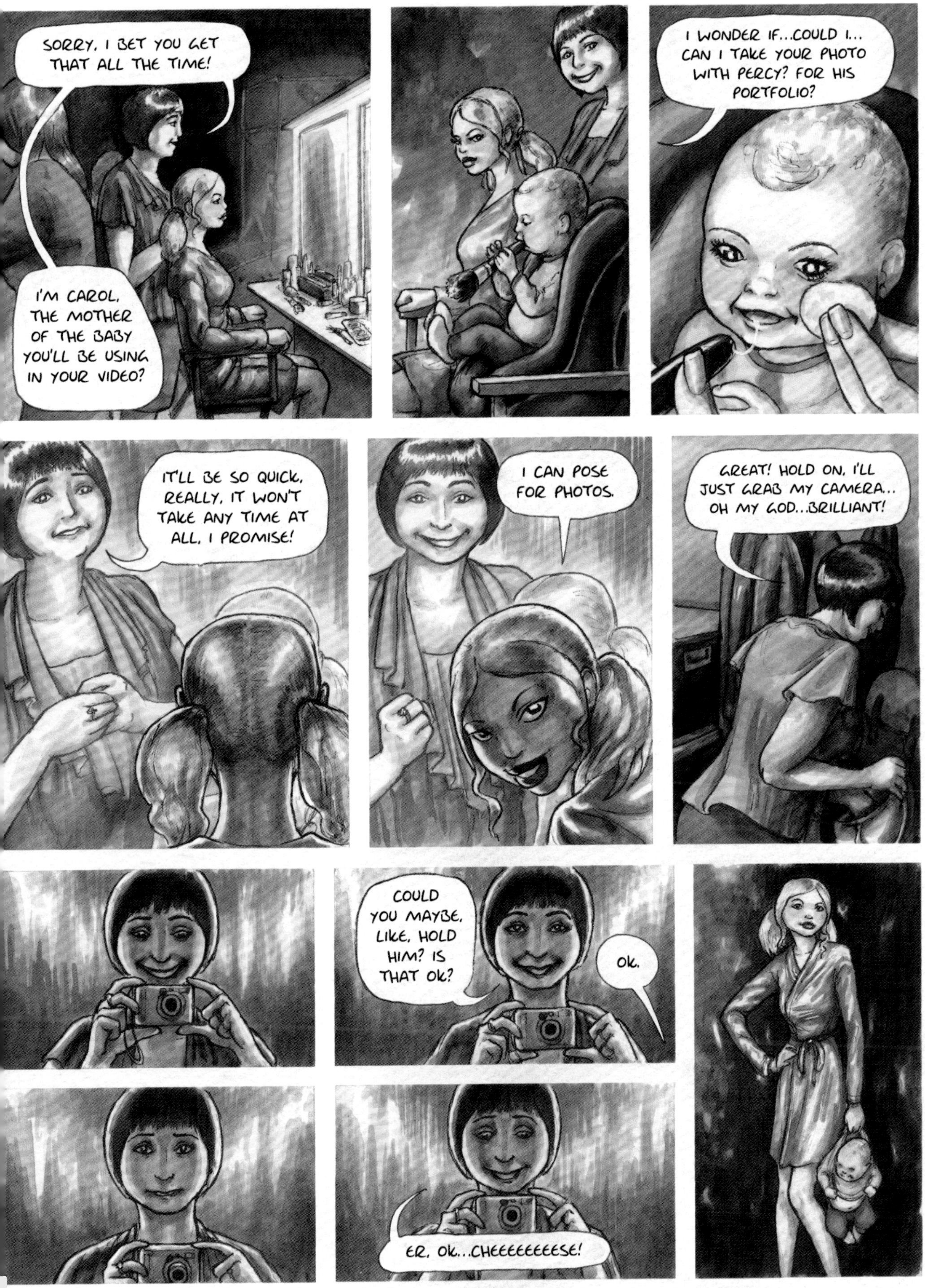
SORRY, I BET YOU GET THAT ALL THE TIME!
I'M CAROL, THE MOTHER OF THE BABY YOU'LL BE USING IN YOUR VIDEO?
I WONDER IF...COULD I... CAN I TAKE YOUR PHOTO WITH PERCY? FOR HIS PORTFOLIO?
IT'LL BE SO QUICK, REALLY, IT WON'T TAKE ANY TIME AT ALL, I PROMISE!
I CAN POSE FOR PHOTOS.
GREAT! HOLD ON, I'LL JUST GRAB MY CAMERA... OH MY GOD...BRILLIANT!
COULD YOU MAYBE, LIKE, HOLD HIM? IS THAT OK?
OK.
ER, OK...CHEEEEEEEEESE!

CLEM! THEY'RE READY FOR YOU!

"GOOD GIRL"
CLEMENTINE DARLING
ROURKE PRODUCTIONS

It's a bad, bad world
I can see here from your arms

There are bad, bad girls with their charms
Trying to break us with their charms

There are bad, bad men
Who hate on what we do

And do bad, bad when

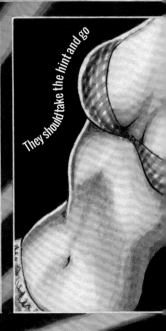

They should take the hint and go

They wanna break us up, shake us up, mess us, try to wake us up

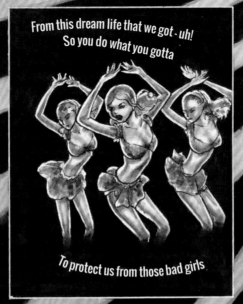

From this dream life that we got - uh!
So you do what you gotta

To protect us from those bad girls

Just remember I'm your good girl!

Take care of all those bad boys

Remember you're my good boy!

I don't care how you deal with it

I know it's for our benefit

Do what it takes to end this threat

And I'll be your good girl forever!

I'll be good to you forever

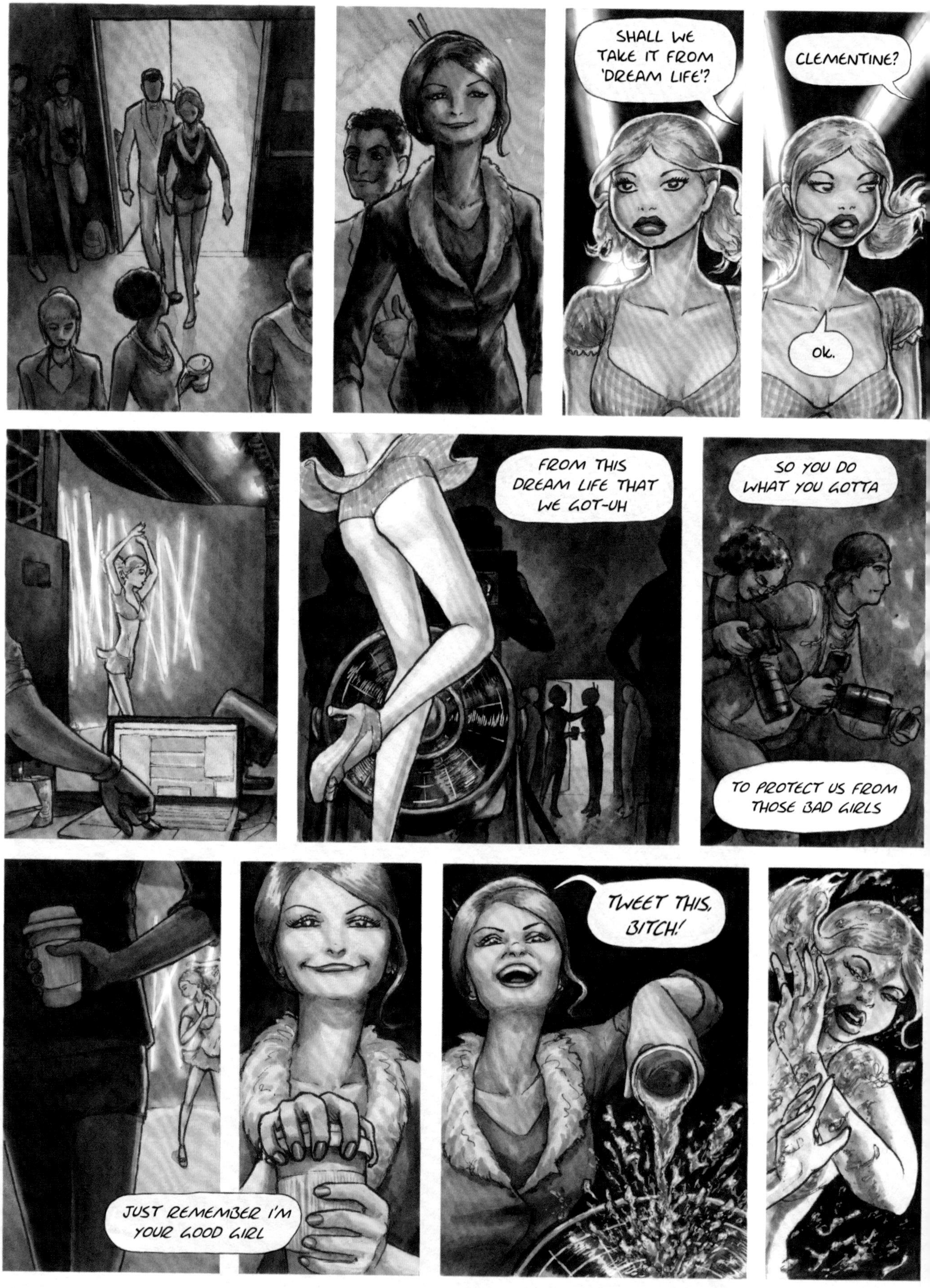
SHALL WE TAKE IT FROM 'DREAM LIFE'?
CLEMENTINE?
OK.
FROM THIS DREAM LIFE THAT WE GOT-UH
SO YOU DO WHAT YOU GOTTA
TO PROTECT US FROM THOSE BAD GIRLS
JUST REMEMBER I'M YOUR GOOD GIRL
TWEET THIS, BITCH!

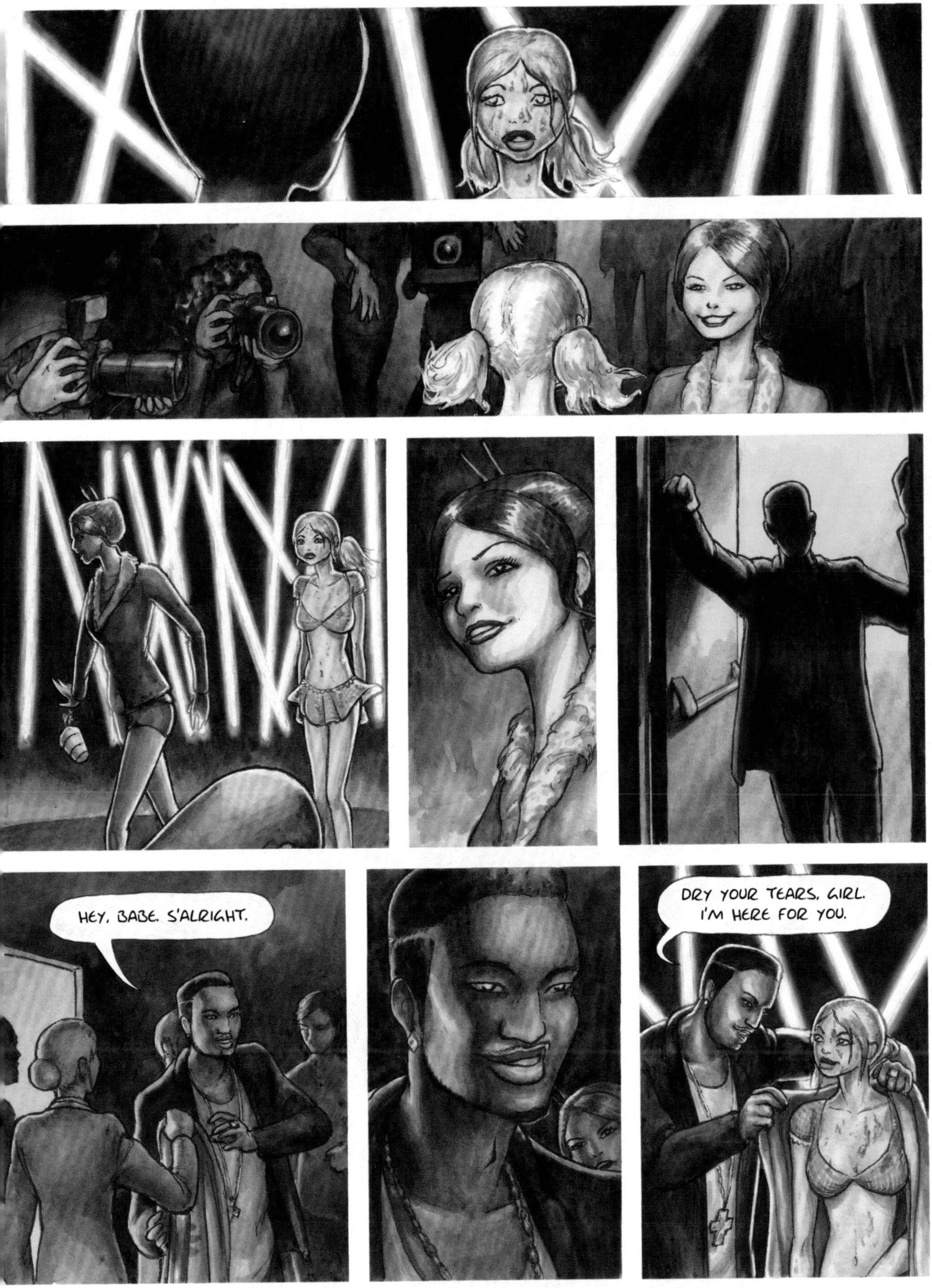
HEY, BABE. S'ALRIGHT.
DRY YOUR TEARS, GIRL. I'M HERE FOR YOU.

GENEVIEVRE

the
lighter
touch

REJUVENISE
RETALIASE
REVITALUX

GENEVIEVRE

CRÈME

MURDER ON THE DANCEFLOOR
Bitter love rival Coral seeks revenge on set of Clementine's latest music video over relationship with Devon Ayre as dramatic love triangle heats up

💬 446 comments

TEARS FOR FREARS
Emotional minister tells the heartbreaking story of one dog and her act of heroism against an 'unstoppable monster'

💬 96 comments

WHAT IS THE NEW HUMAN RIGHTS ACT ALL ABOUT?
In this terrifying new age, how proposed amendments to an outdated law will help us all live in safety and security

PROOF THAT BAD SKINCARE CAN MAKE YOU FAT: a new study finds link between using the wrong skin products and obesity

BAD GAS: singer Nina Malick labelled 'unpatriotic and pathetic' after refusing call to perform at Gas Aid concert

BRITISH PRIDE DAY: as plans are being drawn up to promote 'Britishness', find out what's happening right on your doorstep

SQUIRRELGEDDON: meet the woman who

GENEV

the
ligh
tou

REJUVEN
RETALIA
REVITAL

GENEVIE

CRÈM

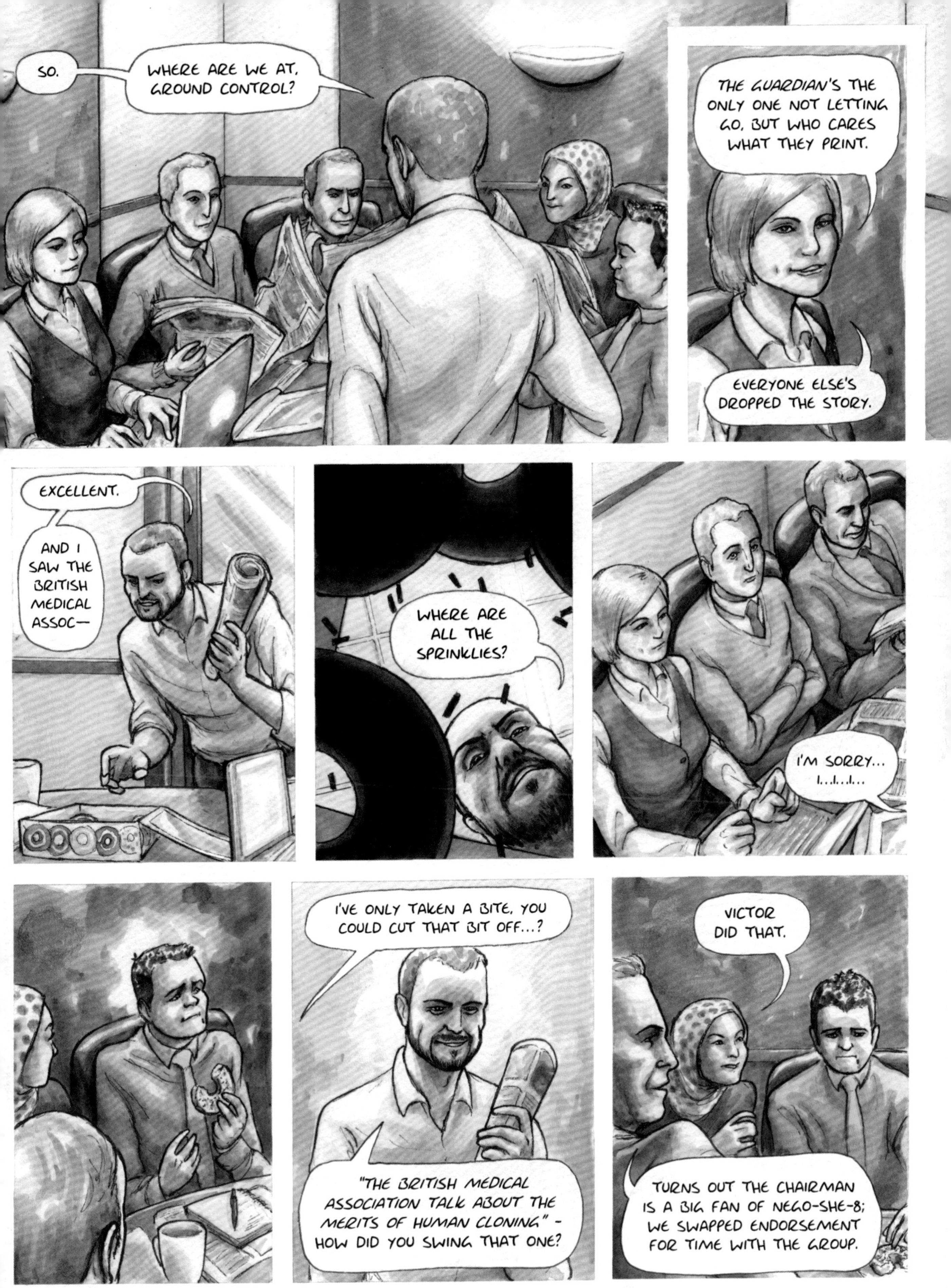
SO.
WHERE ARE WE AT, GROUND CONTROL?
THE GUARDIAN'S THE ONLY ONE NOT LETTING GO, BUT WHO CARES WHAT THEY PRINT.
EVERYONE ELSE'S DROPPED THE STORY.
EXCELLENT.
AND I SAW THE BRITISH MEDICAL ASSOC—
WHERE ARE ALL THE SPRINKLIES?
I'M SORRY... I...I...I...
I'VE ONLY TAKEN A BITE, YOU COULD CUT THAT BIT OFF...?
"THE BRITISH MEDICAL ASSOCIATION TALK ABOUT THE MERITS OF HUMAN CLONING" - HOW DID YOU SWING THAT ONE?
VICTOR DID THAT.
TURNS OUT THE CHAIRMAN IS A BIG FAN OF NEGO-SHE-8; WE SWAPPED ENDORSEMENT FOR TIME WITH THE GROUP.

SO THE PRINT HEADLINES?

ALL TAKEN UP WITH THE CORAL/CLEMENTINE FEUD.

GOOD, GOOD.

WHAT ARE YOU DOING?

IF YOU TAKE THE LAST SPRINKLIE, YOU HAVE TO EAT IT.

EAT

IT

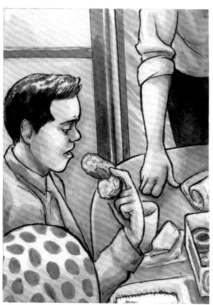

I'VE HAD MARJORIE ON THE PHONE.

THEY'RE CONCERNED THAT THE MINISTER MENTIONED THEM ON LIVE TV. SHOULD THEY BE CONCERNED?

NO ONE SEEMS TO HAVE PICKED UP ON IT...

GOOD. KEEP AN EYE ON SOCIAL ENGINEERING, JUST IN CASE.

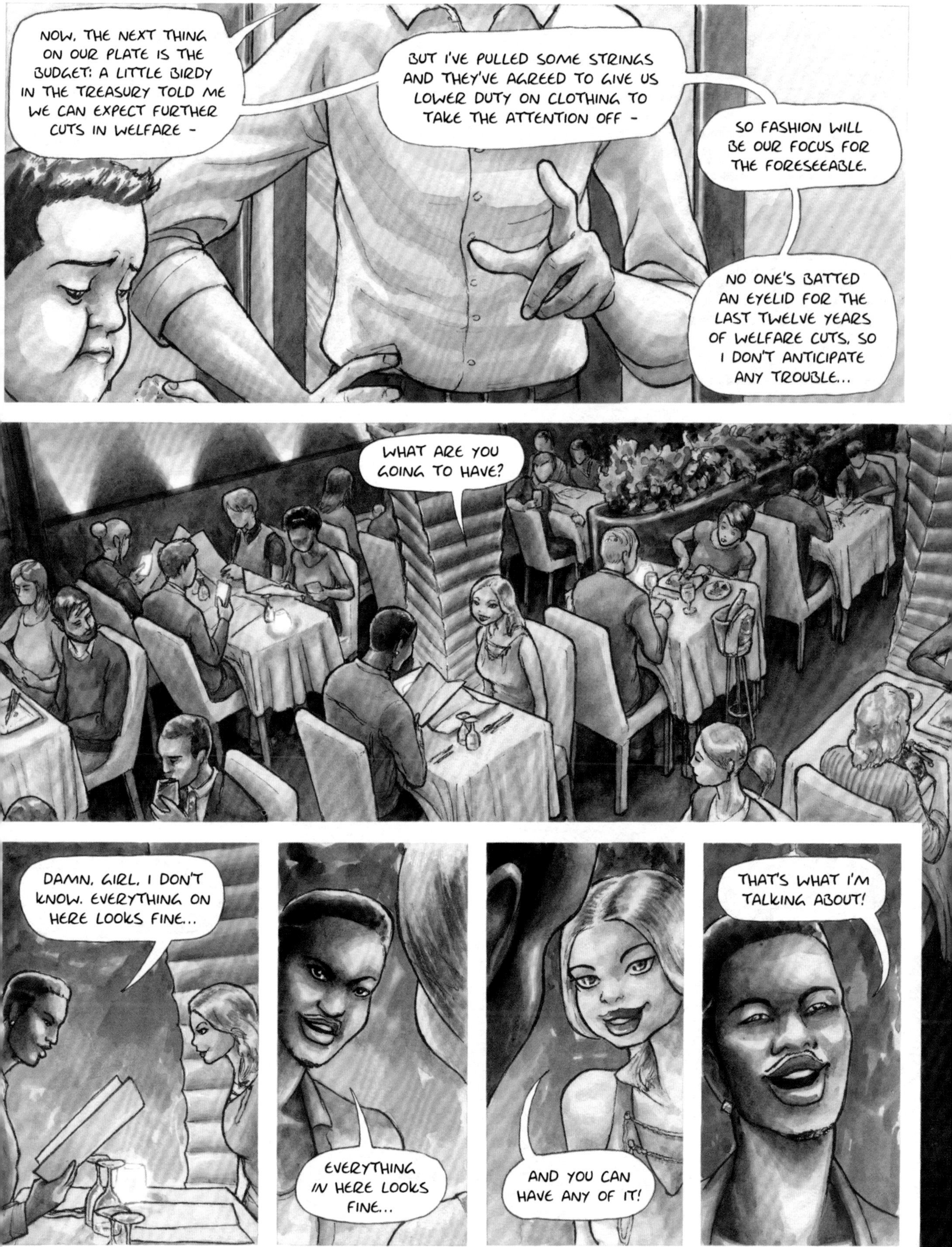
NOW, THE NEXT THING ON OUR PLATE IS THE BUDGET: A LITTLE BIRDY IN THE TREASURY TOLD ME WE CAN EXPECT FURTHER CUTS IN WELFARE -
BUT I'VE PULLED SOME STRINGS AND THEY'VE AGREED TO GIVE US LOWER DUTY ON CLOTHING TO TAKE THE ATTENTION OFF -
SO FASHION WILL BE OUR FOCUS FOR THE FORESEEABLE.
NO ONE'S BATTED AN EYELID FOR THE LAST TWELVE YEARS OF WELFARE CUTS, SO I DON'T ANTICIPATE ANY TROUBLE...
WHAT ARE YOU GOING TO HAVE?
DAMN, GIRL, I DON'T KNOW. EVERYTHING ON HERE LOOKS FINE...
EVERYTHING IN HERE LOOKS FINE...
AND YOU CAN HAVE ANY OF IT!
THAT'S WHAT I'M TALKING ABOUT!

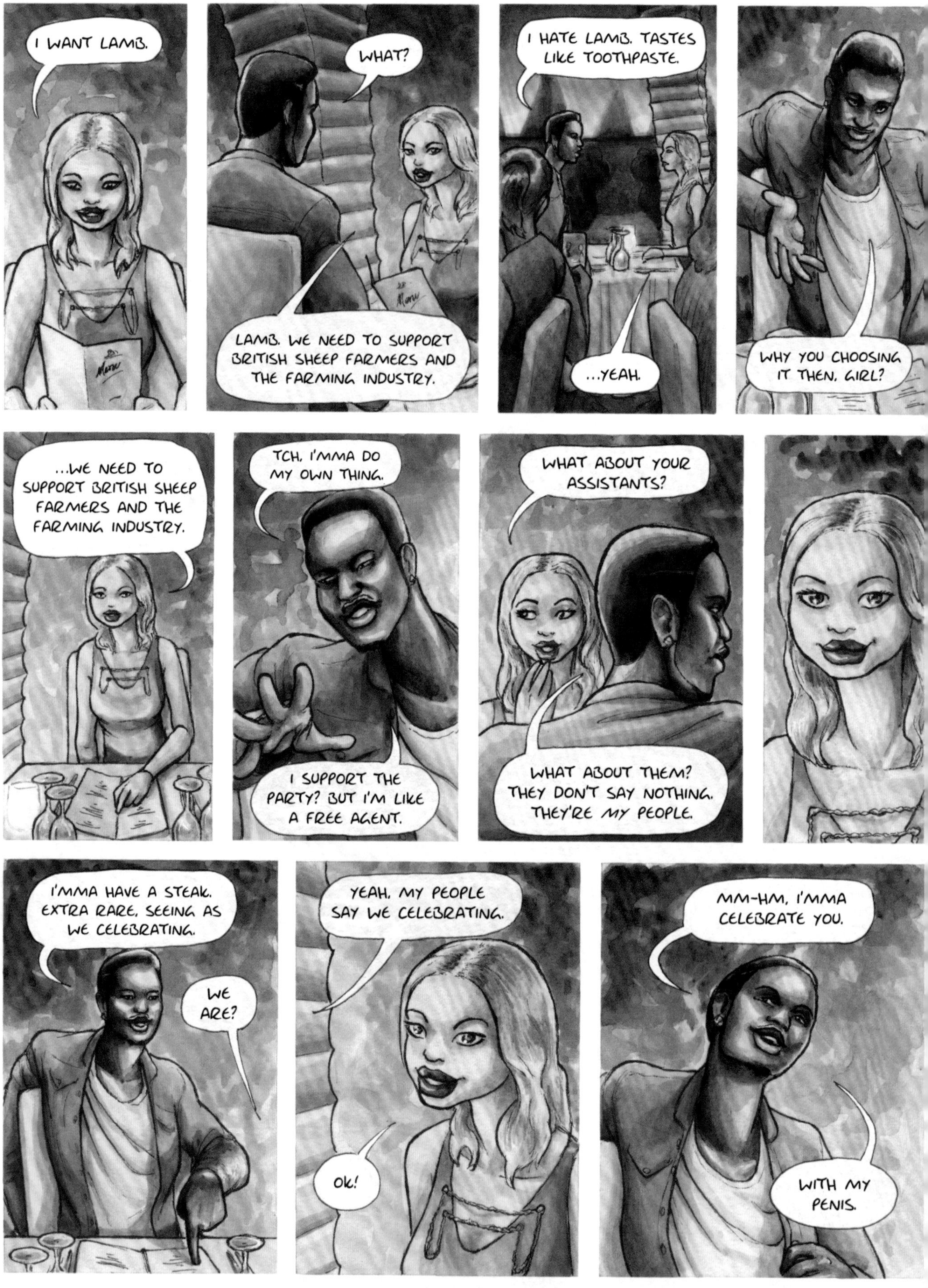
I WANT LAMB.
WHAT?
LAMB. WE NEED TO SUPPORT BRITISH SHEEP FARMERS AND THE FARMING INDUSTRY.
I HATE LAMB. TASTES LIKE TOOTHPASTE.
...YEAH.
WHY YOU CHOOSING IT THEN, GIRL?
...WE NEED TO SUPPORT BRITISH SHEEP FARMERS AND THE FARMING INDUSTRY.
TCH, I'MMA DO MY OWN THING.
I SUPPORT THE PARTY? BUT I'M LIKE A FREE AGENT.
WHAT ABOUT YOUR ASSISTANTS?
WHAT ABOUT THEM? THEY DON'T SAY NOTHING. THEY'RE MY PEOPLE.
I'MMA HAVE A STEAK. EXTRA RARE, SEEING AS WE CELEBRATING.
WE ARE?
YEAH, MY PEOPLE SAY WE CELEBRATING.
OK!
MM-HM, I'MMA CELEBRATE YOU.
WITH MY PENIS.

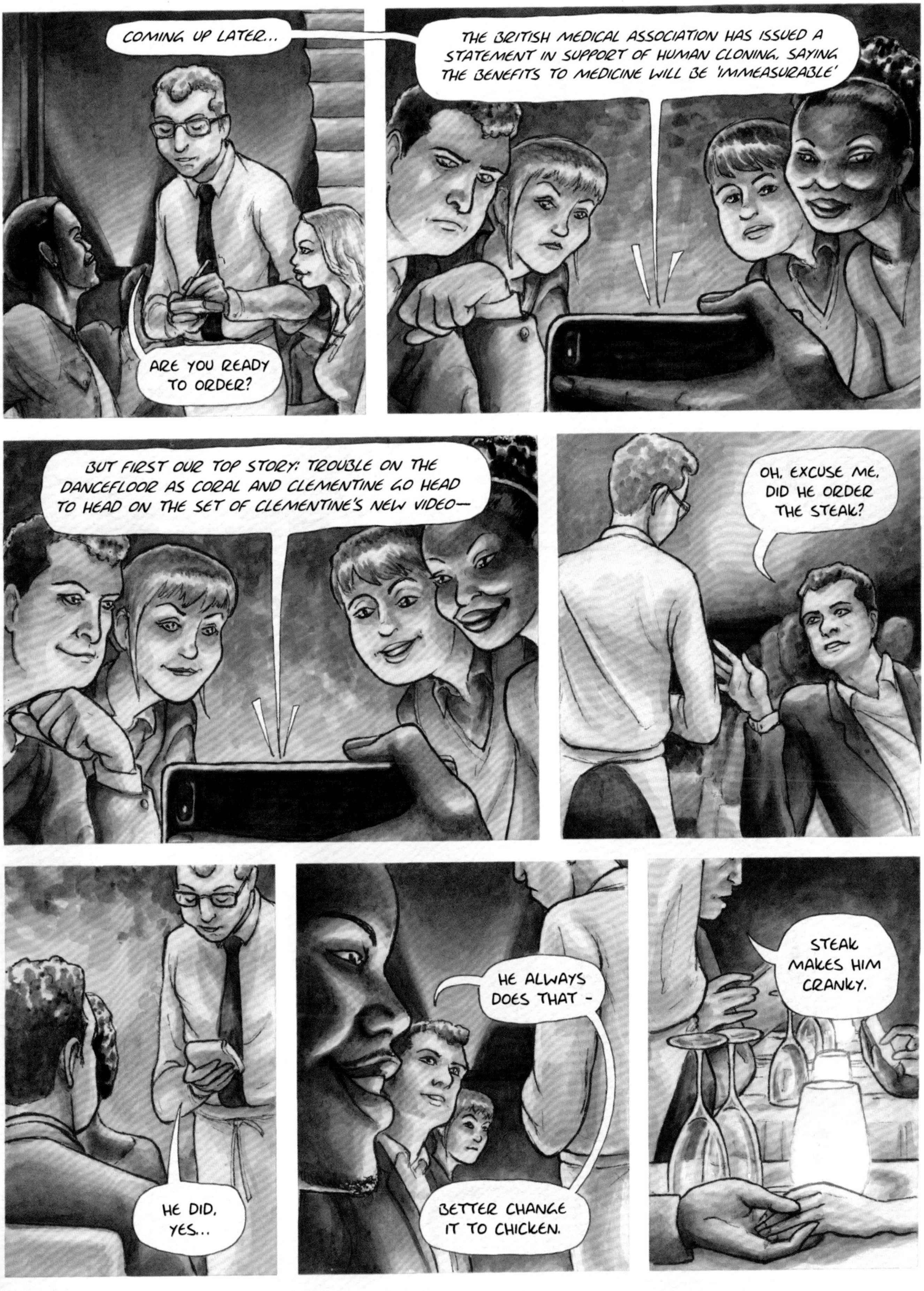
COMING UP LATER...
ARE YOU READY TO ORDER?
THE BRITISH MEDICAL ASSOCIATION HAS ISSUED A STATEMENT IN SUPPORT OF HUMAN CLONING, SAYING THE BENEFITS TO MEDICINE WILL BE 'IMMEASURABLE'
BUT FIRST OUR TOP STORY: TROUBLE ON THE DANCEFLOOR AS CORAL AND CLEMENTINE GO HEAD TO HEAD ON THE SET OF CLEMENTINE'S NEW VIDEO—
OH, EXCUSE ME, DID HE ORDER THE STEAK?
HE DID, YES...
HE ALWAYS DOES THAT -
BETTER CHANGE IT TO CHICKEN.
STEAK MAKES HIM CRANKY.

WHAT'S TRENDING

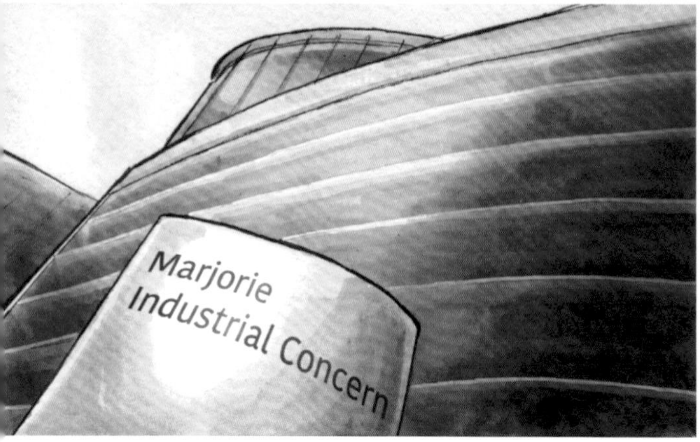

Marjorie Industrial Concern

SECRET MONEY SOURCE UNCOVERED

Derwent Foundation, think tank behind Frankenstein Bill, funded by private scientific research and development giant Marjorie Industrial Concern public interest group finds

129 comments

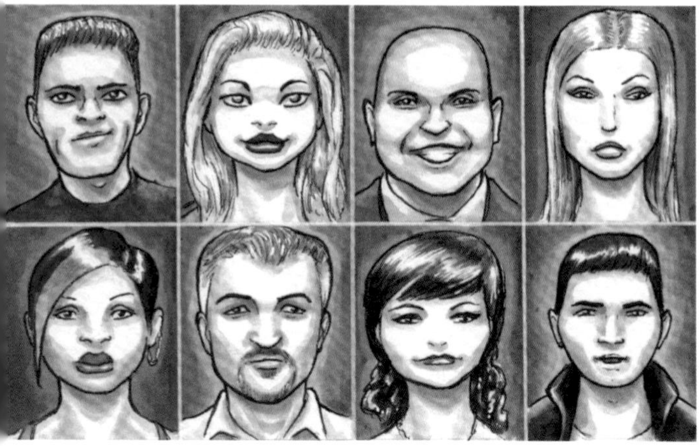

TWAMMY AWARDS

Bookies select their favourites to win big at the prestigious ceremony as speculation reaches fever pitch

303 comments

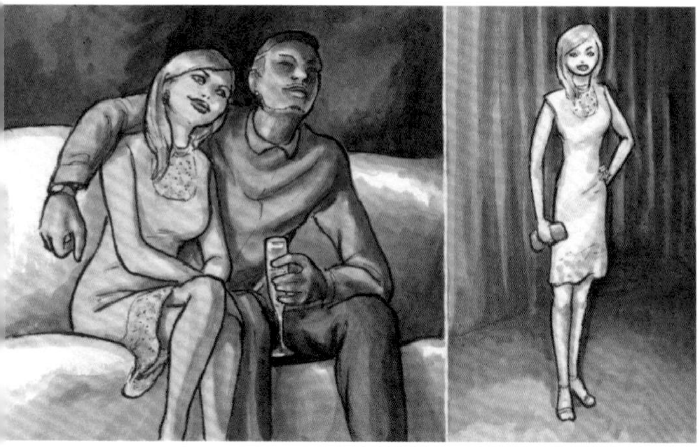

WEDDING BELLS?

Clementine stuns in bridal white on date with Devon - does she know something we don't?

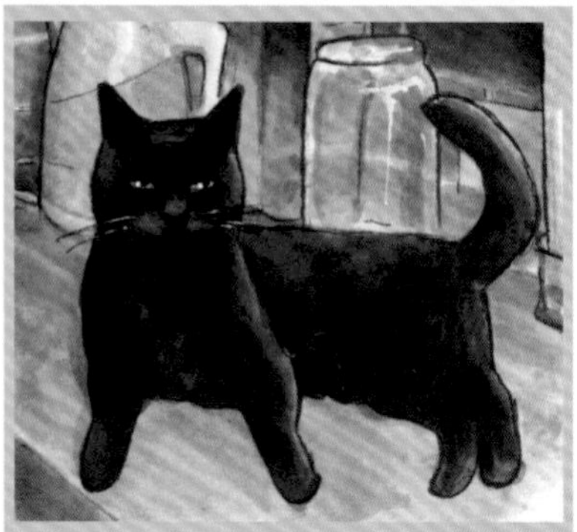

CONVENIENT LIES: the terrorist who we couldn't prosecute...because he had a cat

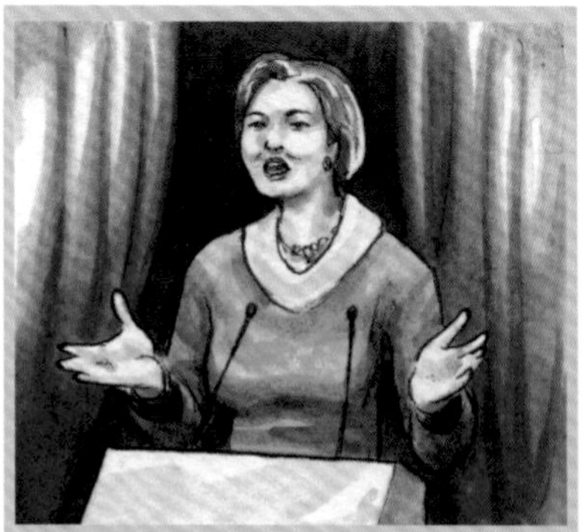

CALAMITY JANE: Chief Commissioner gave important speech to the United Nations while wearing outfit from well-known high-street chain despite £100k salary

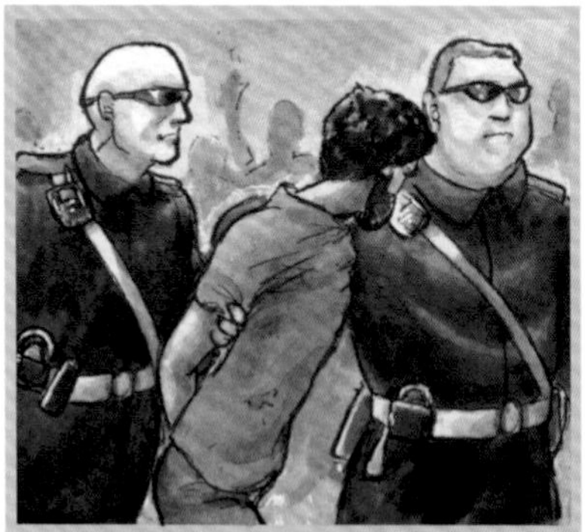

MAKING OUR STREETS 'SAIF'ER: a look at the success of the newly formed Security and Intelligence Force

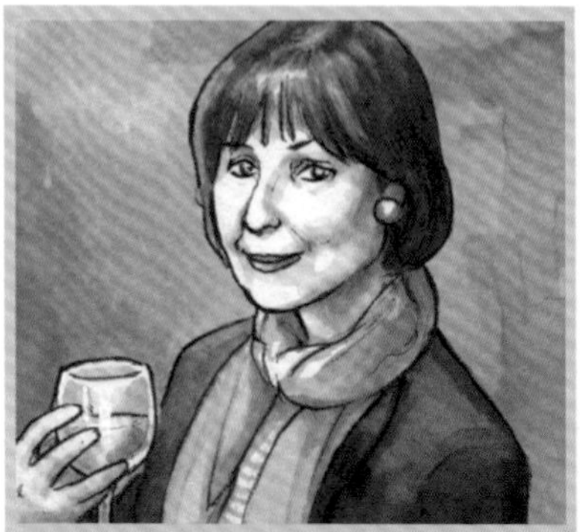

DIRTY LIMERICKS: author delights crowd

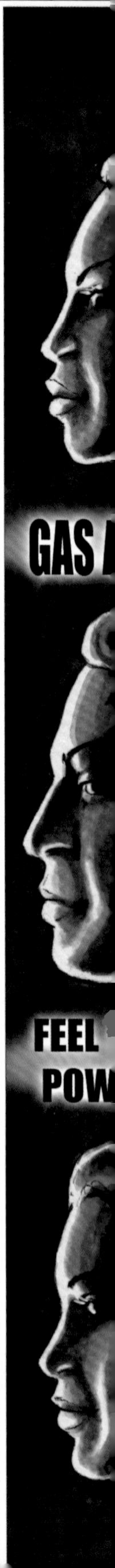

GAS
FEEL
POW

BZZT

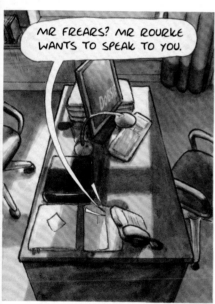

MR FREARS? MR ROURKE WANTS TO SPEAK TO YOU.

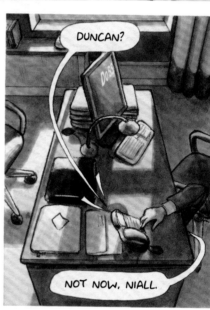

DUNCAN?

NOT NOW, NIALL.

WHAT SHOULD I TELL HIM?

TELL HIM I'M BUSY.

OK...

HE'S VERY INSISTENT THAT HE TALKS TO YOU, THOUGH...

OF COURSE HE WANTS TO TALK TO ME —

HE WANTS TO TALK TO ME LIKE A, A, A VET WANTS TO TALK TO A BLASTED TOMCAT'S TESTICLES!

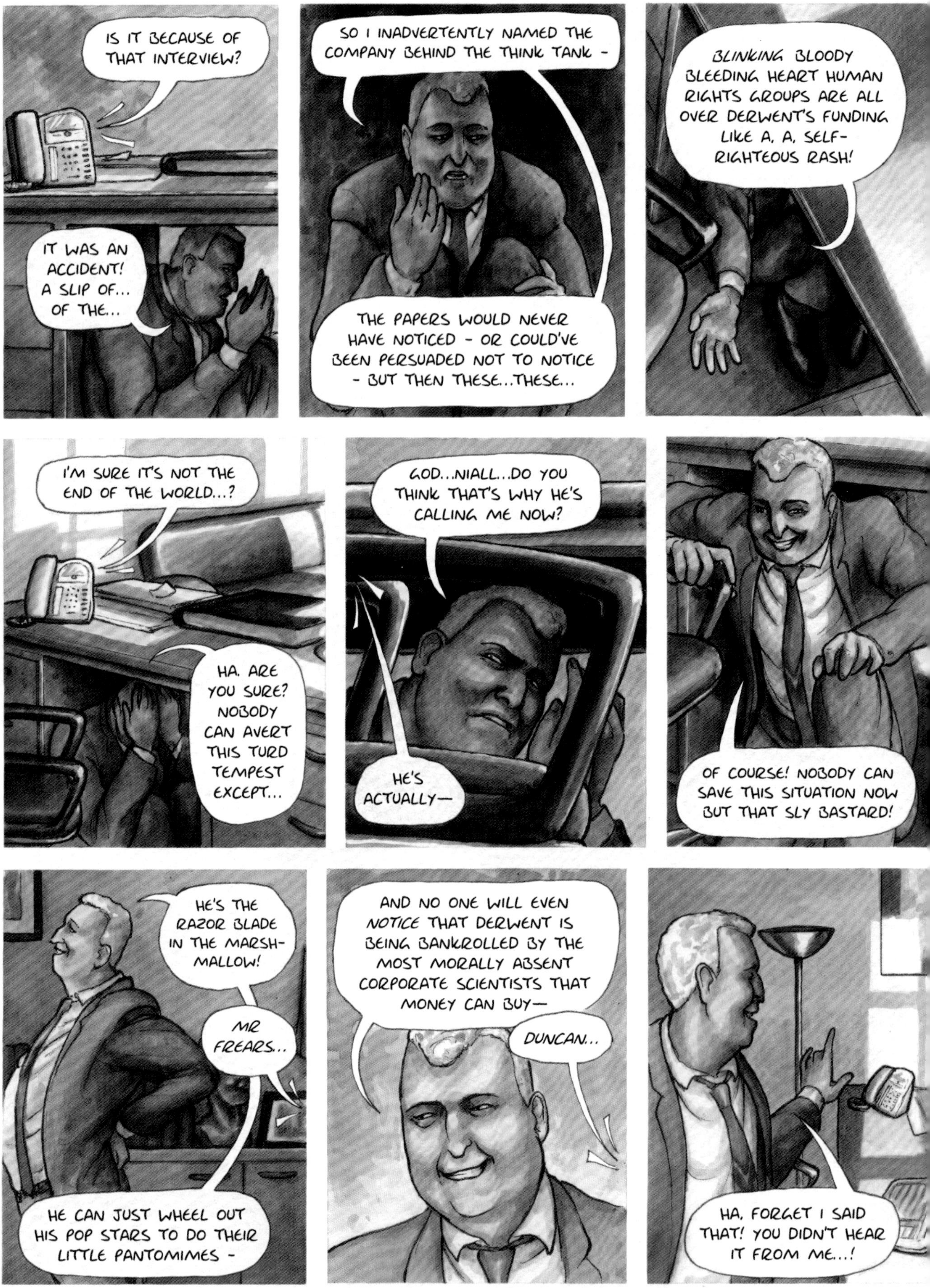
IS IT BECAUSE OF THAT INTERVIEW?
IT WAS AN ACCIDENT! A SLIP OF... OF THE...
SO I INADVERTENTLY NAMED THE COMPANY BEHIND THE THINK TANK -
THE PAPERS WOULD NEVER HAVE NOTICED - OR COULD'VE BEEN PERSUADED NOT TO NOTICE - BUT THEN THESE...THESE...
BLINKING BLOODY BLEEDING HEART HUMAN RIGHTS GROUPS ARE ALL OVER DERWENT'S FUNDING LIKE A, A, SELF-RIGHTEOUS RASH!
I'M SURE IT'S NOT THE END OF THE WORLD...?
HA. ARE YOU SURE? NOBODY CAN AVERT THIS TURD TEMPEST EXCEPT...
GOD...NIALL...DO YOU THINK THAT'S WHY HE'S CALLING ME NOW?
HE'S ACTUALLY—
OF COURSE! NOBODY CAN SAVE THIS SITUATION NOW BUT THAT SLY BASTARD!
HE'S THE RAZOR BLADE IN THE MARSH-MALLOW!
MR FREARS...
HE CAN JUST WHEEL OUT HIS POP STARS TO DO THEIR LITTLE PANTOMIMES -
AND NO ONE WILL EVEN NOTICE THAT DERWENT IS BEING BANKROLLED BY THE MOST MORALLY ABSENT CORPORATE SCIENTISTS THAT MONEY CAN BUY—
DUNCAN...
HA, FORGET I SAID THAT! YOU DIDN'T HEAR IT FROM ME...!

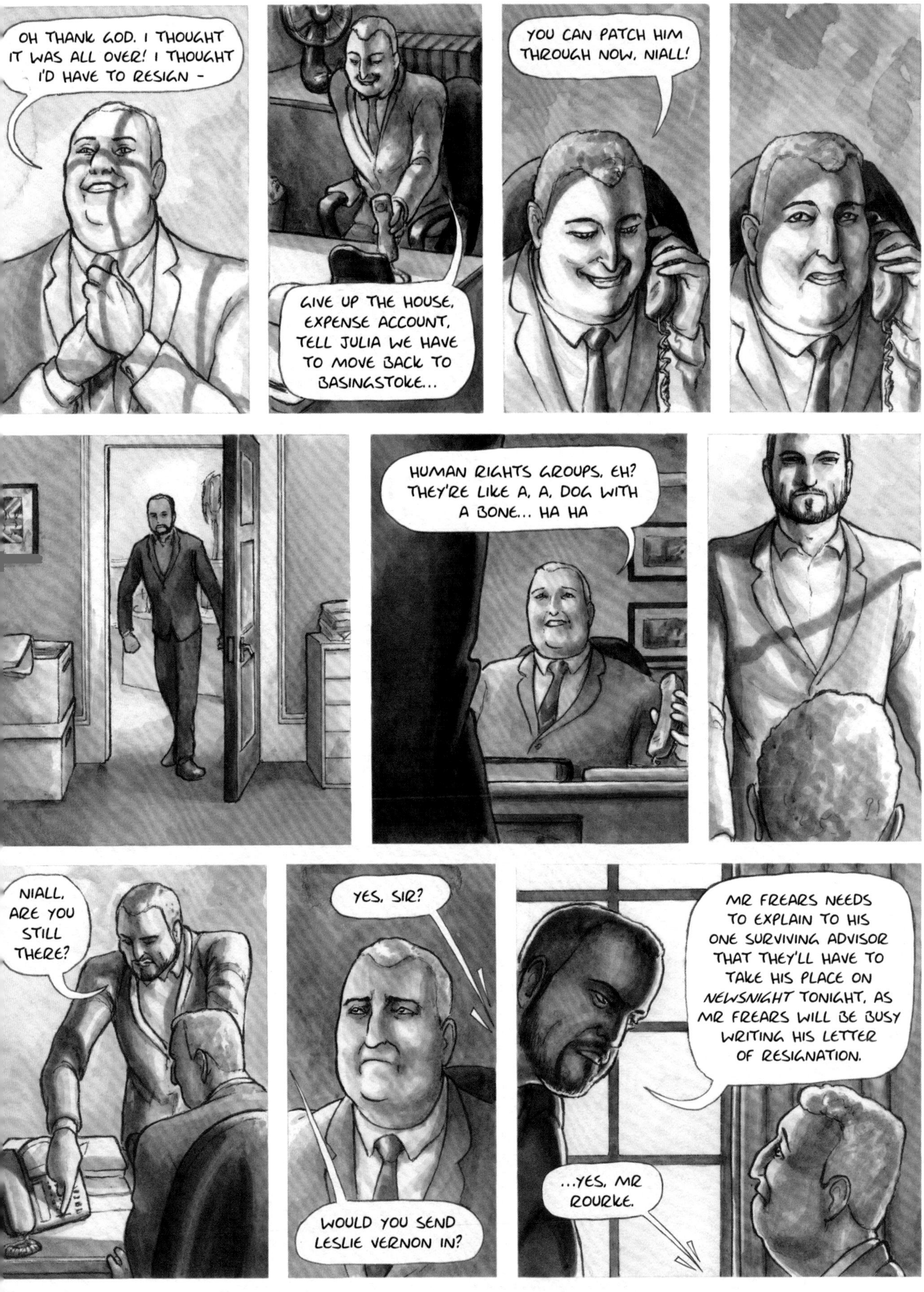

OH THANK GOD. I THOUGHT IT WAS ALL OVER! I THOUGHT I'D HAVE TO RESIGN –
GIVE UP THE HOUSE, EXPENSE ACCOUNT, TELL JULIA WE HAVE TO MOVE BACK TO BASINGSTOKE...
YOU CAN PATCH HIM THROUGH NOW, NIALL!
HUMAN RIGHTS GROUPS, EH? THEY'RE LIKE A, A, DOG WITH A BONE... HA HA
NIALL, ARE YOU STILL THERE?
YES, SIR?
WOULD YOU SEND LESLIE VERNON IN?
MR FREARS NEEDS TO EXPLAIN TO HIS ONE SURVIVING ADVISOR THAT THEY'LL HAVE TO TAKE HIS PLACE ON NEWSNIGHT TONIGHT, AS MR FREARS WILL BE BUSY WRITING HIS LETTER OF RESIGNATION.
...YES, MR ROURKE.

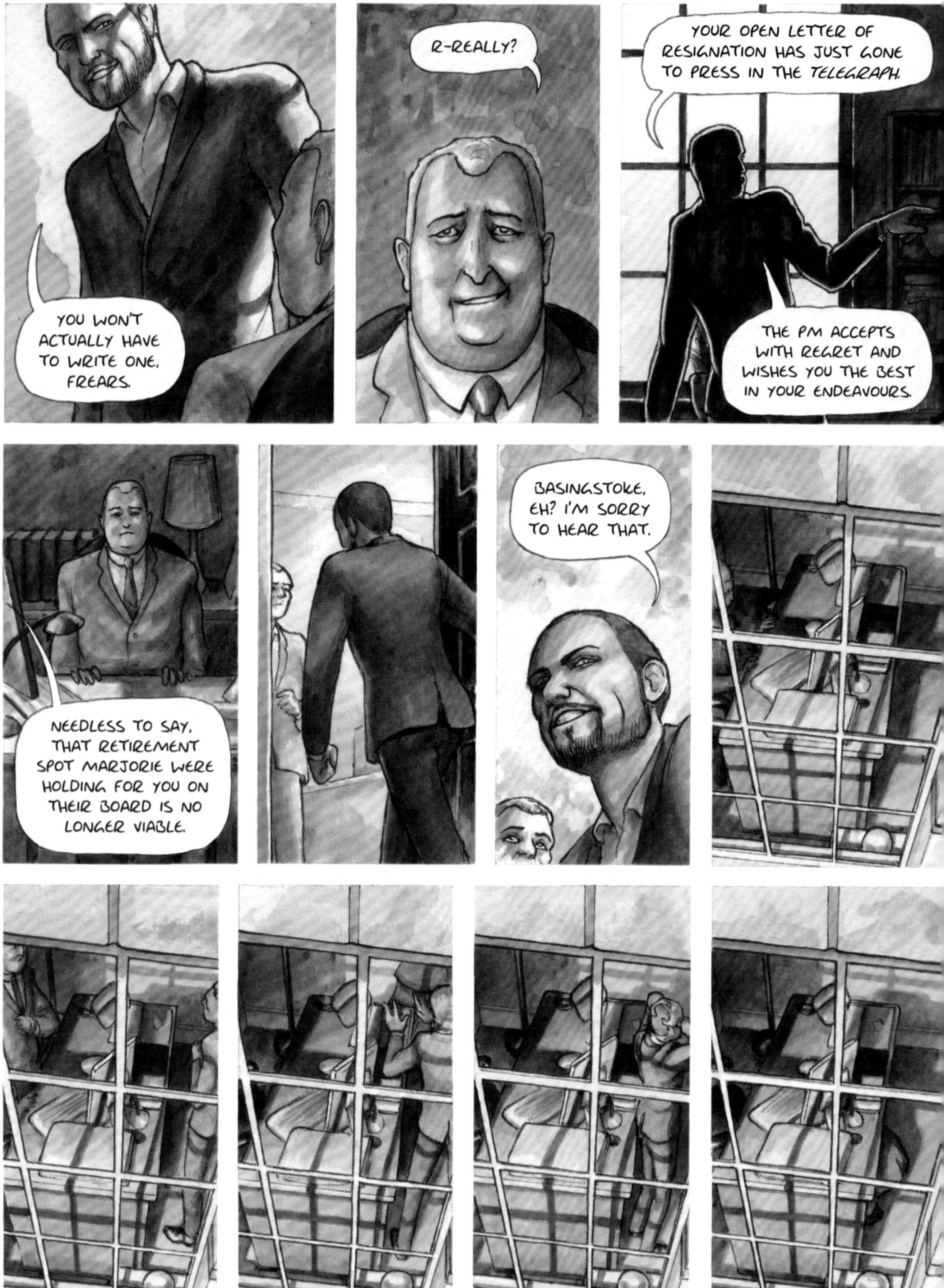
YOU WON'T ACTUALLY HAVE TO WRITE ONE, FREARS.
R-REALLY?
YOUR OPEN LETTER OF RESIGNATION HAS JUST GONE TO PRESS IN THE *TELEGRAPH*.
THE PM ACCEPTS WITH REGRET AND WISHES YOU THE BEST IN YOUR ENDEAVOURS.
NEEDLESS TO SAY, THAT RETIREMENT SPOT MARJORIE WERE HOLDING FOR YOU ON THEIR BOARD IS NO LONGER VIABLE.
BASINGSTOKE, EH? I'M SORRY TO HEAR THAT.

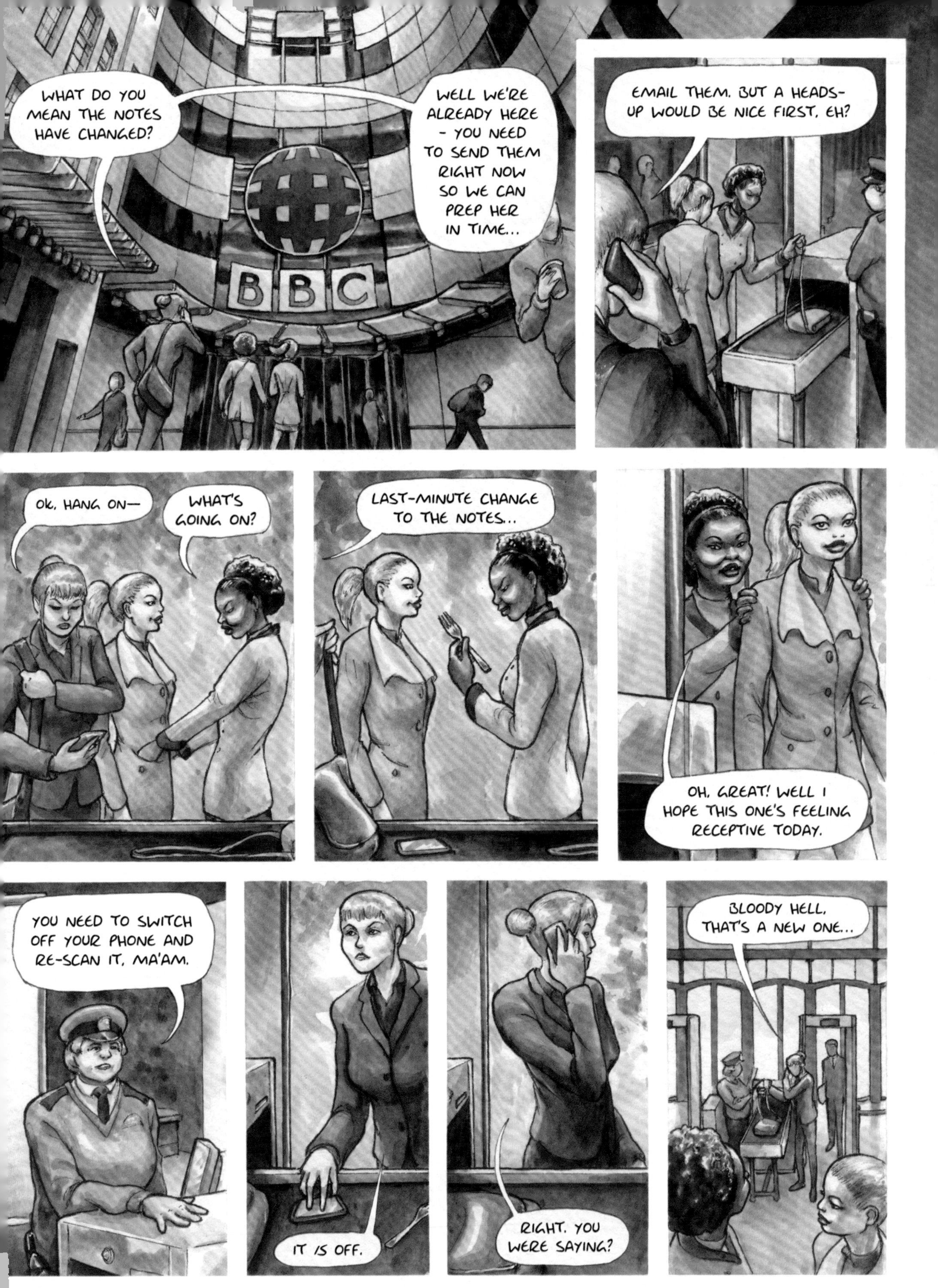
WHAT DO YOU MEAN THE NOTES HAVE CHANGED?
WELL WE'RE ALREADY HERE - YOU NEED TO SEND THEM RIGHT NOW SO WE CAN PREP HER IN TIME...
BBC
EMAIL THEM. BUT A HEADS-UP WOULD BE NICE FIRST, EH?
OK, HANG ON—
WHAT'S GOING ON?
LAST-MINUTE CHANGE TO THE NOTES...
OH, GREAT! WELL I HOPE THIS ONE'S FEELING RECEPTIVE TODAY.
YOU NEED TO SWITCH OFF YOUR PHONE AND RE-SCAN IT, MA'AM.
IT IS OFF.
RIGHT. YOU WERE SAYING?
BLOODY HELL, THAT'S A NEW ONE...

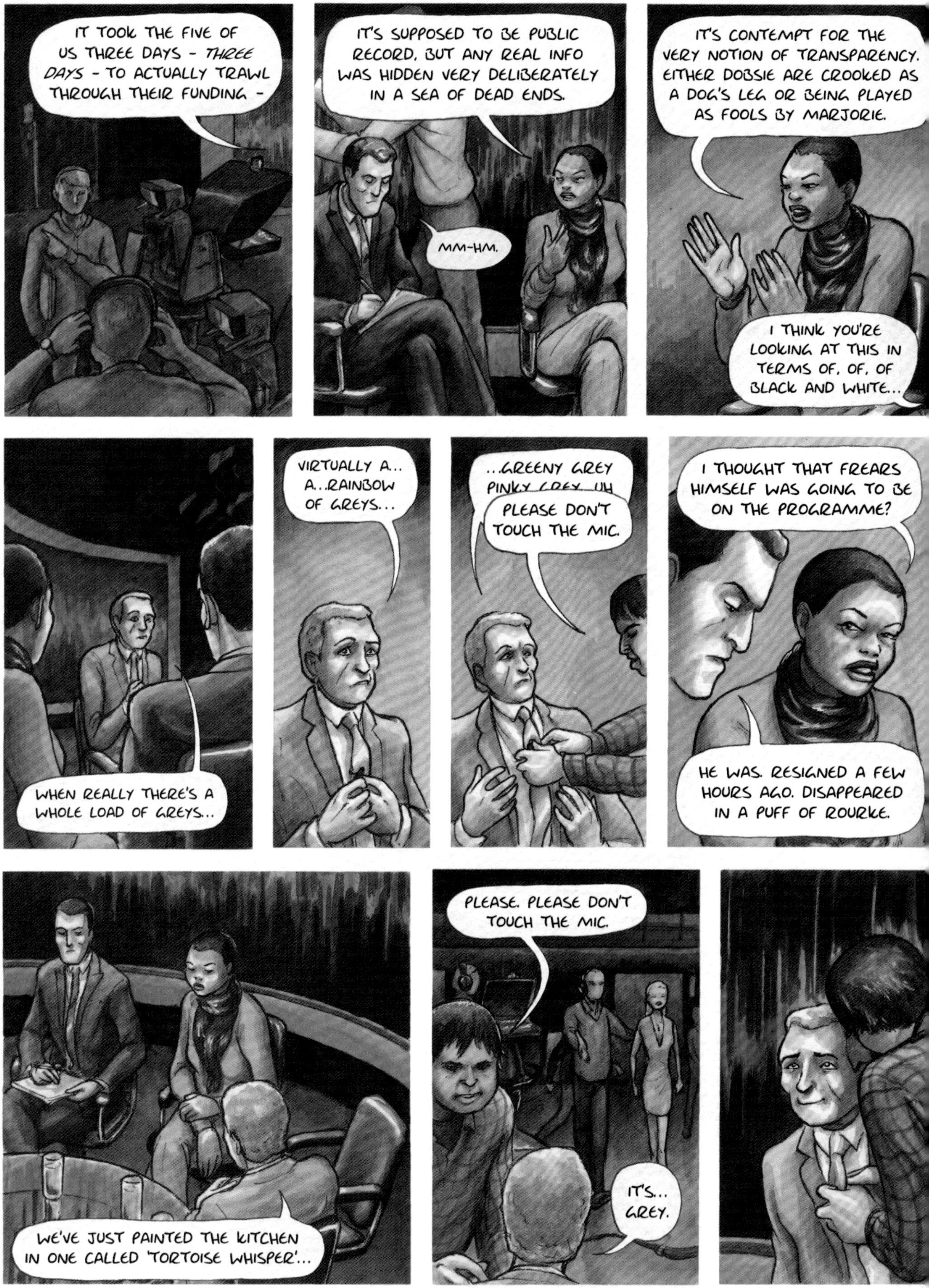
IT TOOK THE FIVE OF US THREE DAYS - *THREE DAYS* - TO ACTUALLY TRAWL THROUGH THEIR FUNDING -
IT'S SUPPOSED TO BE PUBLIC RECORD, BUT ANY REAL INFO WAS HIDDEN VERY DELIBERATELY IN A SEA OF DEAD ENDS.
MM-HM.
IT'S CONTEMPT FOR THE VERY NOTION OF TRANSPARENCY. EITHER DOBSIE ARE CROOKED AS A DOG'S LEG OR BEING PLAYED AS FOOLS BY MARJORIE.
I THINK YOU'RE LOOKING AT THIS IN TERMS OF, OF, OF BLACK AND WHITE...
WHEN REALLY THERE'S A WHOLE LOAD OF GREYS...
VIRTUALLY A... A...RAINBOW OF GREYS...
...GREENY GREY PINKY
PLEASE DON'T TOUCH THE MIC.
I THOUGHT THAT FREARS HIMSELF WAS GOING TO BE ON THE PROGRAMME?
HE WAS. RESIGNED A FEW HOURS AGO. DISAPPEARED IN A PUFF OF ROURKE.
WE'VE JUST PAINTED THE KITCHEN IN ONE CALLED 'TORTOISE WHISPER'...
PLEASE. PLEASE DON'T TOUCH THE MIC.
IT'S... GREY.

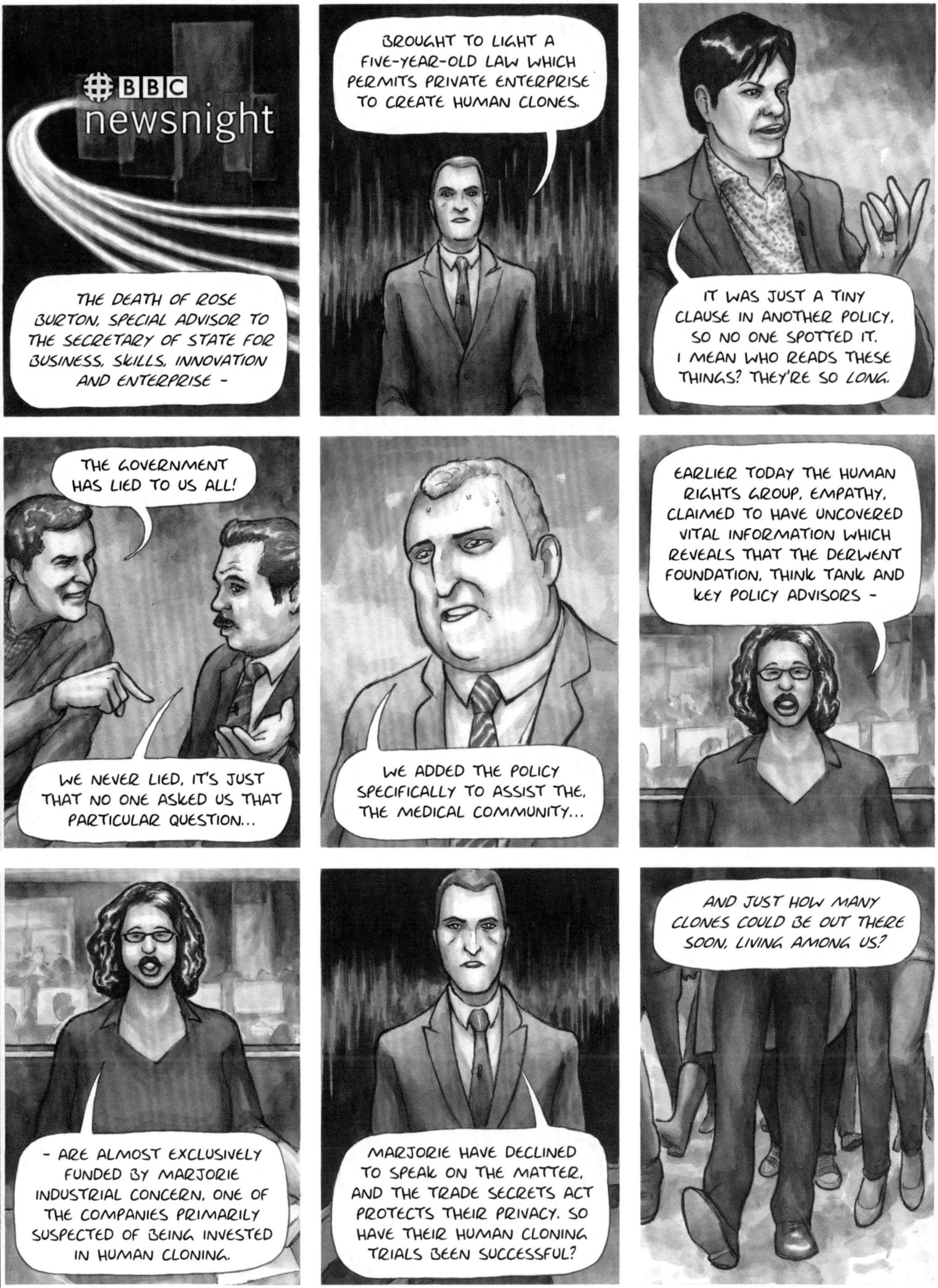
BBC newsnight
THE DEATH OF ROSE BURTON, SPECIAL ADVISOR TO THE SECRETARY OF STATE FOR BUSINESS, SKILLS, INNOVATION AND ENTERPRISE -
BROUGHT TO LIGHT A FIVE-YEAR-OLD LAW WHICH PERMITS PRIVATE ENTERPRISE TO CREATE HUMAN CLONES.
IT WAS JUST A TINY CLAUSE IN ANOTHER POLICY, SO NO ONE SPOTTED IT. I MEAN WHO READS THESE THINGS? THEY'RE SO LONG.
THE GOVERNMENT HAS LIED TO US ALL!
WE NEVER LIED, IT'S JUST THAT NO ONE ASKED US THAT PARTICULAR QUESTION...
WE ADDED THE POLICY SPECIFICALLY TO ASSIST THE, THE MEDICAL COMMUNITY...
EARLIER TODAY THE HUMAN RIGHTS GROUP, EMPATHY, CLAIMED TO HAVE UNCOVERED VITAL INFORMATION WHICH REVEALS THAT THE DERWENT FOUNDATION, THINK TANK AND KEY POLICY ADVISORS -
- ARE ALMOST EXCLUSIVELY FUNDED BY MARJORIE INDUSTRIAL CONCERN, ONE OF THE COMPANIES PRIMARILY SUSPECTED OF BEING INVESTED IN HUMAN CLONING.
MARJORIE HAVE DECLINED TO SPEAK ON THE MATTER, AND THE TRADE SECRETS ACT PROTECTS THEIR PRIVACY. SO HAVE THEIR HUMAN CLONING TRIALS BEEN SUCCESSFUL?
AND JUST HOW MANY CLONES COULD BE OUT THERE SOON, LIVING AMONG US?

IS THE GOVERNMENT JUST A PAWN OF BIG BUSINESS? HOW CLOSE MIGHT MARJORIE BE TO CLONING HUMANS? AND ARE WE ALL SAFE?

TONIGHT WE'LL BE TALKING TO LESLIE VERNON, SPECIAL ADVISOR AT DOBSIE TO THE RECENTLY RESIGNED DUNCAN FREARS;

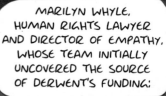

MARILYN WHYLE, HUMAN RIGHTS LAWYER AND DIRECTOR OF EMPATHY, WHOSE TEAM INITIALLY UNCOVERED THE SOURCE OF DERWENT'S FUNDING;

AND CLEMENTINE DARLING, WHO HAS JUST BEEN NOMINATED *AGAIN* FOR THE PRESTIGIOUS MELLY KANE AWARD FOR BEST FEMALE SINGER AND POLITICAL SPOKESPERSON AT THE TWAMMIES –

WELL DONE, CLEMENTINE!

THANK YOU, I'M LITERALLY BESIDE MYSELF!

SO, NOW, LESLIE VERNON. WHEN CAN YOU FIRST RECALL REALISING YOUR DEPARTMENT WERE...WHAT'S THE PHRASE I'M LOOKING FOR...

CORPORATE SHILLS?

MY DEPARTMENT OF DOBSIE... MY DOBSIE... MY...W-WE WORK TO REPRESENT THE, THE COUNTRY'S BEST INTERESTS IN THE FIELD OF

SCIENCE AND EVEN IF THESE, THESE, THESE INTERESTS COINCIDE WITH INTERESTS OF A PARTICULAR COMPANY, THAT DOESN'T NECESSARILY MEAN THAT WE ARE CORPORATE SH– ER...

IT'S JUST A COINCIDENCE THAT WE HAPPEN TO HAVE THE SAME AIMS AS M...

...AS ANY COMPANY WISHING TO FURTHER MEDICAL SCIENCE...

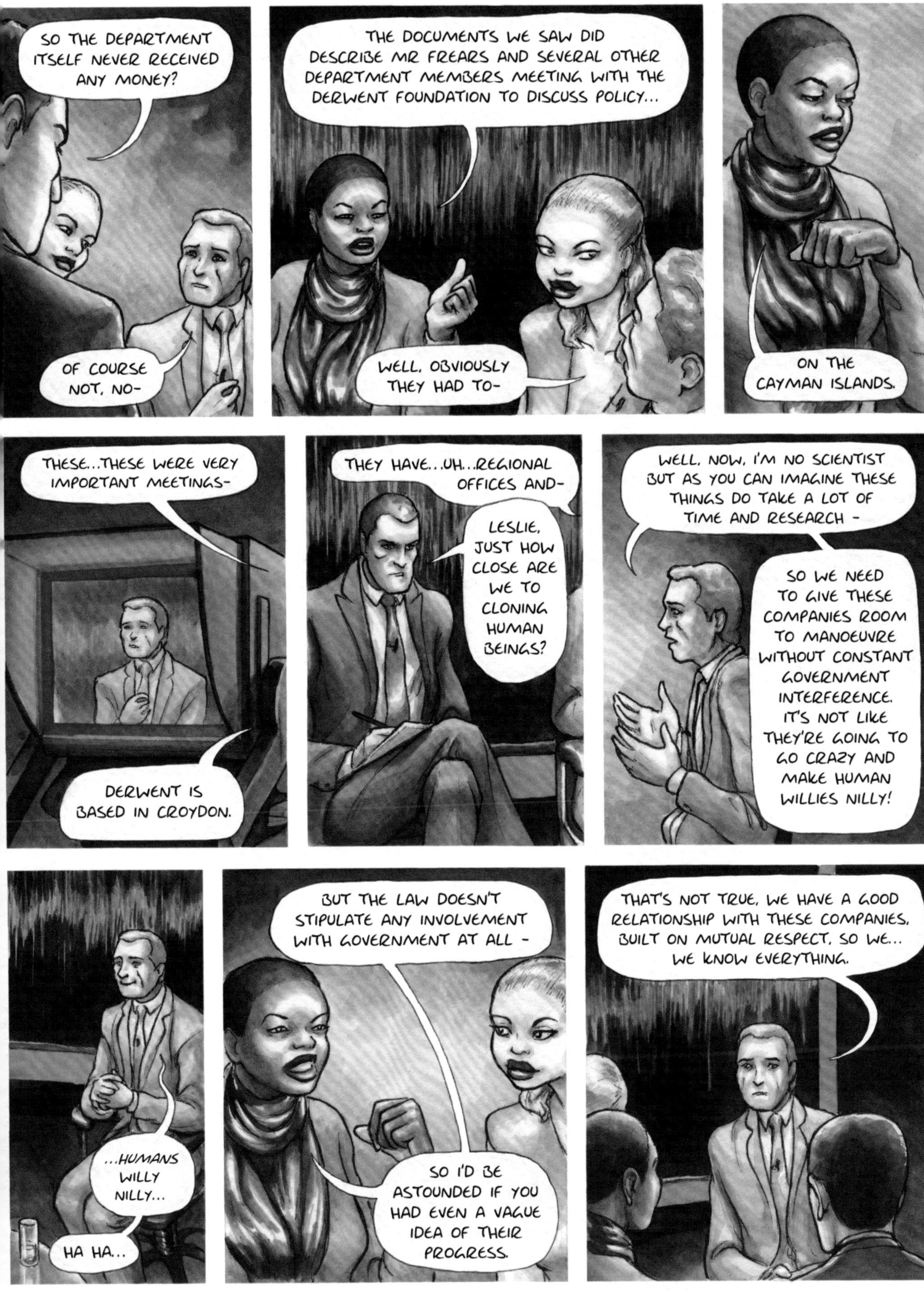
SO THE DEPARTMENT ITSELF NEVER RECEIVED ANY MONEY?
OF COURSE NOT, NO-
THE DOCUMENTS WE SAW DID DESCRIBE MR FREARS AND SEVERAL OTHER DEPARTMENT MEMBERS MEETING WITH THE DERWENT FOUNDATION TO DISCUSS POLICY...
WELL, OBVIOUSLY THEY HAD TO-
ON THE CAYMAN ISLANDS.
THESE...THESE WERE VERY IMPORTANT MEETINGS-
DERWENT IS BASED IN CROYDON.
THEY HAVE...UH...REGIONAL OFFICES AND-
LESLIE, JUST HOW CLOSE ARE WE TO CLONING HUMAN BEINGS?
WELL, NOW, I'M NO SCIENTIST BUT AS YOU CAN IMAGINE THESE THINGS DO TAKE A LOT OF TIME AND RESEARCH -
SO WE NEED TO GIVE THESE COMPANIES ROOM TO MANOEUVRE WITHOUT CONSTANT GOVERNMENT INTERFERENCE. IT'S NOT LIKE THEY'RE GOING TO GO CRAZY AND MAKE HUMAN WILLIES NILLY!
...HUMANS WILLY NILLY...
HA HA...
BUT THE LAW DOESN'T STIPULATE ANY INVOLVEMENT WITH GOVERNMENT AT ALL -
SO I'D BE ASTOUNDED IF YOU HAD EVEN A VAGUE IDEA OF THEIR PROGRESS.
THAT'S NOT TRUE, WE HAVE A GOOD RELATIONSHIP WITH THESE COMPANIES, BUILT ON MUTUAL RESPECT, SO WE... WE KNOW EVERYTHING.

ACCORDING TO INFORMATION LEAKED IN THE SO-CALLED 'EMAIL GATE' SCANDAL THERE WERE TWO COMPANIES WORKING IN THIS FIELD, IS THAT THE CASE?

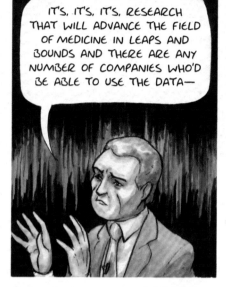

IT'S, IT'S, IT'S, RESEARCH THAT WILL ADVANCE THE FIELD OF MEDICINE IN LEAPS AND BOUNDS AND THERE ARE ANY NUMBER OF COMPANIES WHO'D BE ABLE TO USE THE DATA—

TWO KEY COMPANIES: GOLDSTEIFF GLEIMAN AND OF COURSE MARJORIE. HAS MARJORIE SUCCESSFULLY CREATED HUMAN CLONES?

NOW, LOOK, I'M NOT GOING TO SIT HERE AND RUN THROUGH ALL THE PARTICULARS OF WHO HAS DONE WHAT AND WHEN, BECAUSE THAT WOULD TAKE FAR TOO LONG –

BUT WHAT I'D LIKE TO DO IS—

HAS MARJORIE SUCCESSFULLY CREATED ANY HUMAN CLONES?

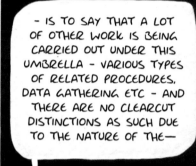

– IS TO SAY THAT A LOT OF OTHER WORK IS BEING CARRIED OUT UNDER THIS UMBRELLA – VARIOUS TYPES OF RELATED PROCEDURES, DATA GATHERING ETC – AND THERE ARE NO CLEARCUT DISTINCTIONS AS SUCH DUE TO THE NATURE OF THE—

WHAT ABOUT GOLDSTEIFF GLEIMAN, HAVE THEY SUCCESSFULLY CREATED ANY HUMAN CLONES?

NO.

I'M PREGNANT!

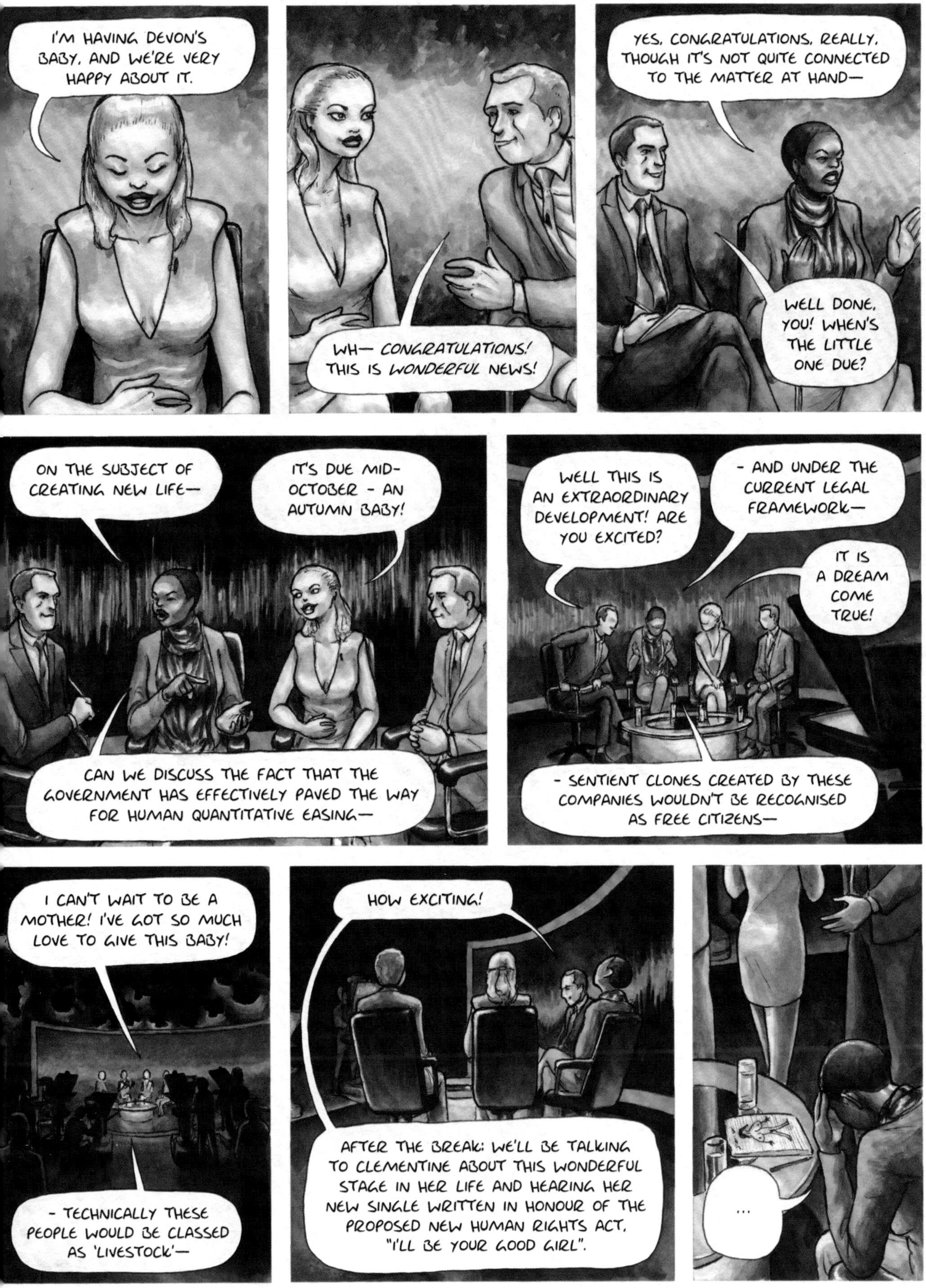
I'M HAVING DEVON'S BABY, AND WE'RE VERY HAPPY ABOUT IT.
WH— CONGRATULATIONS! THIS IS WONDERFUL NEWS!
YES, CONGRATULATIONS, REALLY, THOUGH IT'S NOT QUITE CONNECTED TO THE MATTER AT HAND—
WELL DONE, YOU! WHEN'S THE LITTLE ONE DUE?
ON THE SUBJECT OF CREATING NEW LIFE—
IT'S DUE MID-OCTOBER - AN AUTUMN BABY!
CAN WE DISCUSS THE FACT THAT THE GOVERNMENT HAS EFFECTIVELY PAVED THE WAY FOR HUMAN QUANTITATIVE EASING—
WELL THIS IS AN EXTRAORDINARY DEVELOPMENT! ARE YOU EXCITED?
- AND UNDER THE CURRENT LEGAL FRAMEWORK—
IT IS A DREAM COME TRUE!
- SENTIENT CLONES CREATED BY THESE COMPANIES WOULDN'T BE RECOGNISED AS FREE CITIZENS—
I CAN'T WAIT TO BE A MOTHER! I'VE GOT SO MUCH LOVE TO GIVE THIS BABY!
- TECHNICALLY THESE PEOPLE WOULD BE CLASSED AS 'LIVESTOCK'—
HOW EXCITING!
AFTER THE BREAK: WE'LL BE TALKING TO CLEMENTINE ABOUT THIS WONDERFUL STAGE IN HER LIFE AND HEARING HER NEW SINGLE WRITTEN IN HONOUR OF THE PROPOSED NEW HUMAN RIGHTS ACT, "I'LL BE YOUR GOOD GIRL".
...

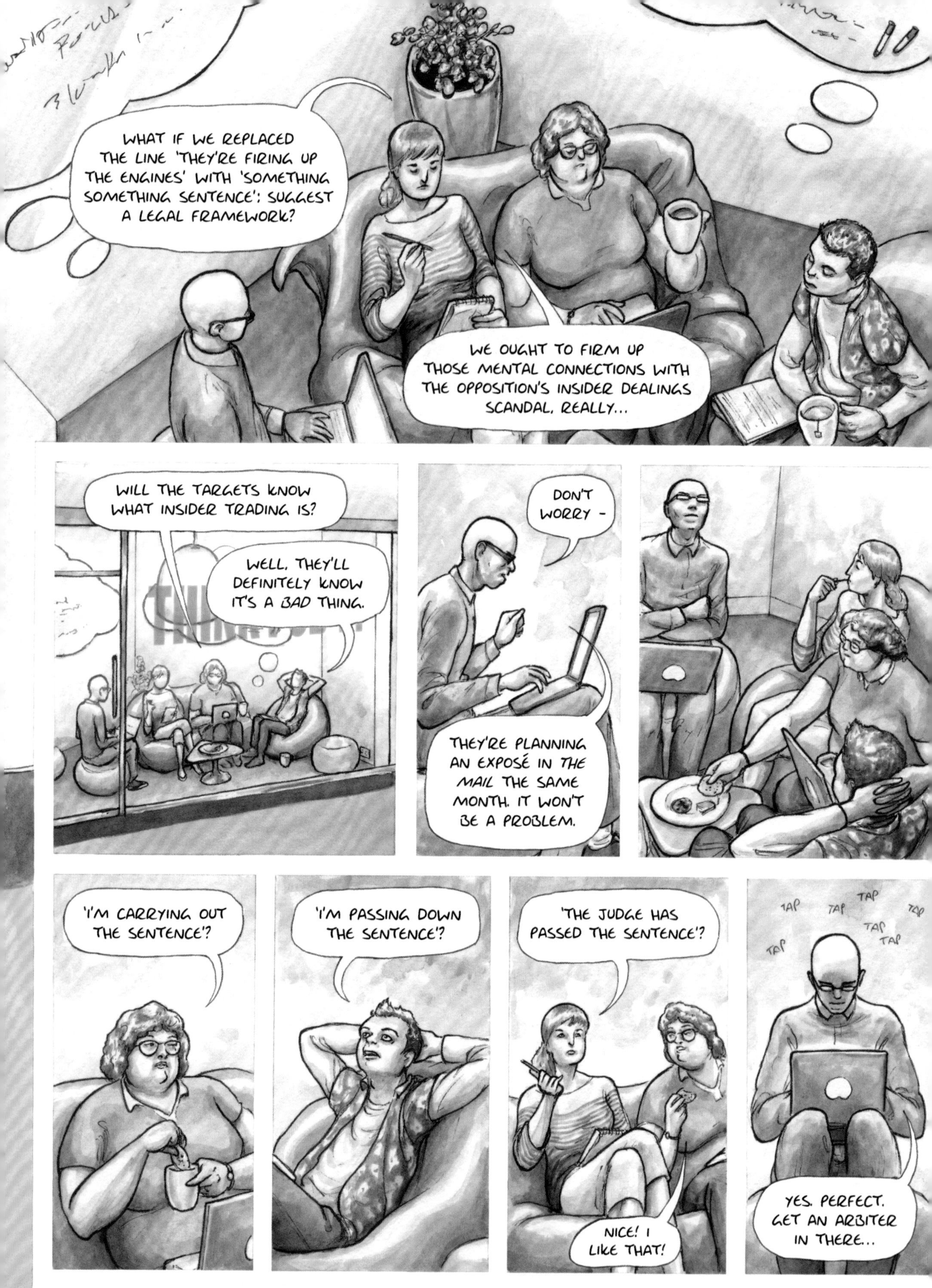
WHAT IF WE REPLACED THE LINE 'THEY'RE FIRING UP THE ENGINES' WITH 'SOMETHING SOMETHING SENTENCE'; SUGGEST A LEGAL FRAMEWORK?
WE OUGHT TO FIRM UP THOSE MENTAL CONNECTIONS WITH THE OPPOSITION'S INSIDER DEALINGS SCANDAL, REALLY...
WILL THE TARGETS KNOW WHAT INSIDER TRADING IS?
WELL, THEY'LL DEFINITELY KNOW IT'S A *BAD* THING.
DON'T WORRY -
THEY'RE PLANNING AN EXPOSÉ IN *THE MAIL* THE SAME MONTH. IT WON'T BE A PROBLEM.
'I'M CARRYING OUT THE SENTENCE'?
'I'M PASSING DOWN THE SENTENCE'?
'THE JUDGE HAS PASSED THE SENTENCE'?
NICE! I LIKE THAT!
TAP TAP TAP TAP TAP TAP TAP
YES. PERFECT. GET AN ARBITER IN THERE...

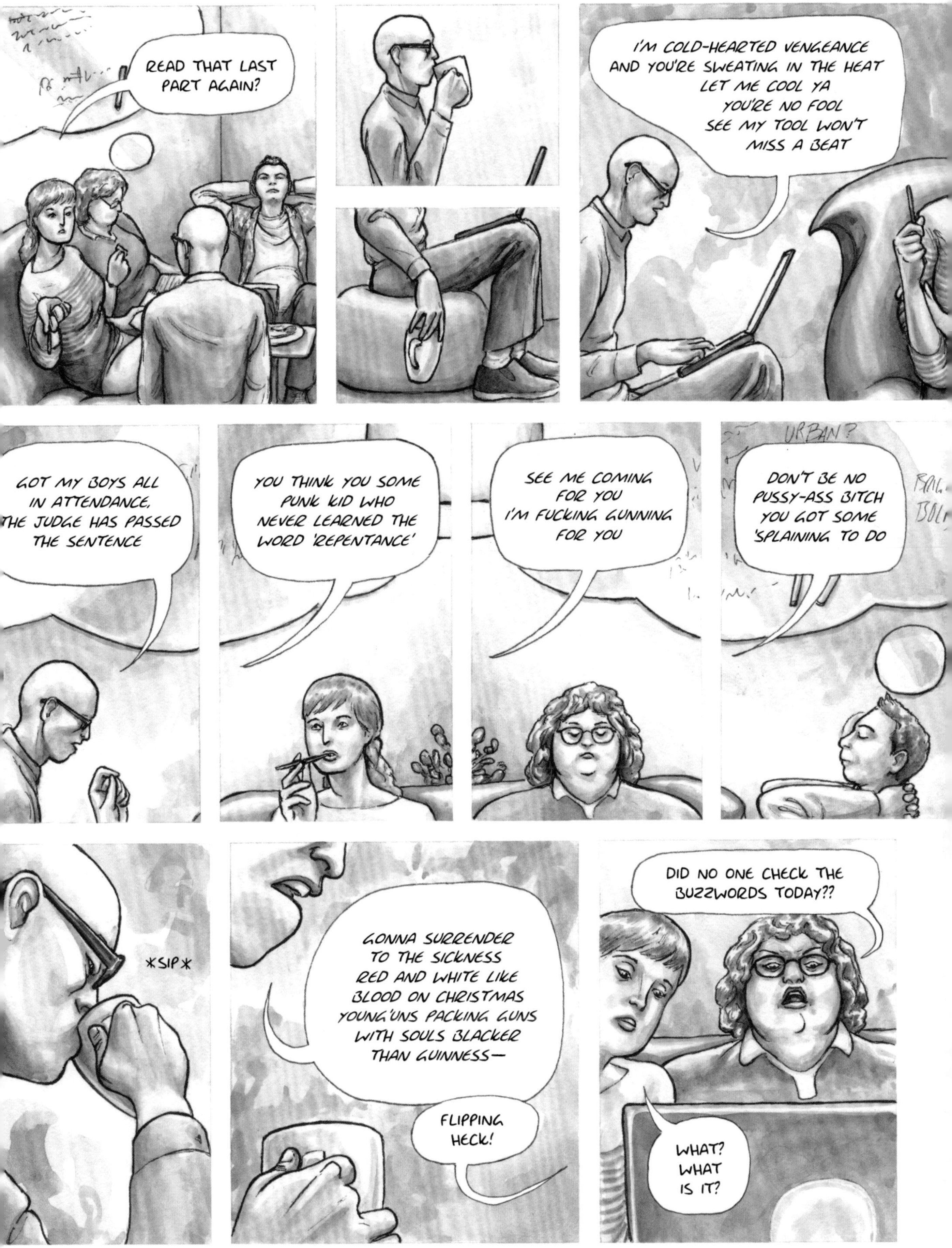
READ THAT LAST PART AGAIN?
I'M COLD-HEARTED VENGEANCE AND YOU'RE SWEATING IN THE HEAT LET ME COOL YA YOU'RE NO FOOL SEE MY TOOL WON'T MISS A BEAT
GOT MY BOYS ALL IN ATTENDANCE, THE JUDGE HAS PASSED THE SENTENCE
YOU THINK YOU SOME PUNK KID WHO NEVER LEARNED THE WORD 'REPENTANCE'
SEE ME COMING FOR YOU I'M FUCKING GUNNING FOR YOU
URBAN?
DON'T BE NO PUSSY-ASS BITCH YOU GOT SOME 'SPLAINING TO DO
SIP
GONNA SURRENDER TO THE SICKNESS RED AND WHITE LIKE BLOOD ON CHRISTMAS YOUNG'UNS PACKING GUNS WITH SOULS BLACKER THAN GUINNESS—
FLIPPING HECK!
DID NO ONE CHECK THE BUZZWORDS TODAY??
WHAT? WHAT IS IT?

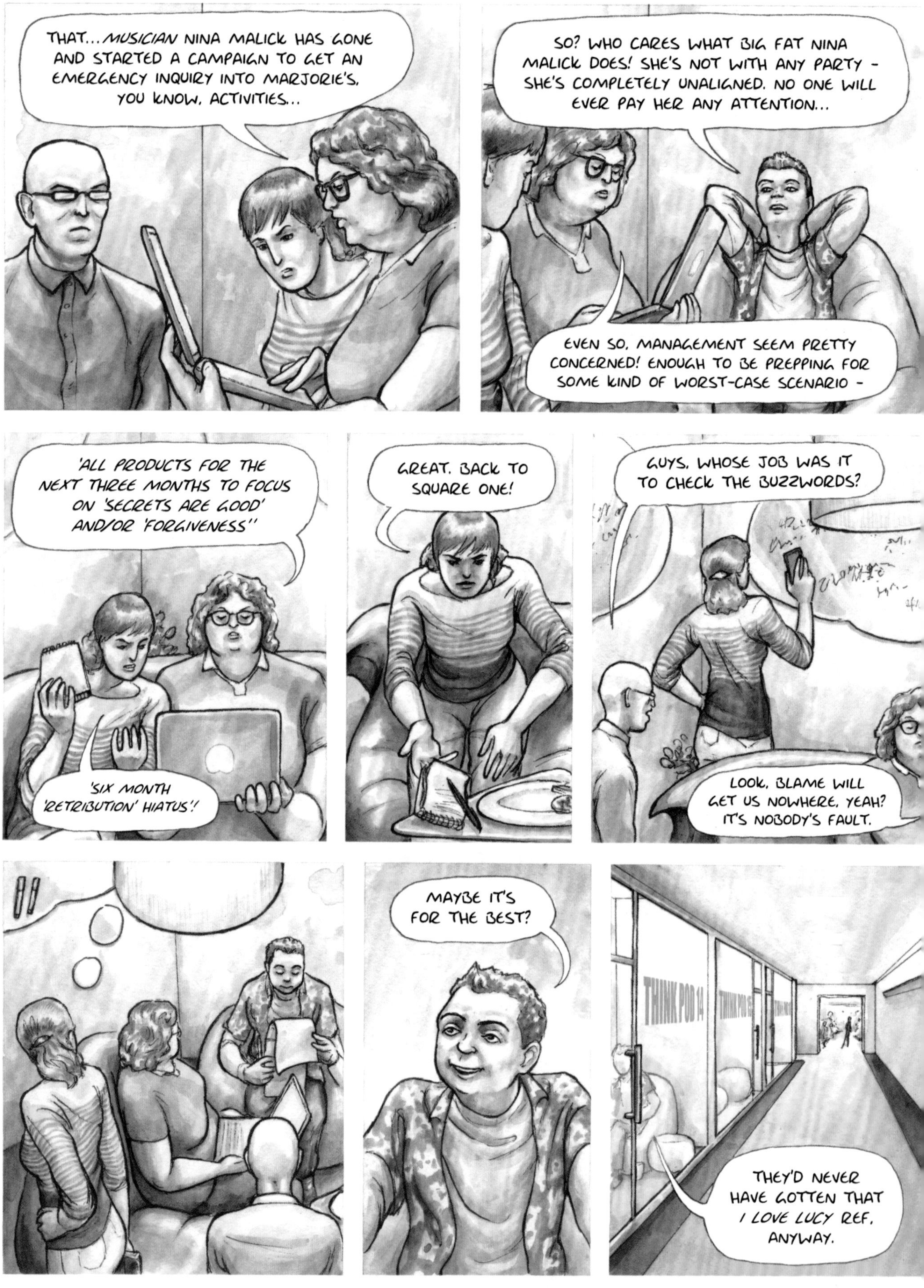
THAT... MUSICIAN NINA MALICK HAS GONE AND STARTED A CAMPAIGN TO GET AN EMERGENCY INQUIRY INTO MARJORIE'S, YOU KNOW, ACTIVITIES...
SO? WHO CARES WHAT BIG FAT NINA MALICK DOES! SHE'S NOT WITH ANY PARTY - SHE'S COMPLETELY UNALIGNED. NO ONE WILL EVER PAY HER ANY ATTENTION...
EVEN SO, MANAGEMENT SEEM PRETTY CONCERNED! ENOUGH TO BE PREPPING FOR SOME KIND OF WORST-CASE SCENARIO -
'ALL PRODUCTS FOR THE NEXT THREE MONTHS TO FOCUS ON 'SECRETS ARE GOOD' AND/OR 'FORGIVENESS''
'SIX MONTH 'RETRIBUTION' HIATUS'!
GREAT. BACK TO SQUARE ONE!
GUYS, WHOSE JOB WAS IT TO CHECK THE BUZZWORDS?
LOOK, BLAME WILL GET US NOWHERE, YEAH? IT'S NOBODY'S FAULT.
MAYBE IT'S FOR THE BEST?
THINK POD 14
THEY'D NEVER HAVE GOTTEN THAT I LOVE LUCY REF. ANYWAY.

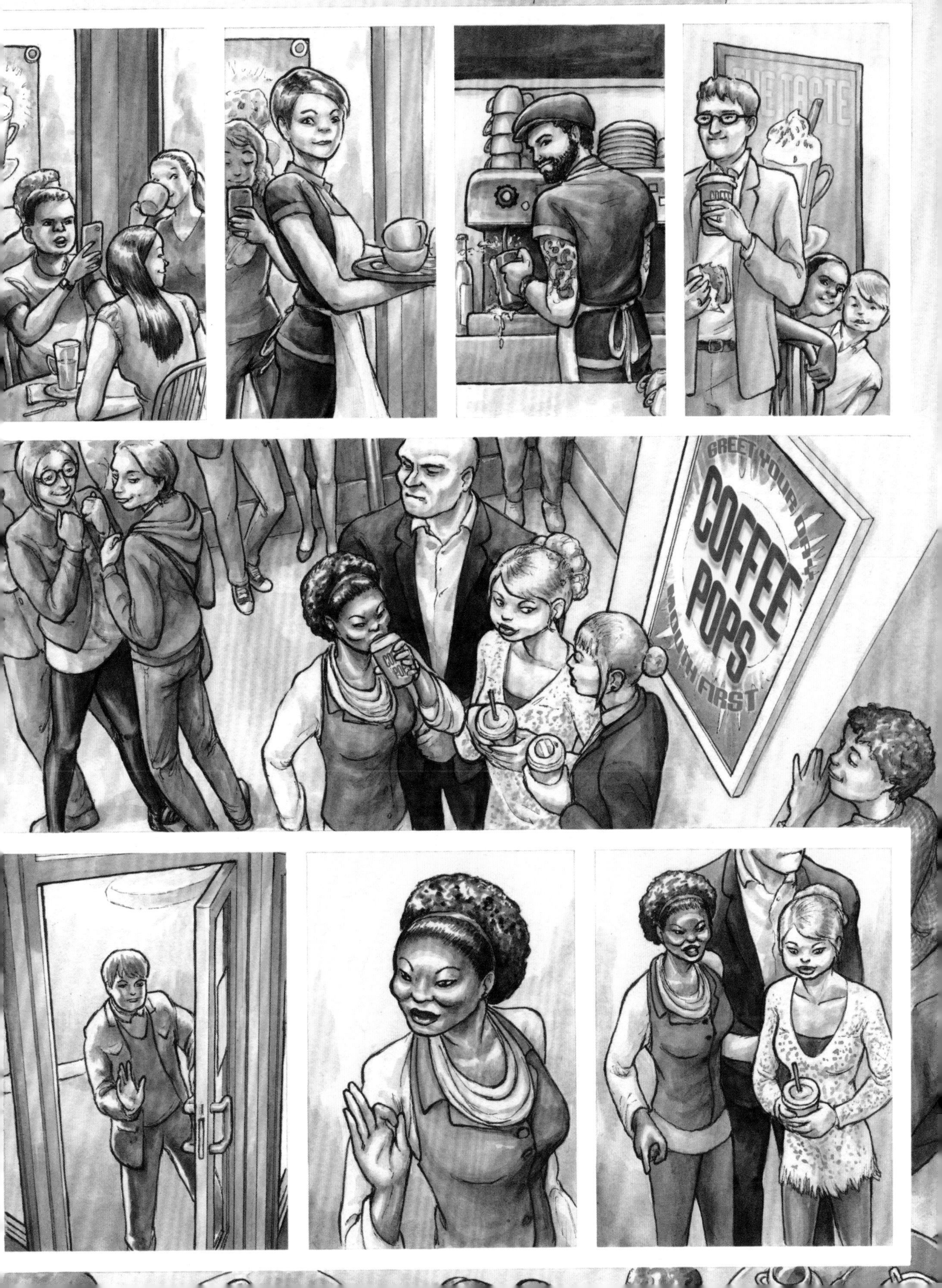
GREET YOUR
COFFEE POPS
MOUTH FIRST

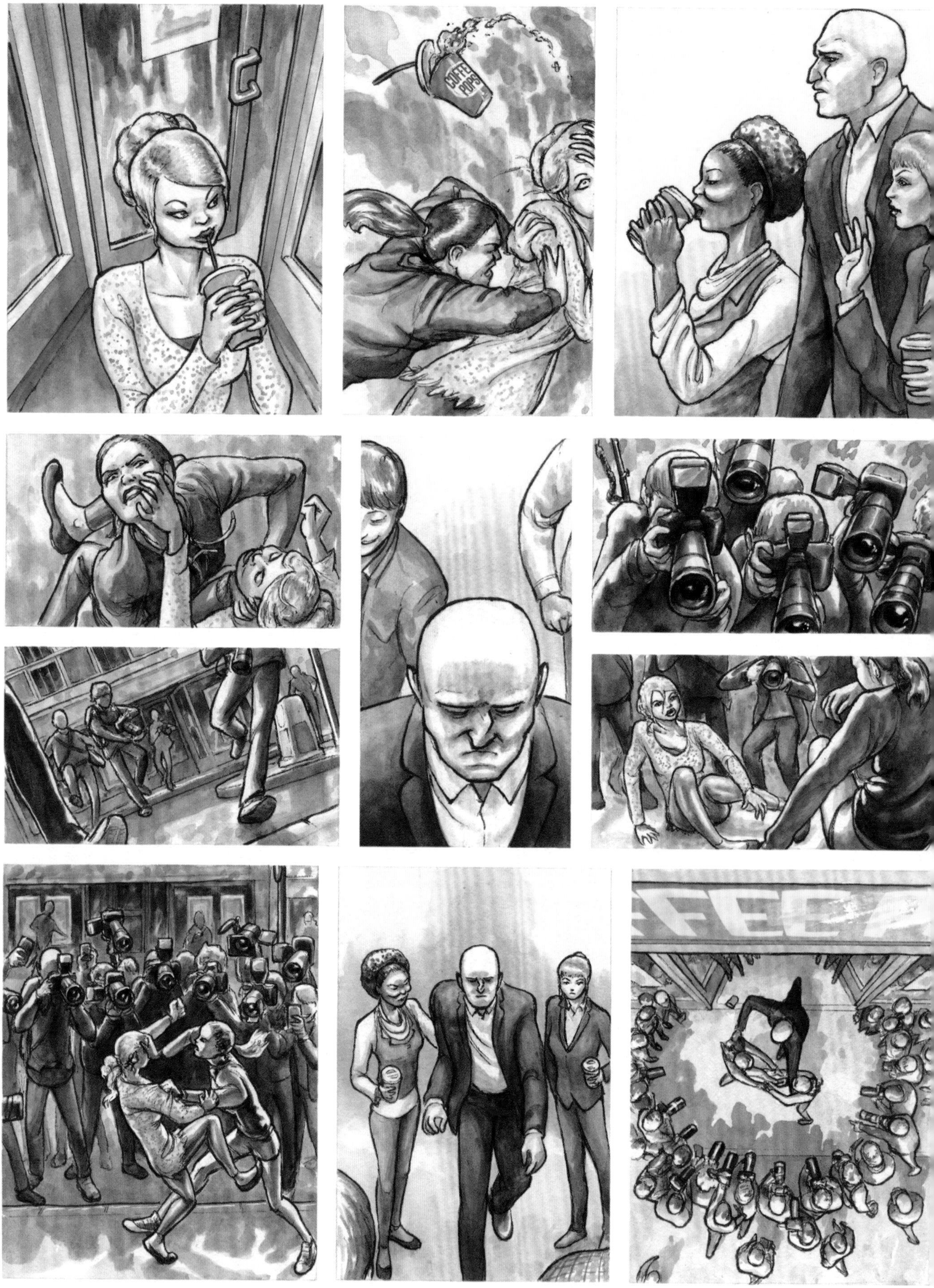
POPS

WHAT'S TRENDING

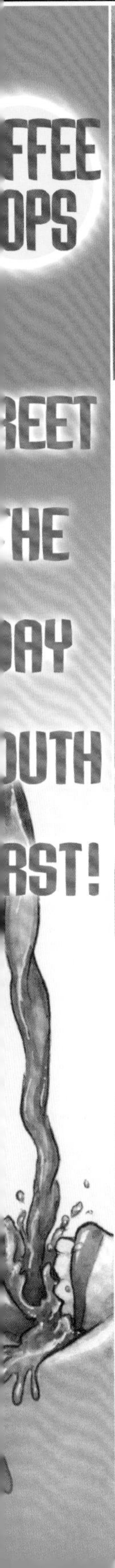
FFEE
OPS
REET
HE
AY
UTH
RST!

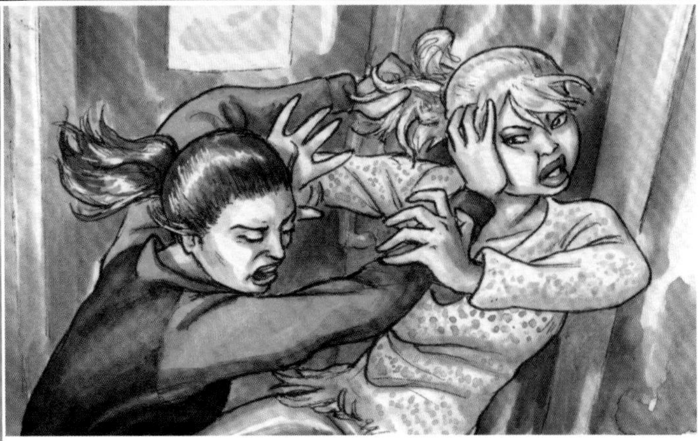

CORAL AND CLEMENTINE'S CAT FIGHT

The pair dressed in stylish but casual streetwear shocked onlookers in an explosive brawl after Clementine announces she is carrying Devon's baby

578 comments

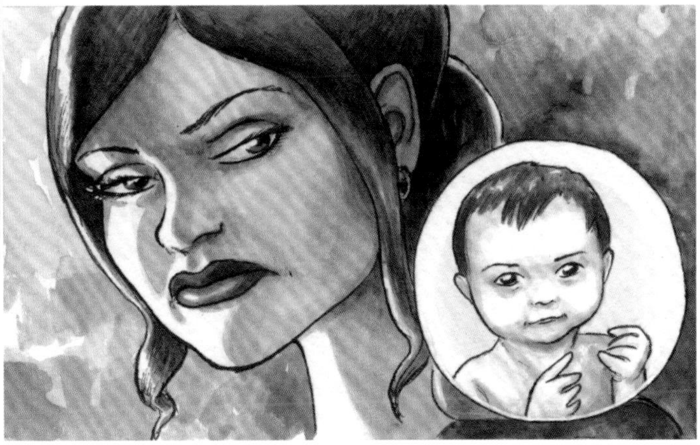

'WHAT CORAL WANTS MOST IS A FAMILY'

Exclusive: Coral's close friend breaks silence on star's desperation to have a child of her own

322 comments

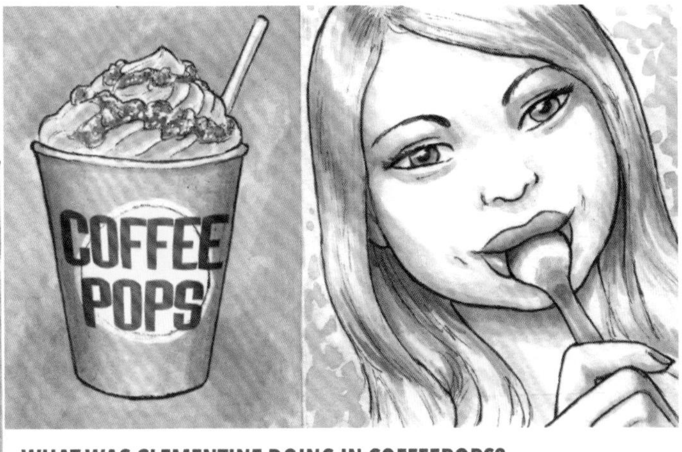
COFFEE
POPS

WHAT WAS CLEMENTINE DOING IN COFFEEPOPS?

Sweet-toothed Clementine drawn to high-street favourite's recently launched new line of delicious jam-flavoured coffees

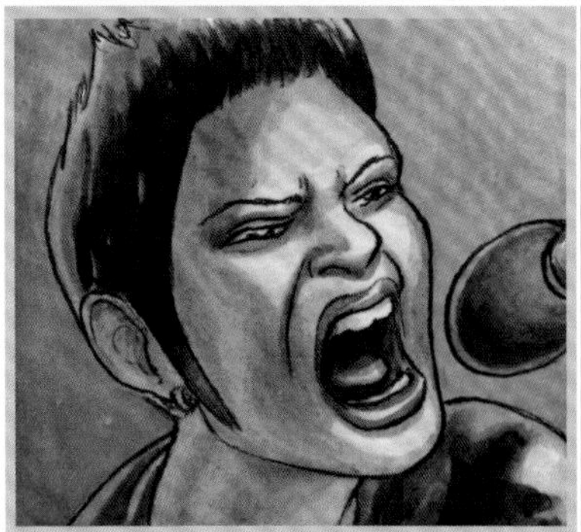

NINA WADES IN: singer Malick stirring up trouble with petition demanding immediate investigation into Marjorie's human cloning activities

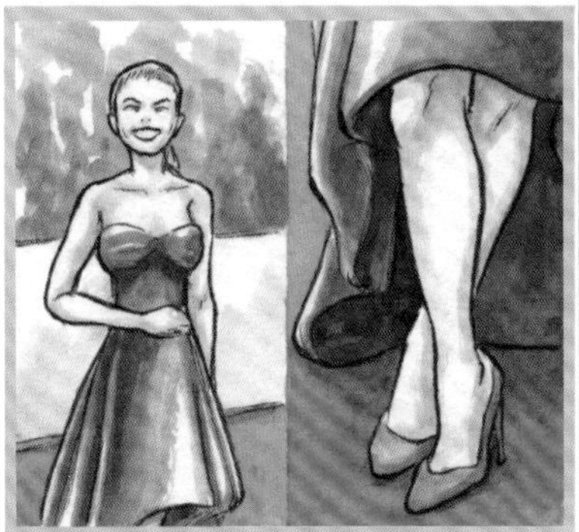

WASTING AWAY: Giselle's closest friends talk of concern over star's sudden weight-loss in wake of 'bloating' criticism

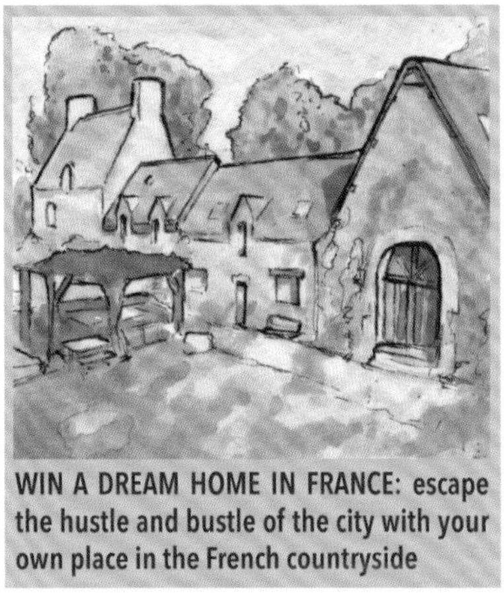

WIN A DREAM HOME IN FRANCE: escape the hustle and bustle of the city with your own place in the French countryside

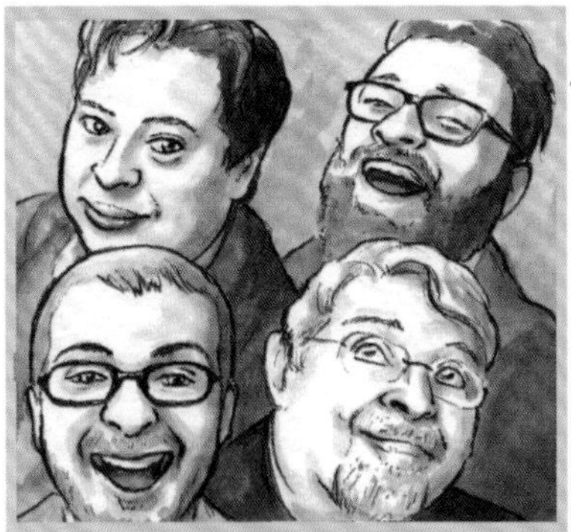

GOOD GOOD ADVENTURES: these boys are

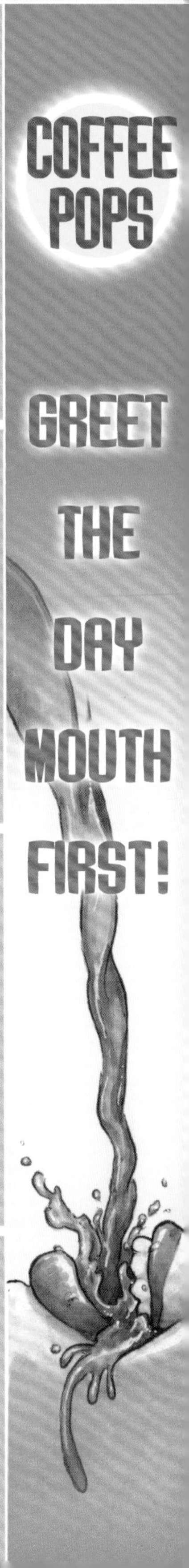
COFFEE
POPS
GREET
THE
DAY
MOUTH
FIRST!

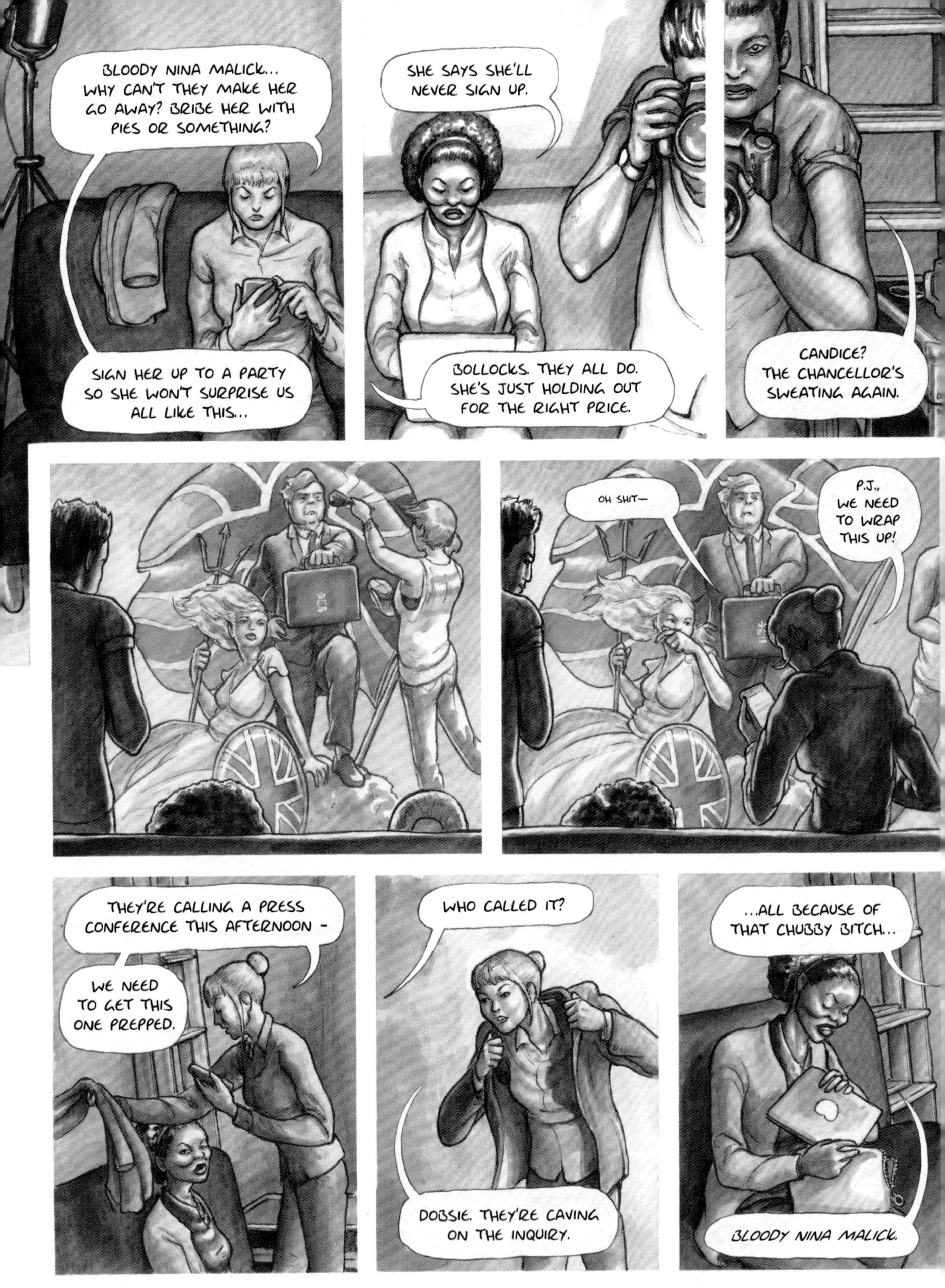
BLOODY NINA MALICK... WHY CAN'T THEY MAKE HER GO AWAY? BRIBE HER WITH PIES OR SOMETHING?
SIGN HER UP TO A PARTY SO SHE WON'T SURPRISE US ALL LIKE THIS...
SHE SAYS SHE'LL NEVER SIGN UP.
BOLLOCKS. THEY ALL DO. SHE'S JUST HOLDING OUT FOR THE RIGHT PRICE.
CANDICE? THE CHANCELLOR'S SWEATING AGAIN.
OH SHIT—
P.J., WE NEED TO WRAP THIS UP!
THEY'RE CALLING A PRESS CONFERENCE THIS AFTERNOON -
WE NEED TO GET THIS ONE PREPPED.
WHO CALLED IT?
DOBSIE. THEY'RE CAVING ON THE INQUIRY.
...ALL BECAUSE OF THAT CHUBBY BITCH...
BLOODY NINA MALICK.

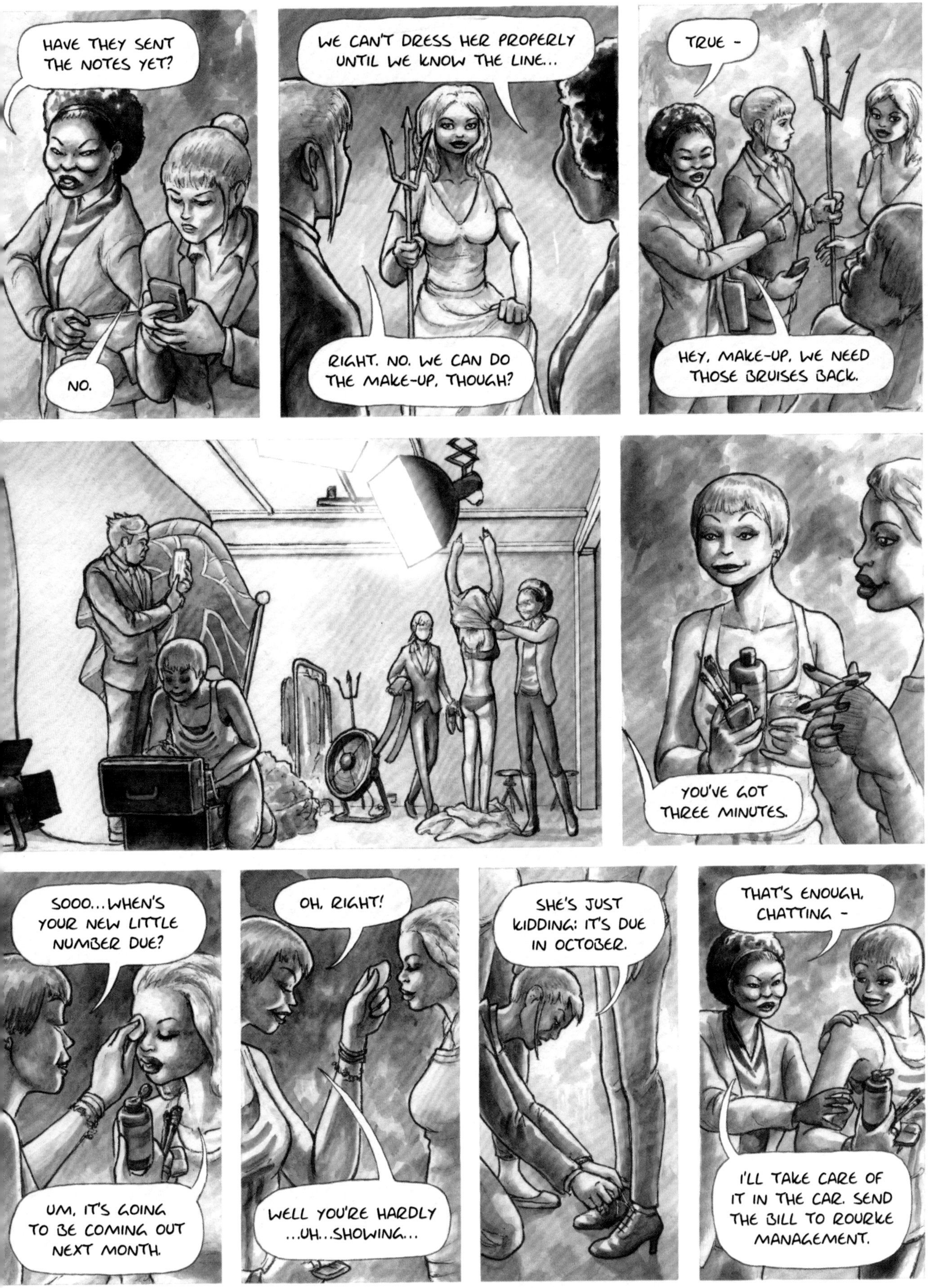
HAVE THEY SENT THE NOTES YET?
NO.
WE CAN'T DRESS HER PROPERLY UNTIL WE KNOW THE LINE...
RIGHT. NO. WE CAN DO THE MAKE-UP, THOUGH?
TRUE -
HEY, MAKE-UP, WE NEED THOSE BRUISES BACK.
YOU'VE GOT THREE MINUTES.
SOOO... WHEN'S YOUR NEW LITTLE NUMBER DUE?
UM, IT'S GOING TO BE COMING OUT NEXT MONTH.
OH, RIGHT!
WELL YOU'RE HARDLY ...UH...SHOWING...
SHE'S JUST KIDDING: IT'S DUE IN OCTOBER.
THAT'S ENOUGH. CHATTING -
I'LL TAKE CARE OF IT IN THE CAR. SEND THE BILL TO ROURKE MANAGEMENT.

BUT IT'S DUE OUT NEXT MONTH, SELINA?

SHE WASN'T TALKING ABOUT THE SINGLE, CLEM. SHE WAS TALKING ABOUT YOUR BABY.

RIIIIIN*

OH. OK.

MR RO—?

YOU'VE HEARD ABOUT THE PRESS CONFERENCE? WELL IT'S EXACTLY WHAT YOU THINK IT'S FOR —

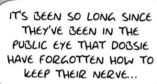

IT'S BEEN SO LONG SINCE THEY'VE BEEN IN THE PUBLIC EYE THAT DOBSIE HAVE FORGOTTEN HOW TO KEEP THEIR NERVE...

ARE YOU EN ROUTE?

TOBY PORTRAITS
D FLOOR

YES, THERE IN...FORTY.

PAUL?

WHAT IS IT, POPPET?

IS DEVON HAPPY ABOUT THE BABY?

OF COURSE, CLEM. YOU'RE VERY MUCH IN LOVE.

SELINA, PEN: MAKE SURE THIS ONE'S WELL-PREPPED.

✳CLICK✳

BUT WHAT WILL HIS MOTHER SAY? AND MY FATHER?

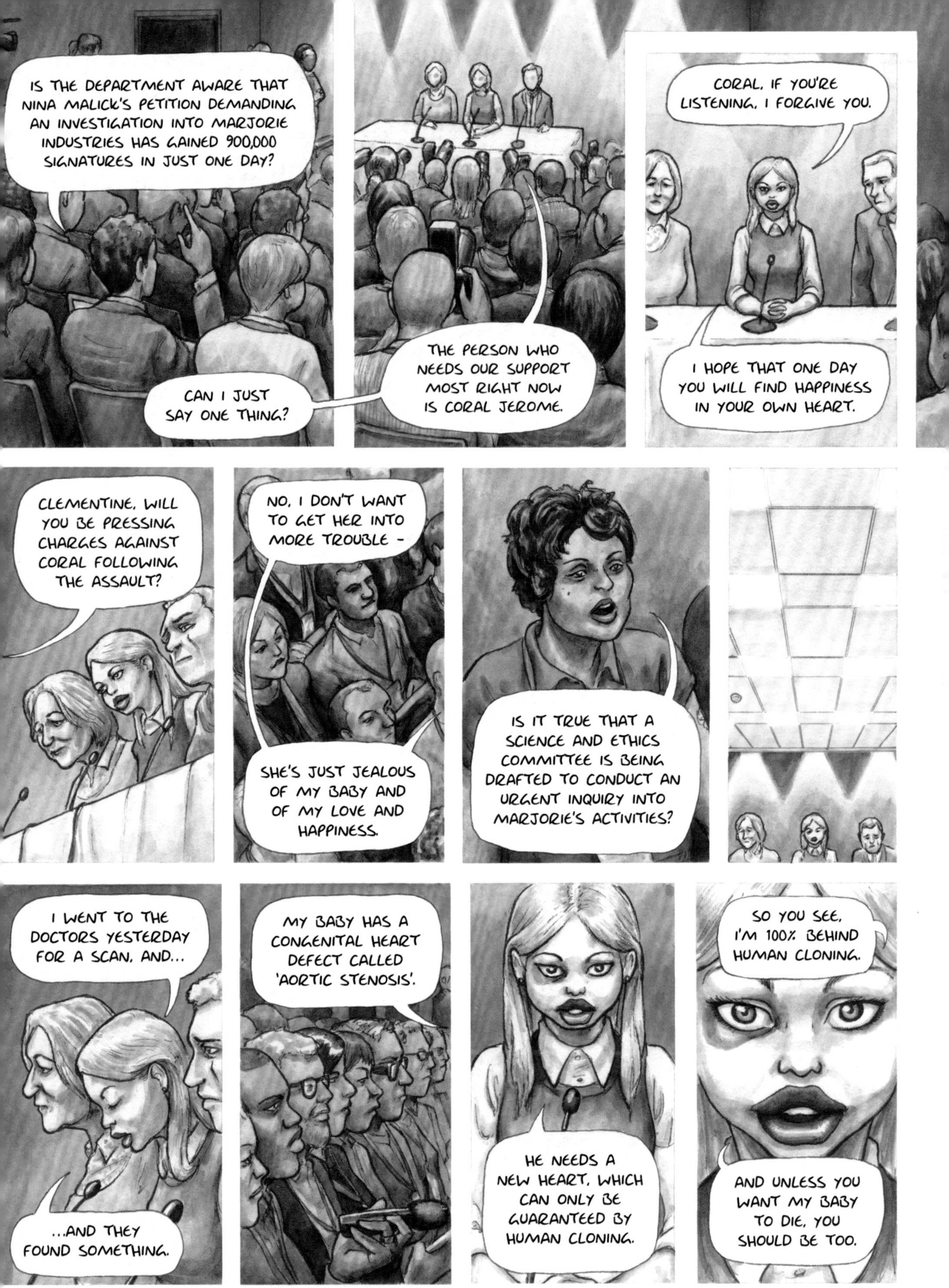
IS THE DEPARTMENT AWARE THAT NINA MALICK'S PETITION DEMANDING AN INVESTIGATION INTO MARJORIE INDUSTRIES HAS GAINED 900,000 SIGNATURES IN JUST ONE DAY?
CAN I JUST SAY ONE THING?
THE PERSON WHO NEEDS OUR SUPPORT MOST RIGHT NOW IS CORAL JEROME.
CORAL, IF YOU'RE LISTENING, I FORGIVE YOU.
I HOPE THAT ONE DAY YOU WILL FIND HAPPINESS IN YOUR OWN HEART.
CLEMENTINE, WILL YOU BE PRESSING CHARGES AGAINST CORAL FOLLOWING THE ASSAULT?
NO, I DON'T WANT TO GET HER INTO MORE TROUBLE -
SHE'S JUST JEALOUS OF MY BABY AND OF MY LOVE AND HAPPINESS.
IS IT TRUE THAT A SCIENCE AND ETHICS COMMITTEE IS BEING DRAFTED TO CONDUCT AN URGENT INQUIRY INTO MARJORIE'S ACTIVITIES?
I WENT TO THE DOCTORS YESTERDAY FOR A SCAN, AND...
...AND THEY FOUND SOMETHING.
MY BABY HAS A CONGENITAL HEART DEFECT CALLED 'AORTIC STENOSIS'.
HE NEEDS A NEW HEART, WHICH CAN ONLY BE GUARANTEED BY HUMAN CLONING.
SO YOU SEE, I'M 100% BEHIND HUMAN CLONING.
AND UNLESS YOU WANT MY BABY TO DIE, YOU SHOULD BE TOO.

WHAT'S TRENDING

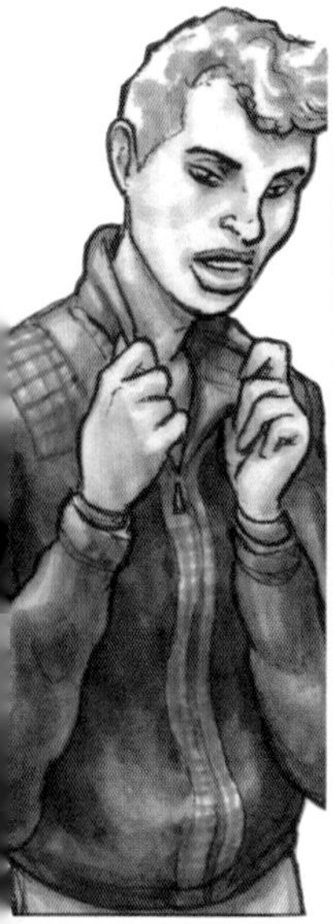

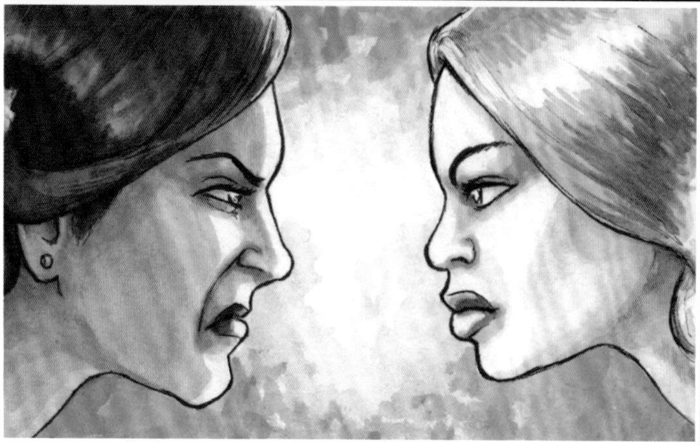

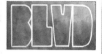

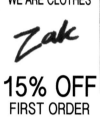

CLEMENTINE'S STRUGGLE

Clementine talks of her feud with Coral and wonders why Nina Malick would want her innocent unborn baby to die

403 comments

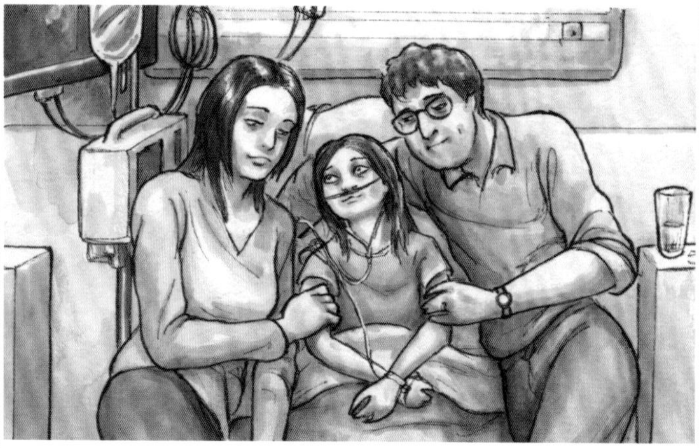

THE GIFT OF LIFE

There are thousands of patients on transplant waiting lists all around the country who will benefit from human cloning, why shouldn't they get a chance at life?

116 comments

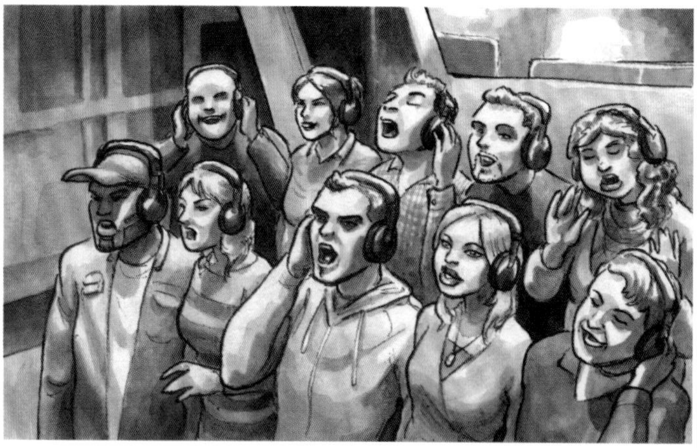

GAS AID PERFORMERS STRIKE CHORD

The story behind the star-studded recording of chart-topping

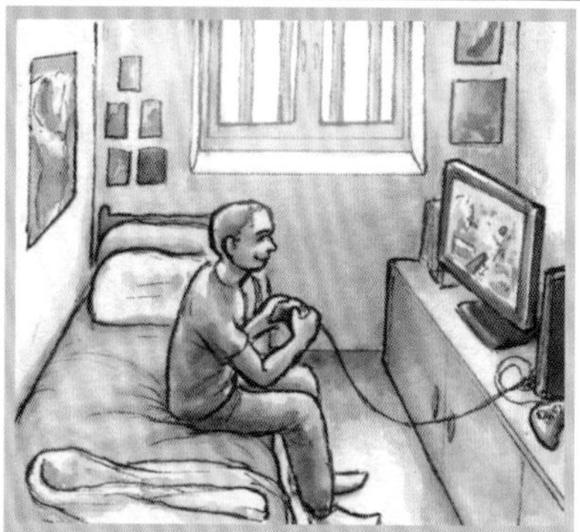

£350 MILLION PER WEEK: the money that could be saved by scrapping outdated Human Rights Act

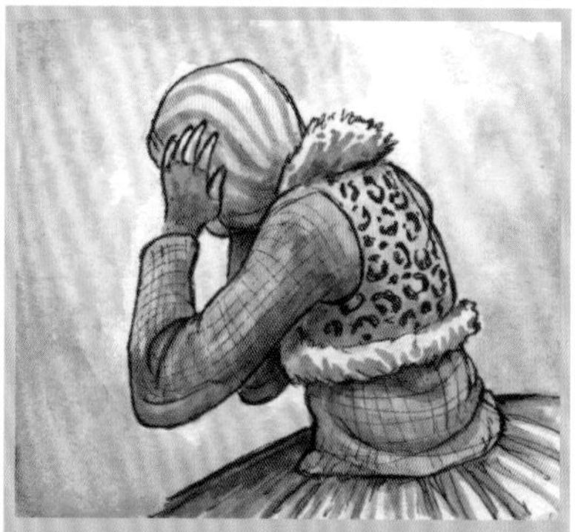

FROCKY HORROR: why wearing the wrong clothing could be ruining your life and what you can do to set it straight

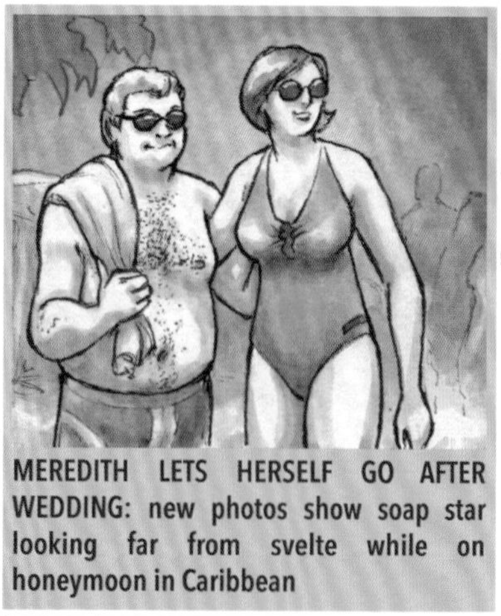

MEREDITH LETS HERSELF GO AFTER WEDDING: new photos show soap star looking far from svelte while on honeymoon in Caribbean

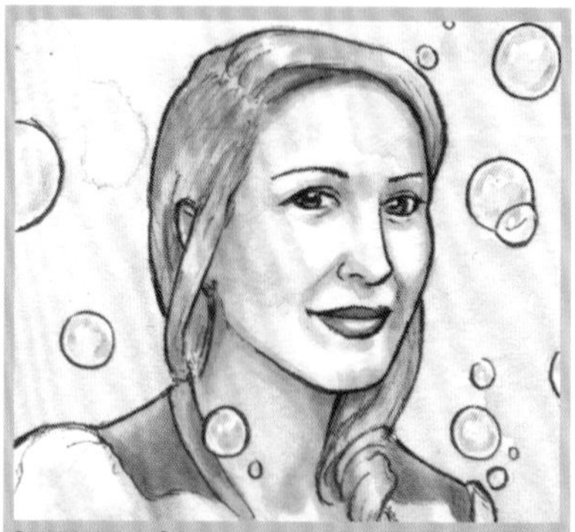

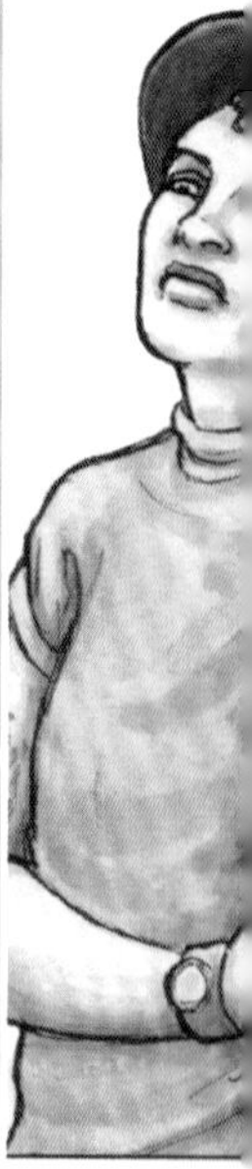

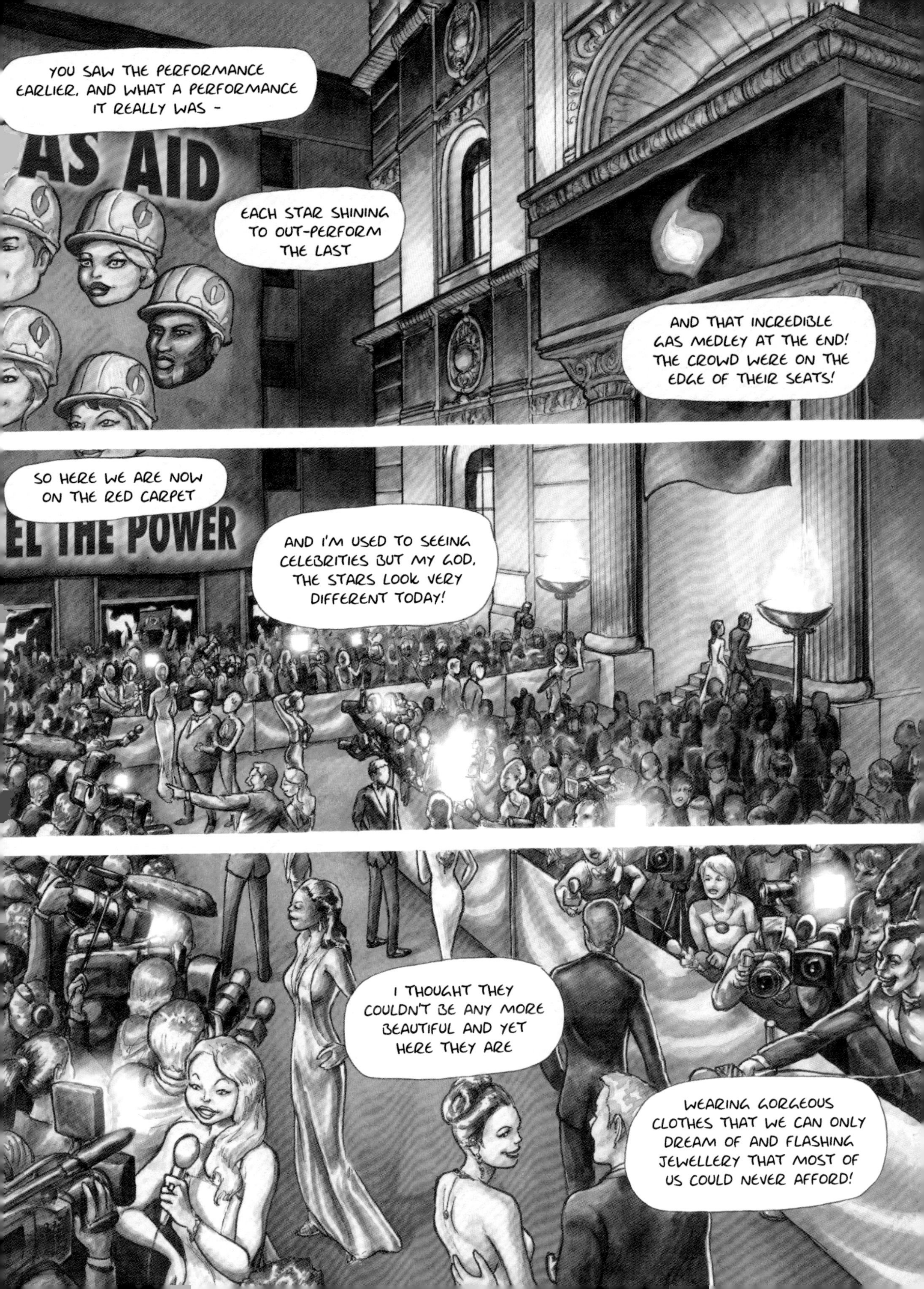
YOU SAW THE PERFORMANCE EARLIER, AND WHAT A PERFORMANCE IT REALLY WAS -
AS AID
EACH STAR SHINING TO OUT-PERFORM THE LAST
AND THAT INCREDIBLE GAS MEDLEY AT THE END! THE CROWD WERE ON THE EDGE OF THEIR SEATS!
SO HERE WE ARE NOW ON THE RED CARPET
EL THE POWER
AND I'M USED TO SEEING CELEBRITIES BUT MY GOD, THE STARS LOOK VERY DIFFERENT TODAY!
I THOUGHT THEY COULDN'T BE ANY MORE BEAUTIFUL AND YET HERE THEY ARE
WEARING GORGEOUS CLOTHES THAT WE CAN ONLY DREAM OF AND FLASHING JEWELLERY THAT MOST OF US COULD NEVER AFFORD!

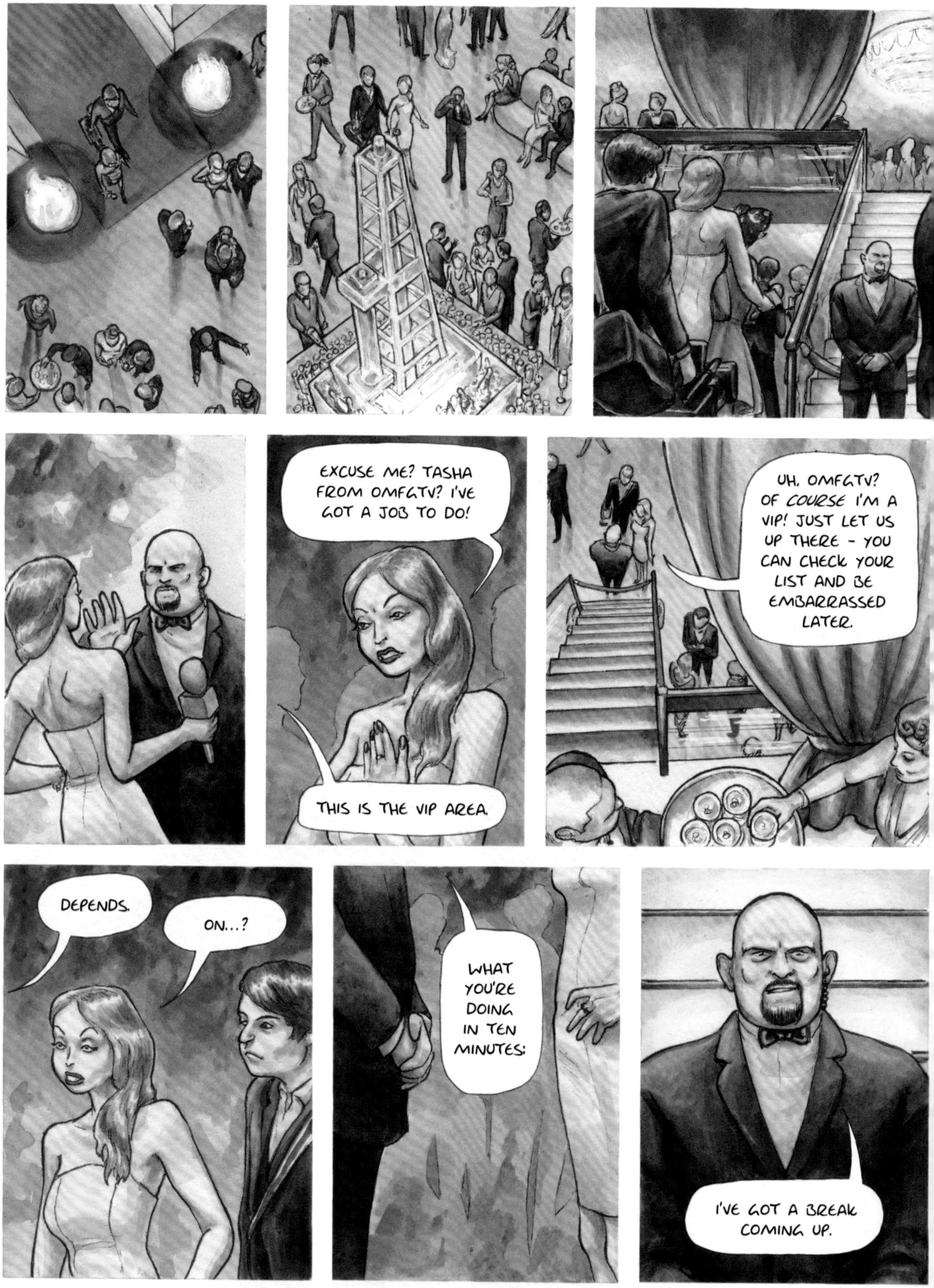
EXCUSE ME? TASHA FROM OMFGTV? I'VE GOT A JOB TO DO!
THIS IS THE VIP AREA.
UH, OMFGTV? OF COURSE I'M A VIP! JUST LET US UP THERE - YOU CAN CHECK YOUR LIST AND BE EMBARRASSED LATER.
DEPENDS.
ON...?
WHAT YOU'RE DOING IN TEN MINUTES:
I'VE GOT A BREAK COMING UP.

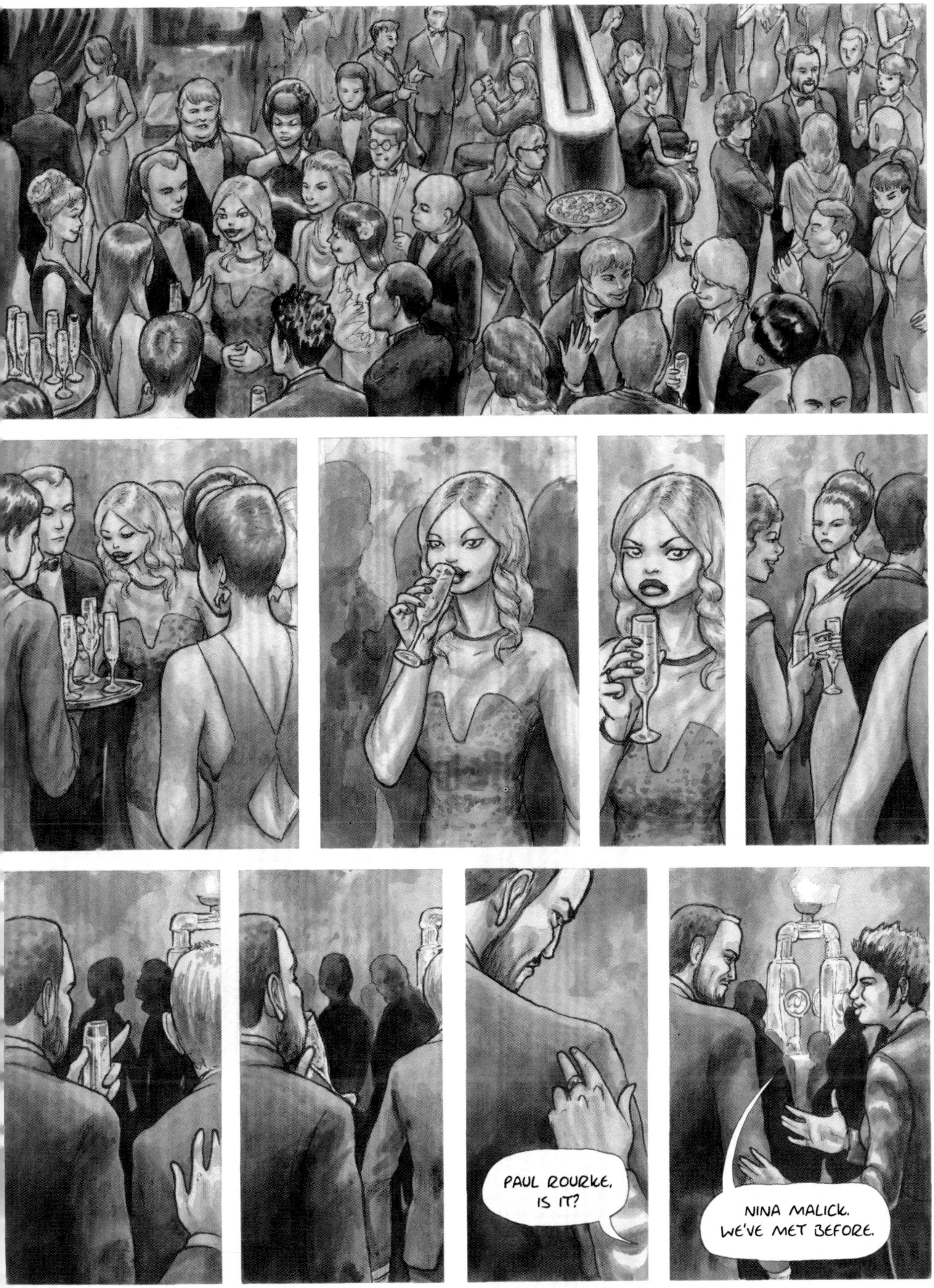
PAUL ROURKE, IS IT?
NINA MALICK. WE'VE MET BEFORE.

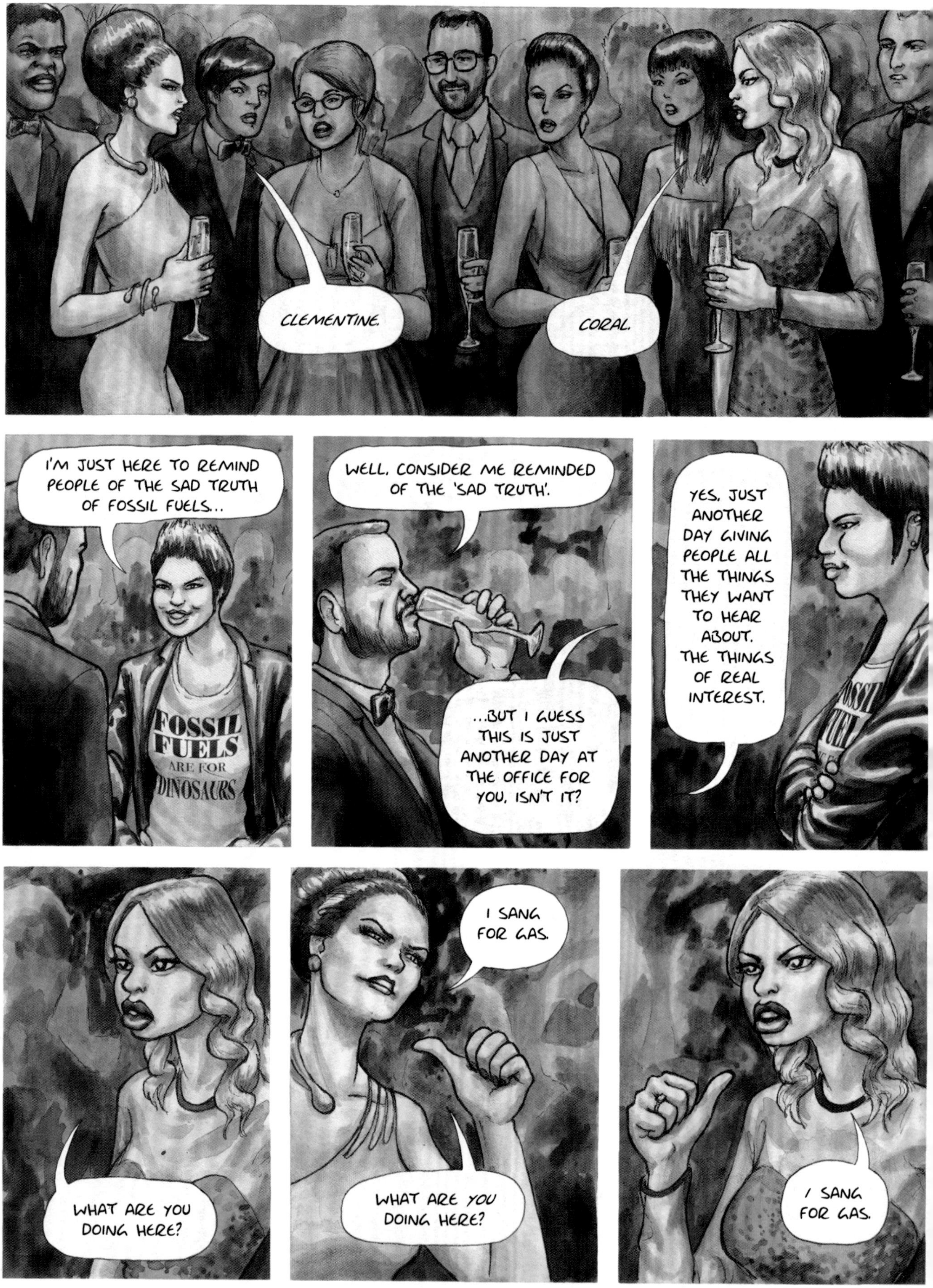
CLEMENTINE.
CORAL.
I'M JUST HERE TO REMIND PEOPLE OF THE SAD TRUTH OF FOSSIL FUELS...
FOSSIL FUELS ARE FOR DINOSAURS
WELL, CONSIDER ME REMINDED OF THE 'SAD TRUTH'.
...BUT I GUESS THIS IS JUST ANOTHER DAY AT THE OFFICE FOR YOU, ISN'T IT?
YES, JUST ANOTHER DAY GIVING PEOPLE ALL THE THINGS THEY WANT TO HEAR ABOUT. THE THINGS OF REAL INTEREST.
WHAT ARE YOU DOING HERE?
I SANG FOR GAS.
WHAT ARE YOU DOING HERE?
I SANG FOR GAS.

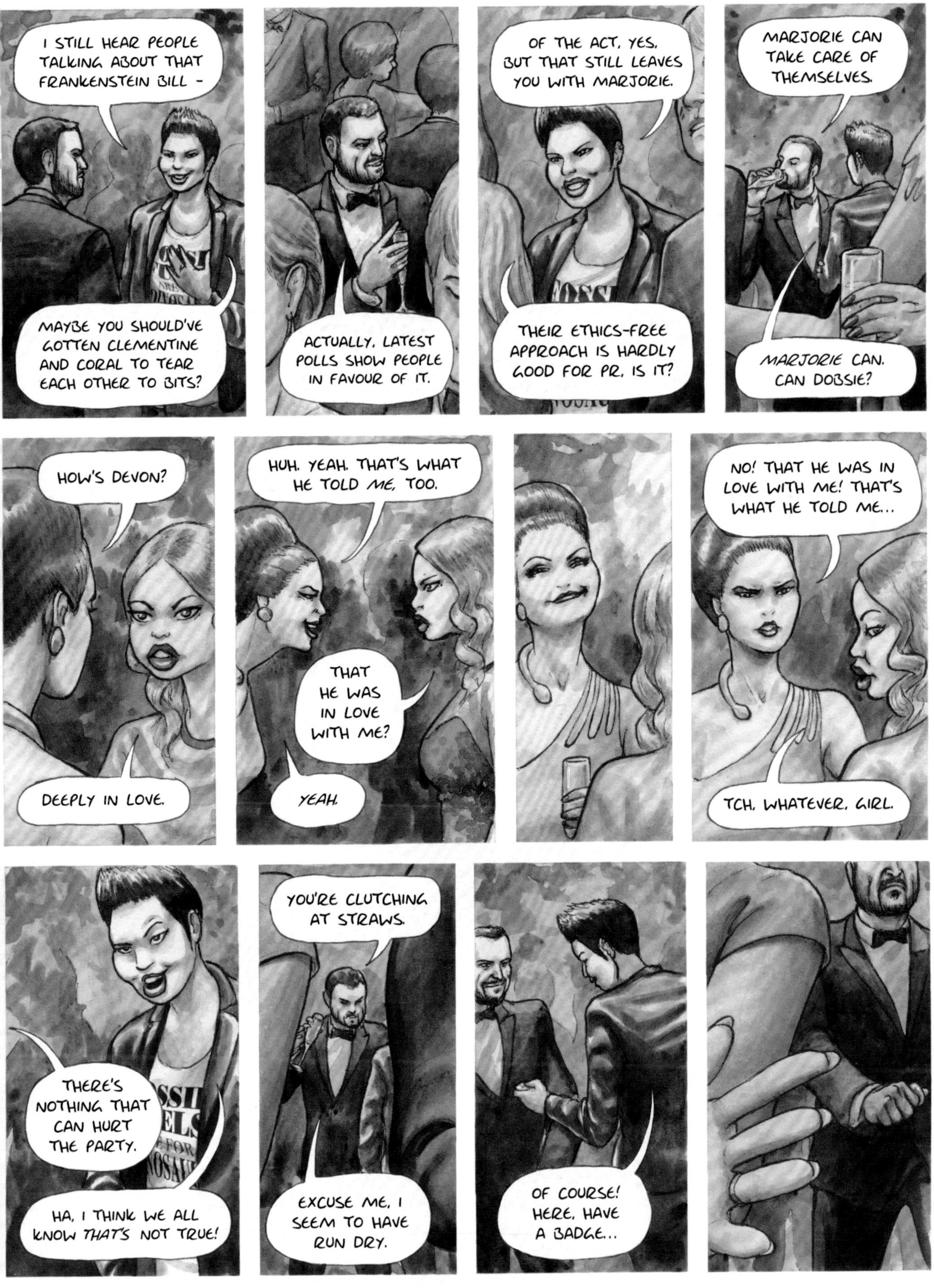

I STILL HEAR PEOPLE TALKING ABOUT THAT FRANKENSTEIN BILL -
MAYBE YOU SHOULD'VE GOTTEN CLEMENTINE AND CORAL TO TEAR EACH OTHER TO BITS?
ACTUALLY, LATEST POLLS SHOW PEOPLE IN FAVOUR OF IT.
OF THE ACT, YES, BUT THAT STILL LEAVES YOU WITH MARJORIE.
THEIR ETHICS-FREE APPROACH IS HARDLY GOOD FOR PR, IS IT?
MARJORIE CAN TAKE CARE OF THEMSELVES.
MARJORIE CAN. CAN DOBSIE?
HOW'S DEVON?
DEEPLY IN LOVE.
HUH. YEAH. THAT'S WHAT HE TOLD *ME*, TOO.
THAT HE WAS IN LOVE WITH ME?
YEAH.
NO! THAT HE WAS IN LOVE WITH ME! THAT'S WHAT HE TOLD ME...
TCH, WHATEVER, GIRL.
THERE'S NOTHING THAT CAN HURT THE PARTY.
HA, I THINK WE ALL KNOW *THAT'S* NOT TRUE!
YOU'RE CLUTCHING AT STRAWS.
EXCUSE ME, I SEEM TO HAVE RUN DRY.
OF COURSE! HERE, HAVE A BADGE...

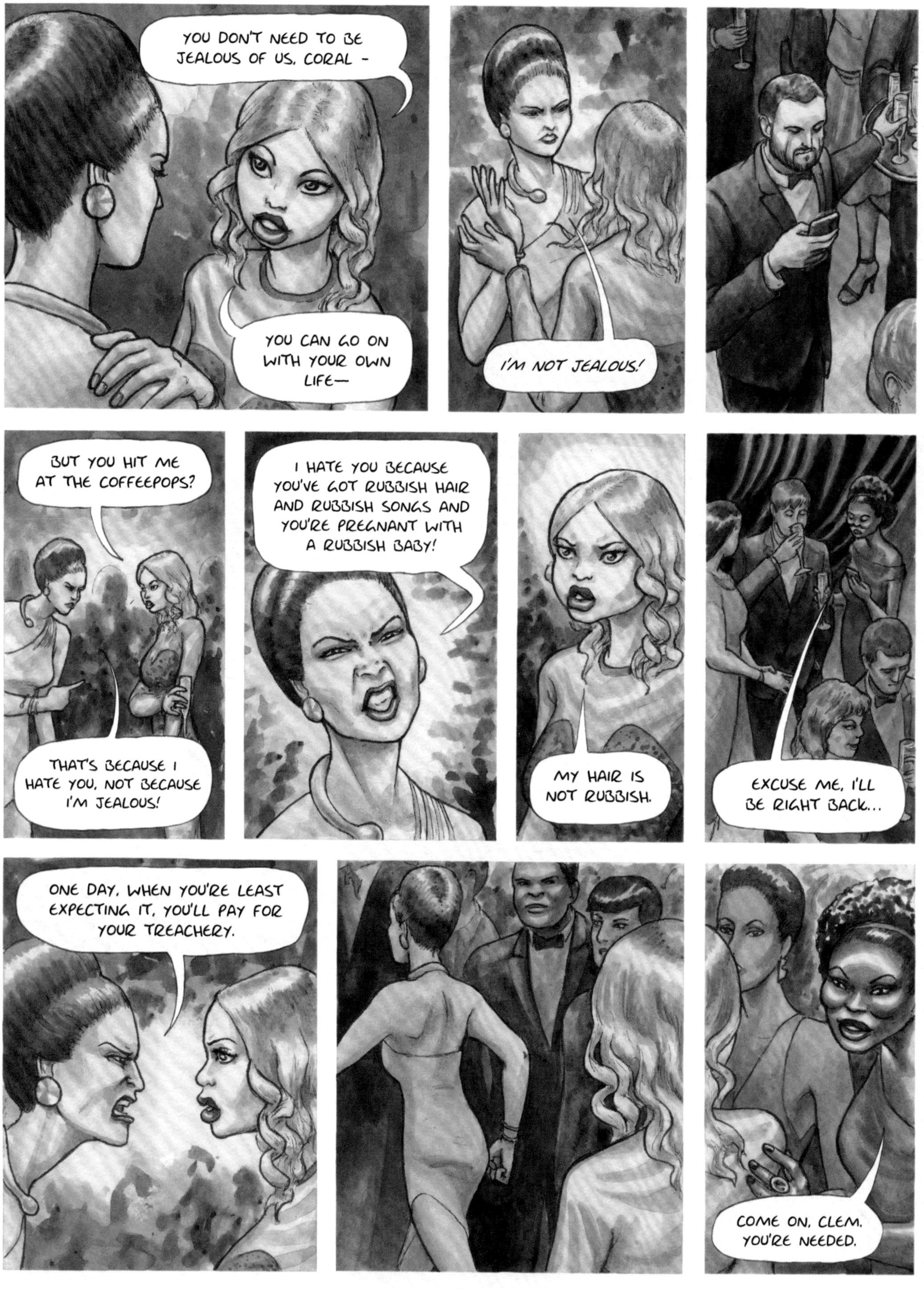
YOU DON'T NEED TO BE JEALOUS OF US, CORAL -
YOU CAN GO ON WITH YOUR OWN LIFE—
I'M NOT JEALOUS!
BUT YOU HIT ME AT THE COFFEEPOPS?
THAT'S BECAUSE I HATE YOU, NOT BECAUSE I'M JEALOUS!
I HATE YOU BECAUSE YOU'VE GOT RUBBISH HAIR AND RUBBISH SONGS AND YOU'RE PREGNANT WITH A RUBBISH BABY!
MY HAIR IS NOT RUBBISH.
EXCUSE ME, I'LL BE RIGHT BACK...
ONE DAY, WHEN YOU'RE LEAST EXPECTING IT, YOU'LL PAY FOR YOUR TREACHERY.
COME ON, CLEM. YOU'RE NEEDED.

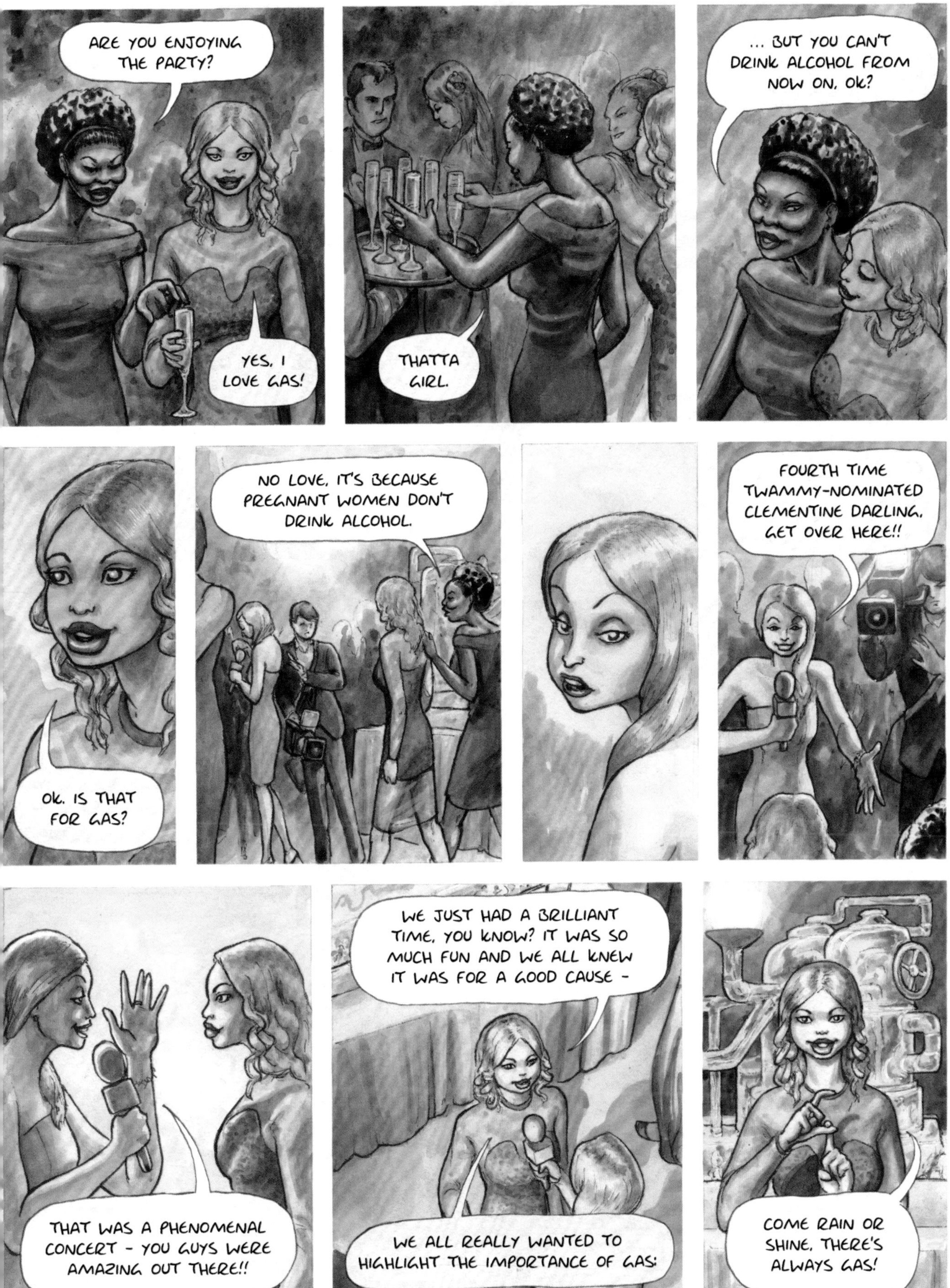
ARE YOU ENJOYING THE PARTY?
YES, I LOVE GAS!
THATTA GIRL.
... BUT YOU CAN'T DRINK ALCOHOL FROM NOW ON, OK?
OK. IS THAT FOR GAS?
NO LOVE, IT'S BECAUSE PREGNANT WOMEN DON'T DRINK ALCOHOL.
FOURTH TIME TWAMMY-NOMINATED CLEMENTINE DARLING, GET OVER HERE!!
THAT WAS A PHENOMENAL CONCERT - YOU GUYS WERE AMAZING OUT THERE!!
WE JUST HAD A BRILLIANT TIME, YOU KNOW? IT WAS SO MUCH FUN AND WE ALL KNEW IT WAS FOR A GOOD CAUSE -
WE ALL REALLY WANTED TO HIGHLIGHT THE IMPORTANCE OF GAS:
COME RAIN OR SHINE, THERE'S ALWAYS GAS!

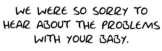

WE WERE SO SORRY TO HEAR ABOUT THE PROBLEMS WITH YOUR BABY.

OH...YEAH, THIS IS A DIFFICULT TIME.

OUR THOUGHTS AND PRAYERS ARE WITH YOU AT THIS DIFFICULT TIME.

THANKS, YOUR WISHES MEAN A LOT TO ME AT THIS DIFFICULT TIME.

SO THE QUESTION ON EVERYONE'S LIPS IS WHAT WIL...

HEY, 'JOURNALISTS'! YOU GUYS WANT A BREAKING STORY?

WHILE THIS LOT SIP GAS-BOUGHT CHAMPAGNE, MARJORIE HAS BEEN MAKING SLAVES:

HUMAN CLONES THAT THEY HAVE COMPLETE OWNERSHIP OF!

WHY DOESN'T THE GOVERNMENT PUT A STOP TO THIS?

WHY DON'T THEY TAKE CONTROL OF THE SITUATION?

ARE THEY HOPING WE'LL ALL LOOK THE OTHER WAY??

WELL, GOOD LUCK WITH THAT!

THIS THURSDAY, WHILE THESE CHUCKLEFUCKS ARE ALL OUT AT THE TWAMMIES, WE'LL BE HOLDING A RALLY IN PARLIAMENT SQUARE!

TRANSPARENCY NOW!

CRACK

WHAT'S TRENDIN

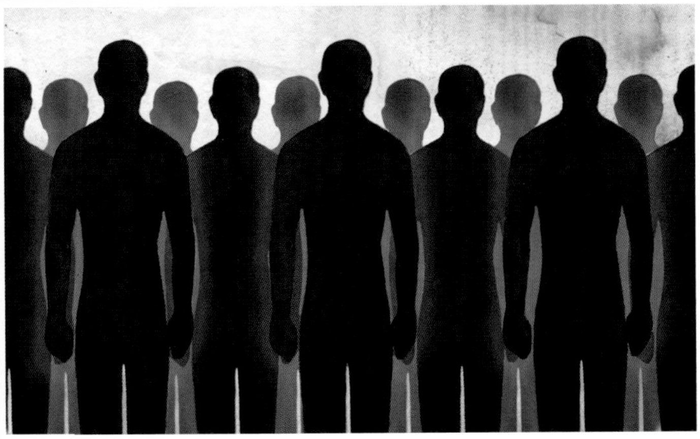

WHAT IS MARJORIE UP TO?

Pressure for public inquiry builds following concern over extent of 'sinister' experiments in human cloning as corporation continues to hide behind trade secrets act

237 comments

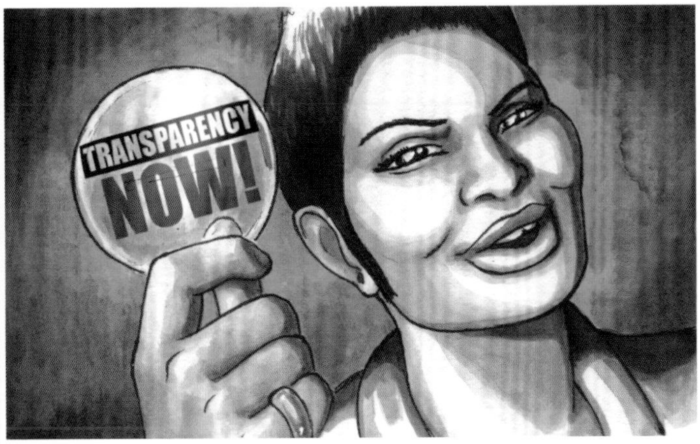
TRANSPARENCY
NOW!

DON'T MESS WITH MALICK

Nina Malick's people-powered protest over human cloning experiments enters records as fastest growing petition ever, currently at nearly 12m signatures

221 comments

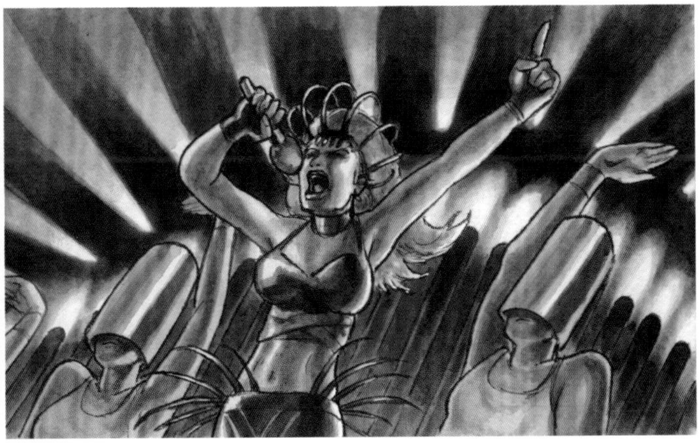

GAS AID RAISES £142m

'Never in our wildest dreams did we hope to raise this much'

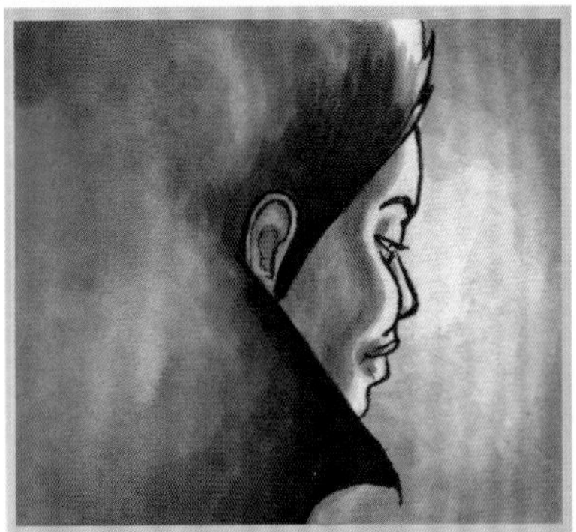

PUBLIC EYE: new tour dates announced after sales soar for Malick's new album SWITCHED BLADE

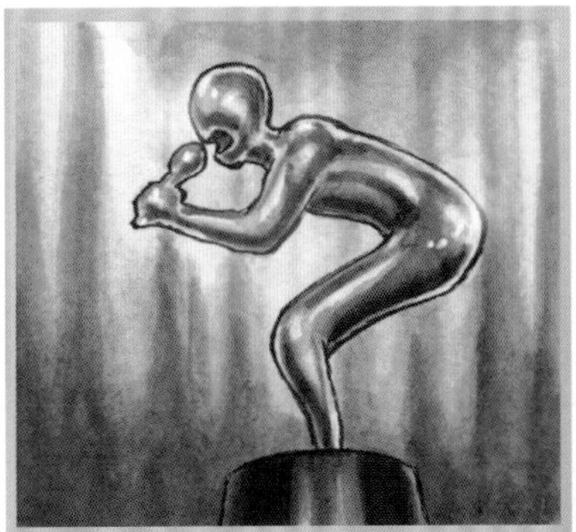

GOING FOR GOLD: preparations underway for this year's Twammy Awards suggest event will be biggest in 15 year history

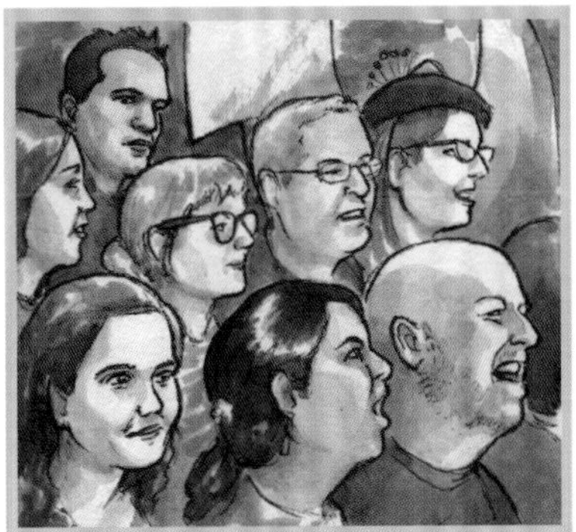

RABBLE ROUSING: huge protest to take place outside parliament in response to secrecy over 'Clone-gate'

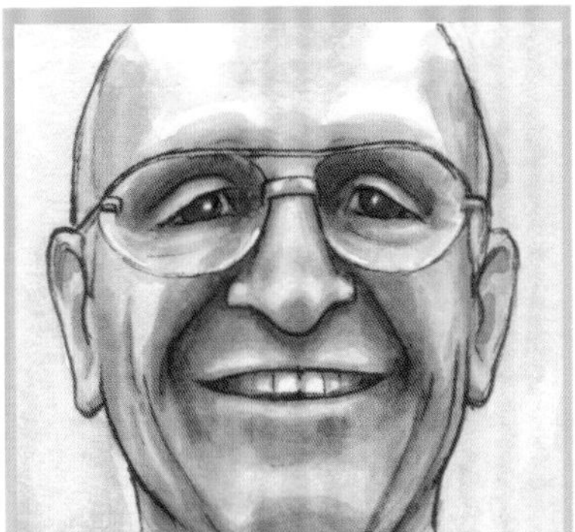

PERVERT ARRESTED: Police have charged a

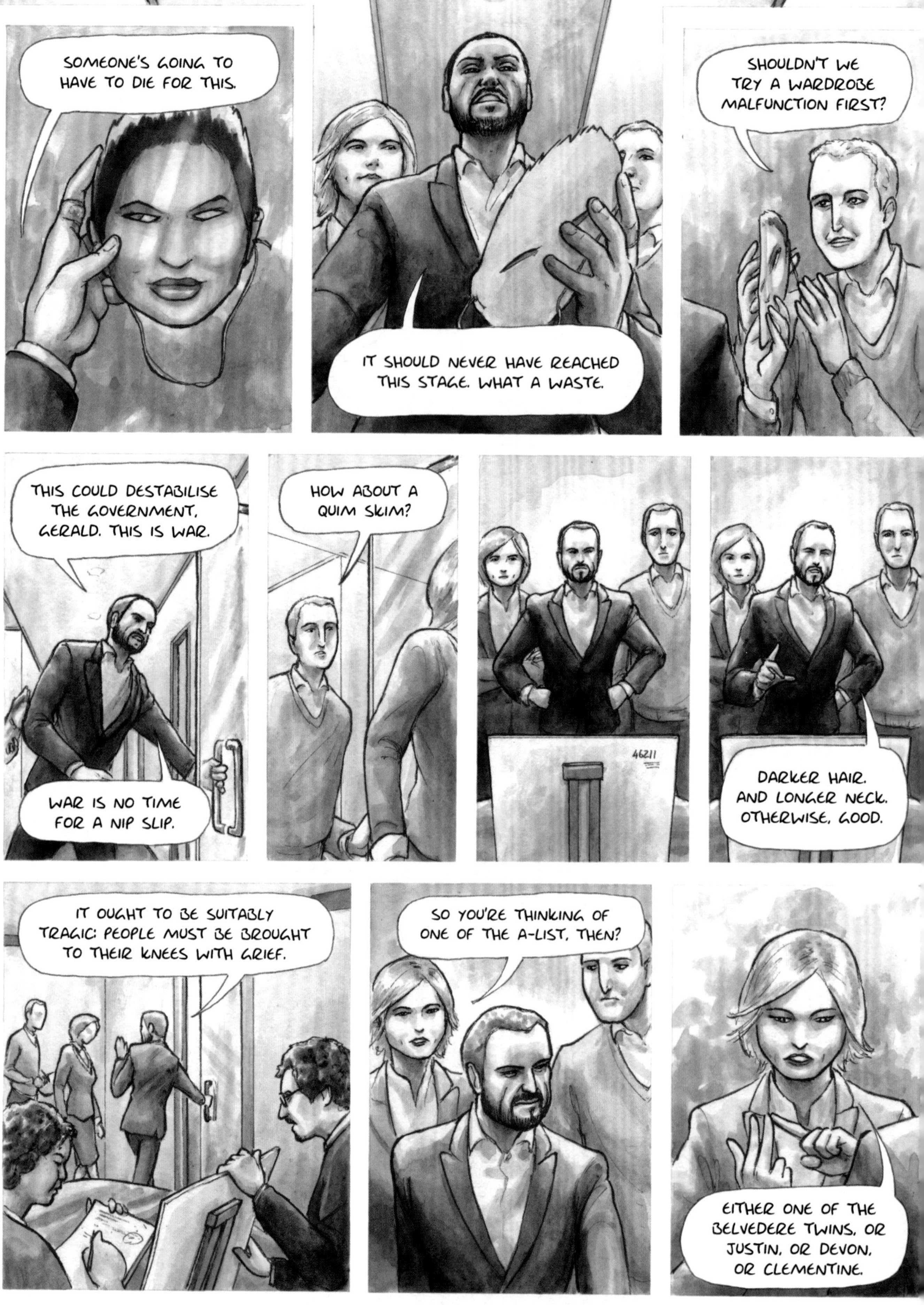
SOMEONE'S GOING TO HAVE TO DIE FOR THIS.
IT SHOULD NEVER HAVE REACHED THIS STAGE. WHAT A WASTE.
SHOULDN'T WE TRY A WARDROBE MALFUNCTION FIRST?
THIS COULD DESTABILISE THE GOVERNMENT, GERALD. THIS IS WAR.
WAR IS NO TIME FOR A NIP SLIP.
HOW ABOUT A QUIM SKIM?
46211
DARKER HAIR. AND LONGER NECK. OTHERWISE, GOOD.
IT OUGHT TO BE SUITABLY TRAGIC: PEOPLE MUST BE BROUGHT TO THEIR KNEES WITH GRIEF.
SO YOU'RE THINKING OF ONE OF THE A-LIST, THEN?
EITHER ONE OF THE BELVEDERE TWINS, OR JUSTIN, OR DEVON, OR CLEMENTINE.

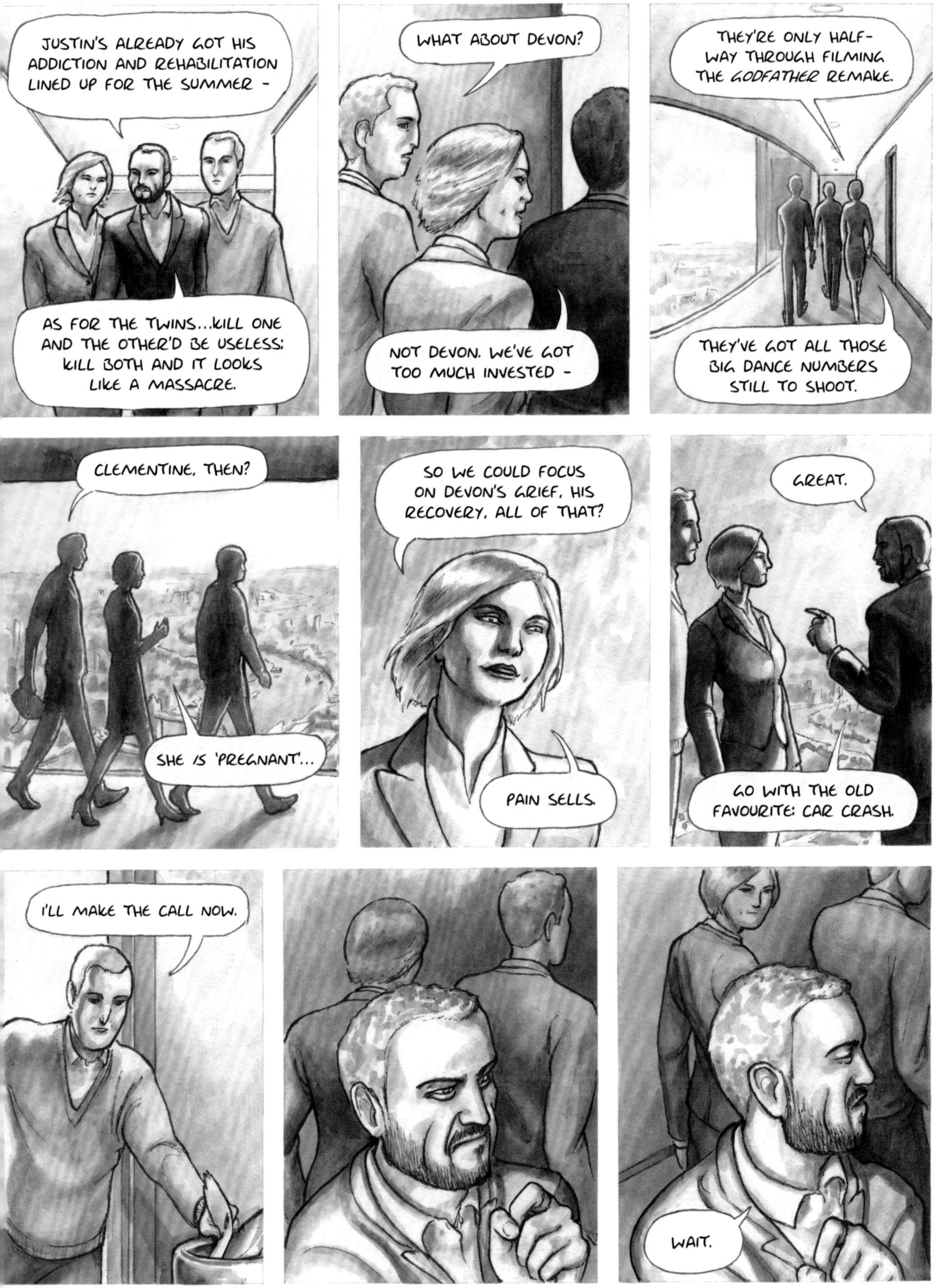
JUSTIN'S ALREADY GOT HIS ADDICTION AND REHABILITATION LINED UP FOR THE SUMMER -
AS FOR THE TWINS...KILL ONE AND THE OTHER'D BE USELESS: KILL BOTH AND IT LOOKS LIKE A MASSACRE.
WHAT ABOUT DEVON?
NOT DEVON. WE'VE GOT TOO MUCH INVESTED -
THEY'RE ONLY HALF-WAY THROUGH FILMING THE *GODFATHER* REMAKE.
THEY'VE GOT ALL THOSE BIG DANCE NUMBERS STILL TO SHOOT.
CLEMENTINE, THEN?
SHE IS 'PREGNANT'...
SO WE COULD FOCUS ON DEVON'S GRIEF, HIS RECOVERY, ALL OF THAT?
PAIN SELLS.
GREAT.
GO WITH THE OLD FAVOURITE: CAR CRASH.
I'LL MAKE THE CALL NOW.
WAIT.

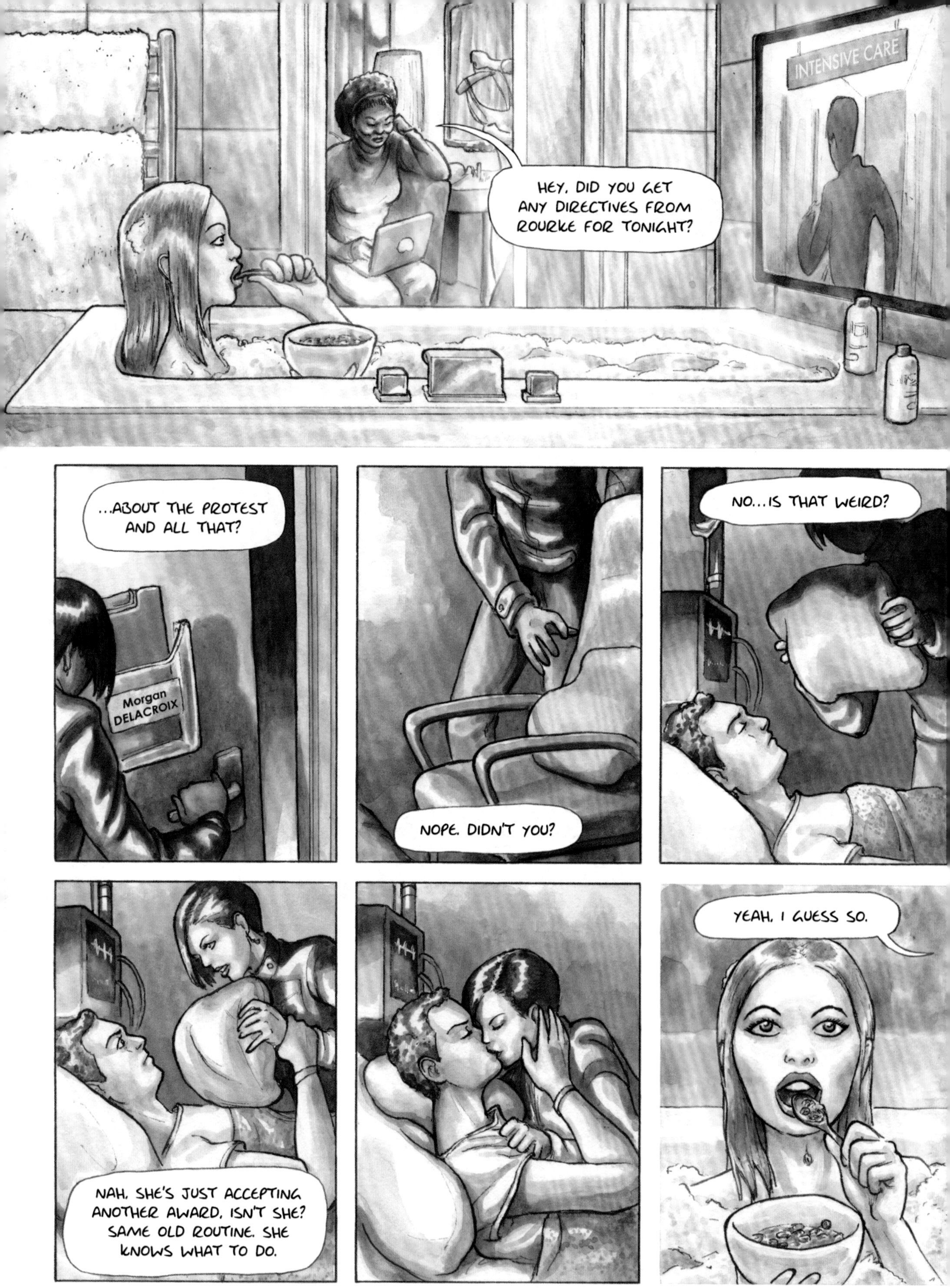
INTENSIVE CARE
HEY, DID YOU GET ANY DIRECTIVES FROM ROURKE FOR TONIGHT?
...ABOUT THE PROTEST AND ALL THAT?
Morgan DELACROIX
NOPE. DIDN'T YOU?
NO... IS THAT WEIRD?
NAH, SHE'S JUST ACCEPTING ANOTHER AWARD, ISN'T SHE? SAME OLD ROUTINE. SHE KNOWS WHAT TO DO.
YEAH, I GUESS SO.

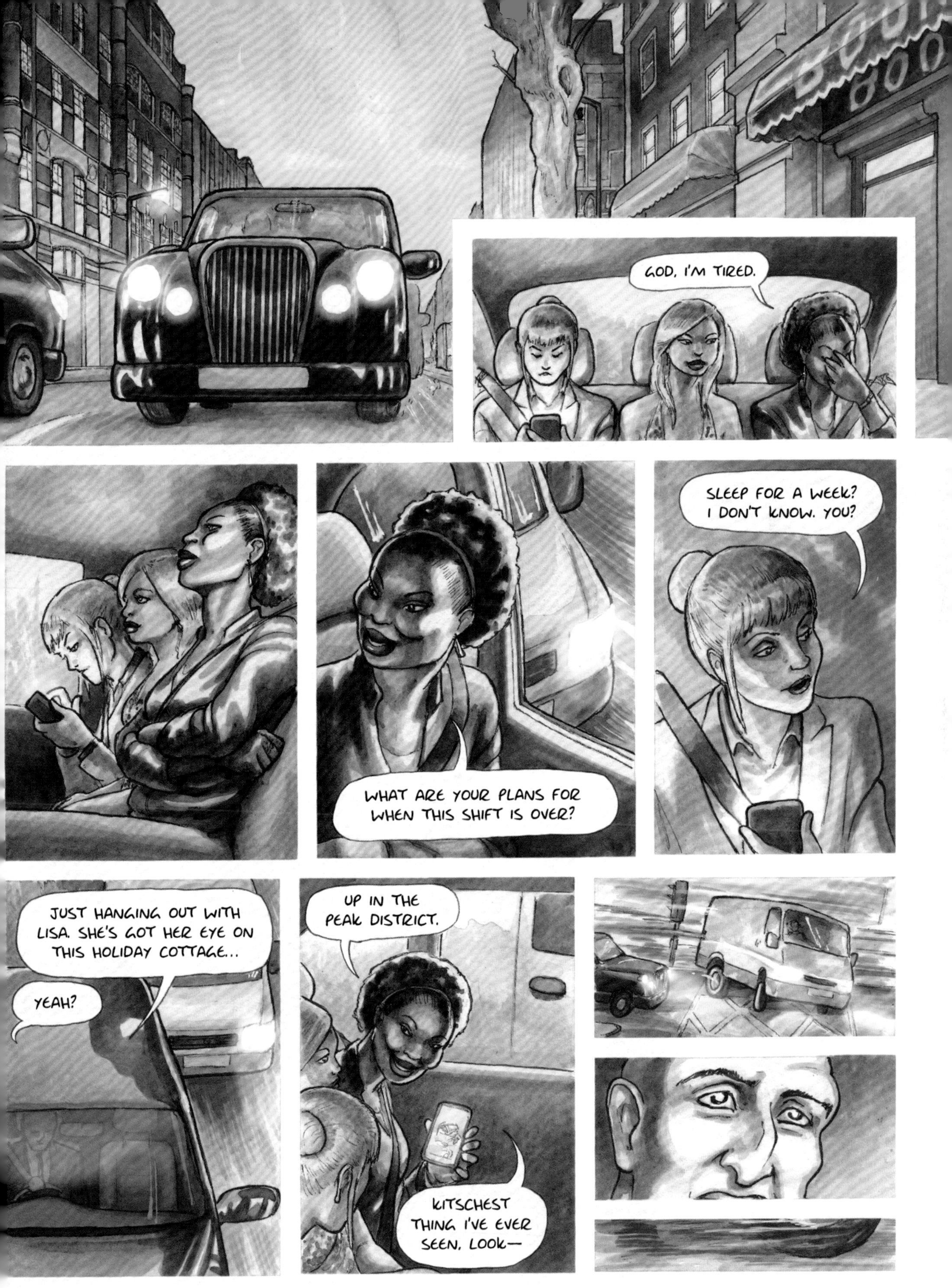
GOD, I'M TIRED.
WHAT ARE YOUR PLANS FOR WHEN THIS SHIFT IS OVER?
SLEEP FOR A WEEK? I DON'T KNOW. YOU?
JUST HANGING OUT WITH LISA. SHE'S GOT HER EYE ON THIS HOLIDAY COTTAGE...
YEAH?
UP IN THE PEAK DISTRICT.
KITSCHEST THING I'VE EVER SEEN, LOOK—

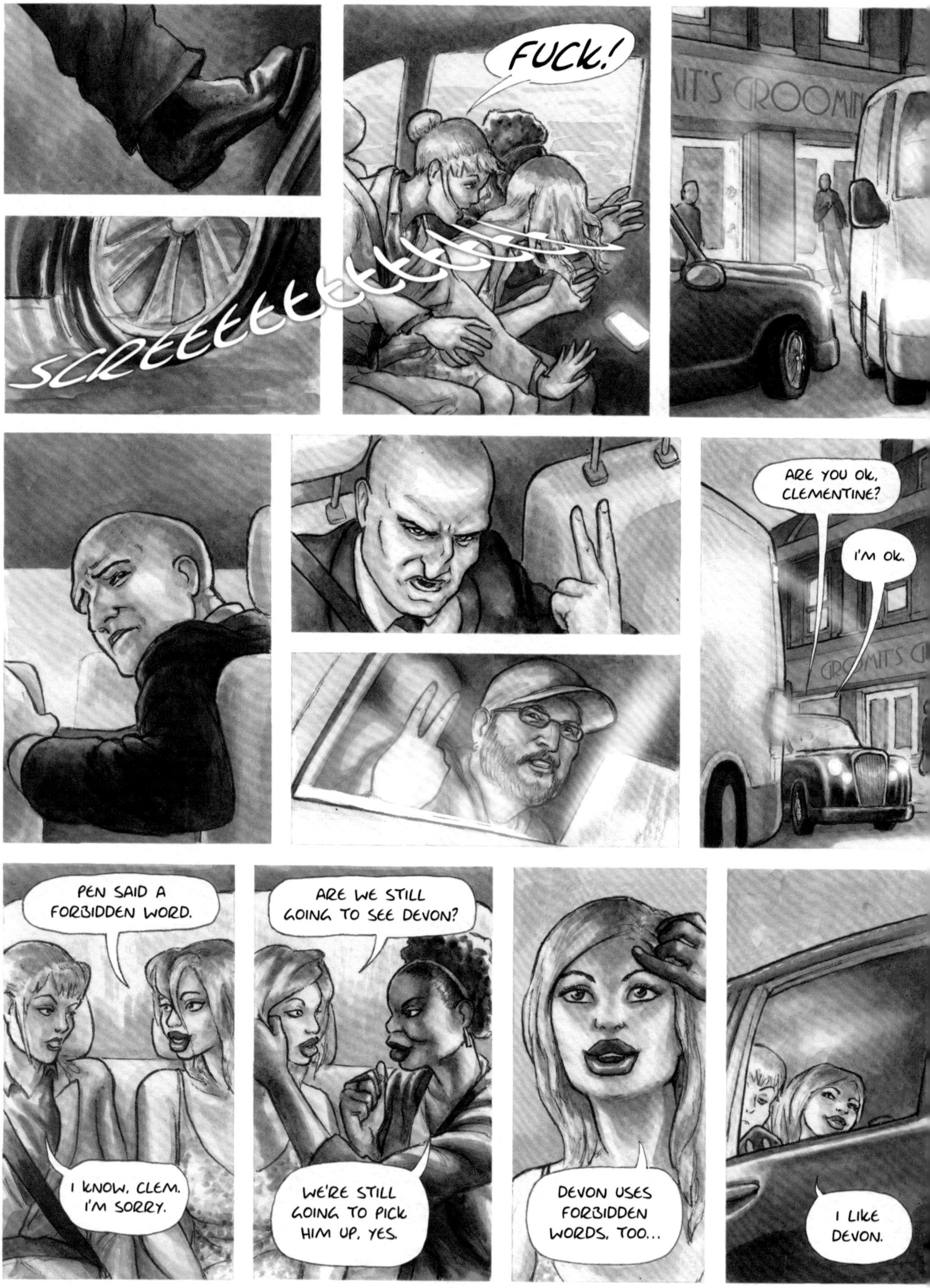
FUCK!
SCREEEEEEEEEE
MIT'S GROOMIN
ARE YOU OK, CLEMENTINE?
I'M OK.
GROMIT'S G
PEN SAID A FORBIDDEN WORD.
I KNOW, CLEM. I'M SORRY.
ARE WE STILL GOING TO SEE DEVON?
WE'RE STILL GOING TO PICK HIM UP, YES.
DEVON USES FORBIDDEN WORDS, TOO...
I LIKE DEVON.

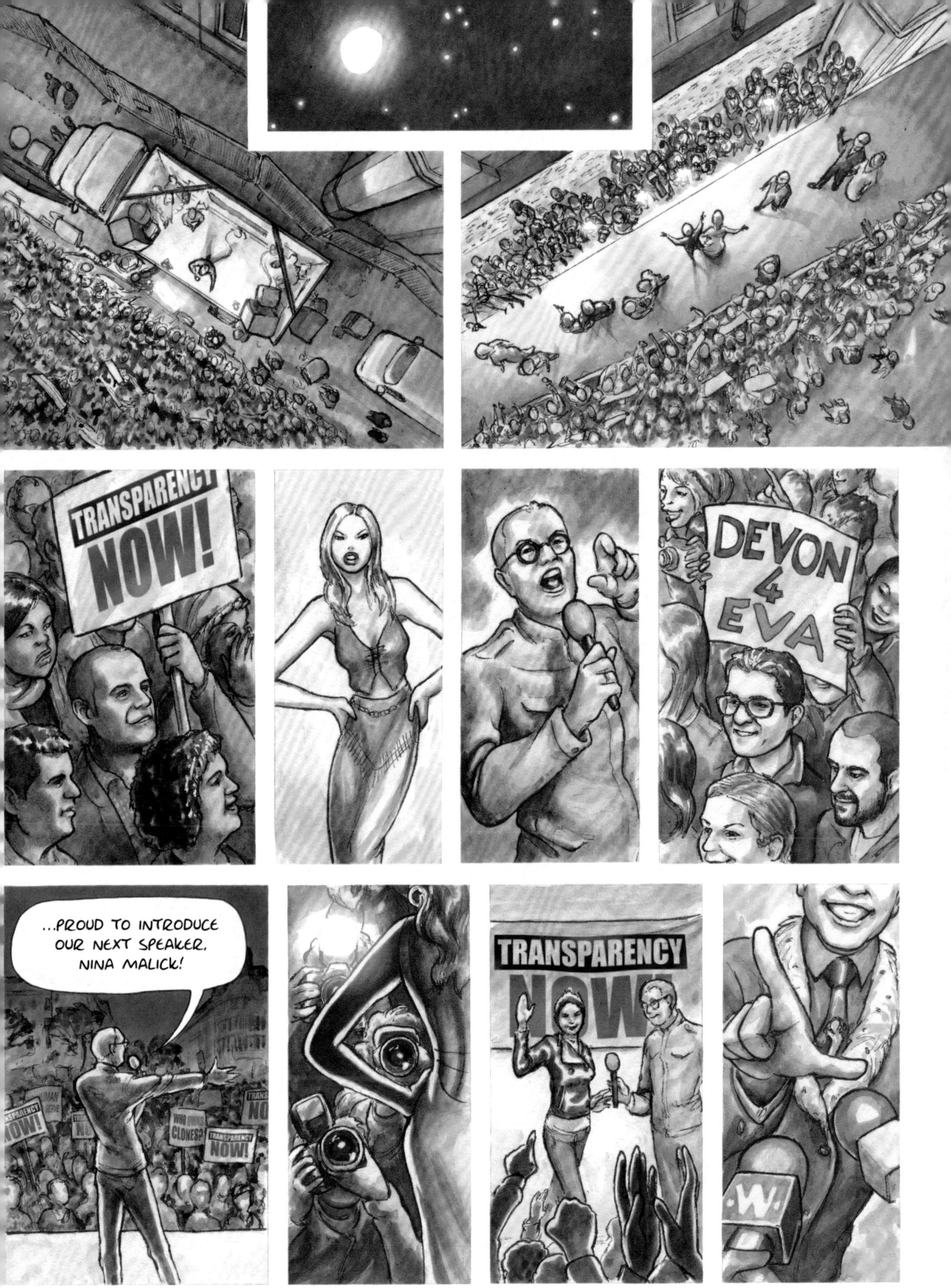
TRANSPARENCY NOW!
DEVON 4 EVA
...PROUD TO INTRODUCE OUR NEXT SPEAKER, NINA MALICK!
WHO OWNS CLONES?
TRANSPARENCY NOW!
TRANSPARENCY

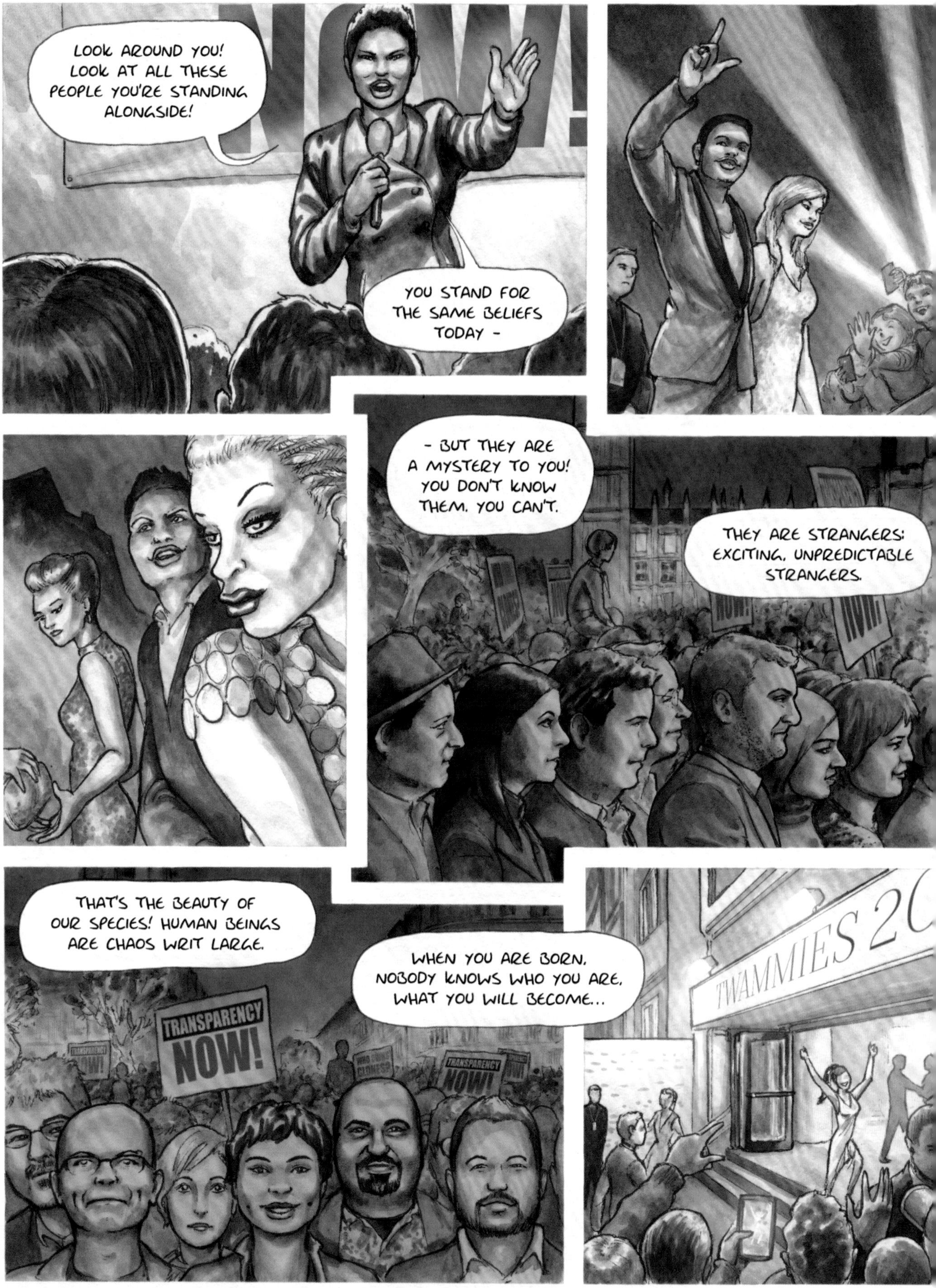
LOOK AROUND YOU! LOOK AT ALL THESE PEOPLE YOU'RE STANDING ALONGSIDE!
YOU STAND FOR THE SAME BELIEFS TODAY -
- BUT THEY ARE A MYSTERY TO YOU! YOU DON'T KNOW THEM. YOU CAN'T.
THEY ARE STRANGERS: EXCITING, UNPREDICTABLE STRANGERS.
THAT'S THE BEAUTY OF OUR SPECIES! HUMAN BEINGS ARE CHAOS WRIT LARGE.
WHEN YOU ARE BORN, NOBODY KNOWS WHO YOU ARE, WHAT YOU WILL BECOME...
TRANSPARENCY NOW!
TWAMMIES

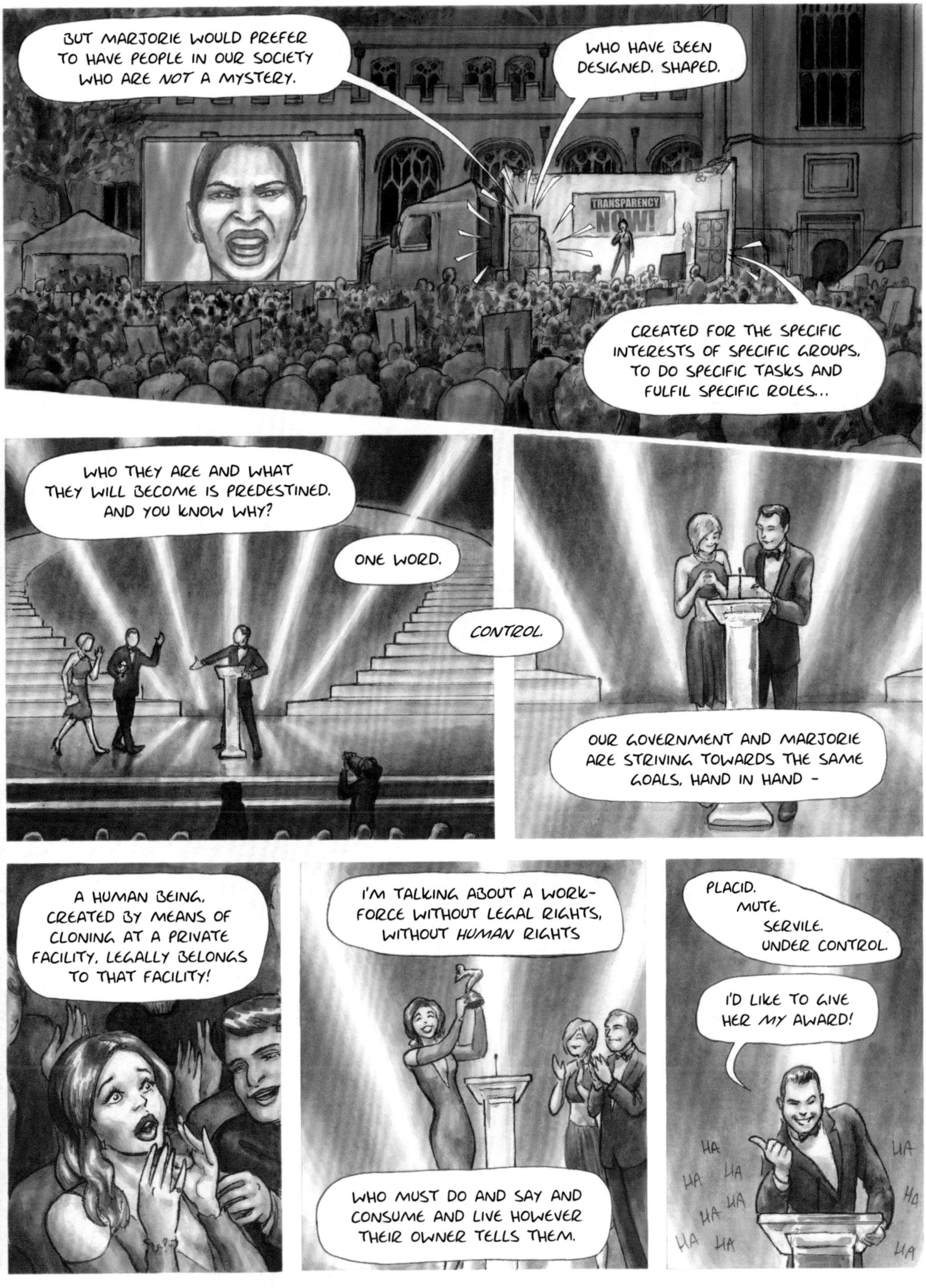

BUT MARJORIE WOULD PREFER TO HAVE PEOPLE IN OUR SOCIETY WHO ARE *NOT* A MYSTERY.
WHO HAVE BEEN DESIGNED. SHAPED.
TRANSPARENCY NOW!
CREATED FOR THE SPECIFIC INTERESTS OF SPECIFIC GROUPS, TO DO SPECIFIC TASKS AND FULFIL SPECIFIC ROLES...
WHO THEY ARE AND WHAT THEY WILL BECOME IS PREDESTINED. AND YOU KNOW WHY?
ONE WORD.
CONTROL.
OUR GOVERNMENT AND MARJORIE ARE STRIVING TOWARDS THE SAME GOALS, HAND IN HAND –
A HUMAN BEING, CREATED BY MEANS OF CLONING AT A PRIVATE FACILITY, LEGALLY BELONGS TO THAT FACILITY!
I'M TALKING ABOUT A WORK-FORCE WITHOUT LEGAL RIGHTS, WITHOUT *HUMAN* RIGHTS
WHO MUST DO AND SAY AND CONSUME AND LIVE HOWEVER THEIR OWNER TELLS THEM.
PLACID. MUTE. SERVILE. UNDER CONTROL.
I'D LIKE TO GIVE HER *MY* AWARD!
HA HA HA HA HA HA HA HA HA HA

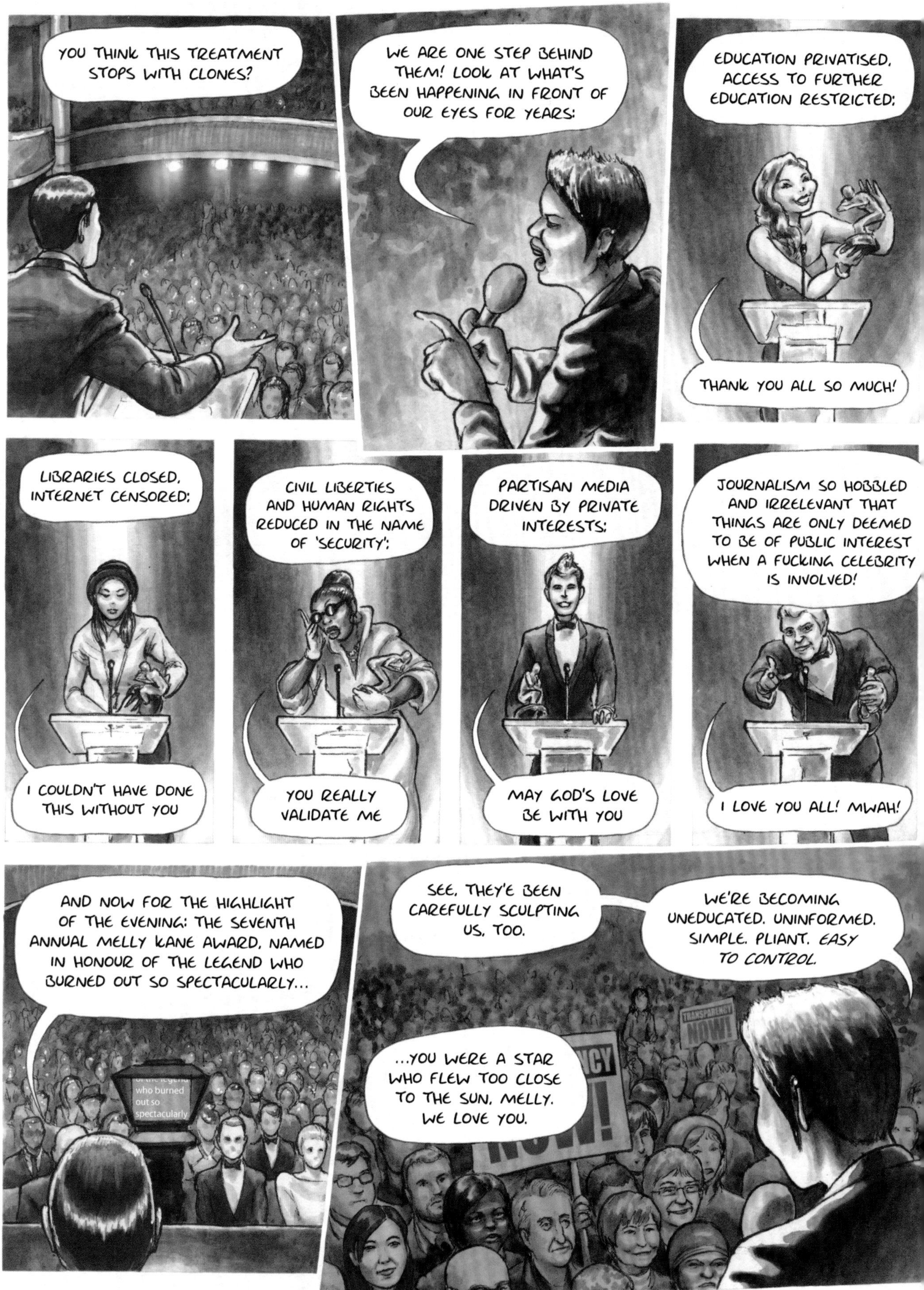
YOU THINK THIS TREATMENT STOPS WITH CLONES?
WE ARE ONE STEP BEHIND THEM! LOOK AT WHAT'S BEEN HAPPENING IN FRONT OF OUR EYES FOR YEARS:
EDUCATION PRIVATISED. ACCESS TO FURTHER EDUCATION RESTRICTED;
THANK YOU ALL SO MUCH!
LIBRARIES CLOSED, INTERNET CENSORED;
I COULDN'T HAVE DONE THIS WITHOUT YOU
CIVIL LIBERTIES AND HUMAN RIGHTS REDUCED IN THE NAME OF 'SECURITY';
YOU REALLY VALIDATE ME
PARTISAN MEDIA DRIVEN BY PRIVATE INTERESTS;
MAY GOD'S LOVE BE WITH YOU
JOURNALISM SO HOBBLED AND IRRELEVANT THAT THINGS ARE ONLY DEEMED TO BE OF PUBLIC INTEREST WHEN A FUCKING CELEBRITY IS INVOLVED!
I LOVE YOU ALL! MWAH!
AND NOW FOR THE HIGHLIGHT OF THE EVENING: THE SEVENTH ANNUAL MELLY KANE AWARD, NAMED IN HONOUR OF THE LEGEND WHO BURNED OUT SO SPECTACULARLY...
who burned out so spectacularly
SEE, THEY'E BEEN CAREFULLY SCULPTING US, TOO.
WE'RE BECOMING UNEDUCATED. UNINFORMED. SIMPLE. PLIANT. EASY TO CONTROL.
TRANSPARENCY NOW!
...YOU WERE A STAR WHO FLEW TOO CLOSE TO THE SUN, MELLY. WE LOVE YOU.

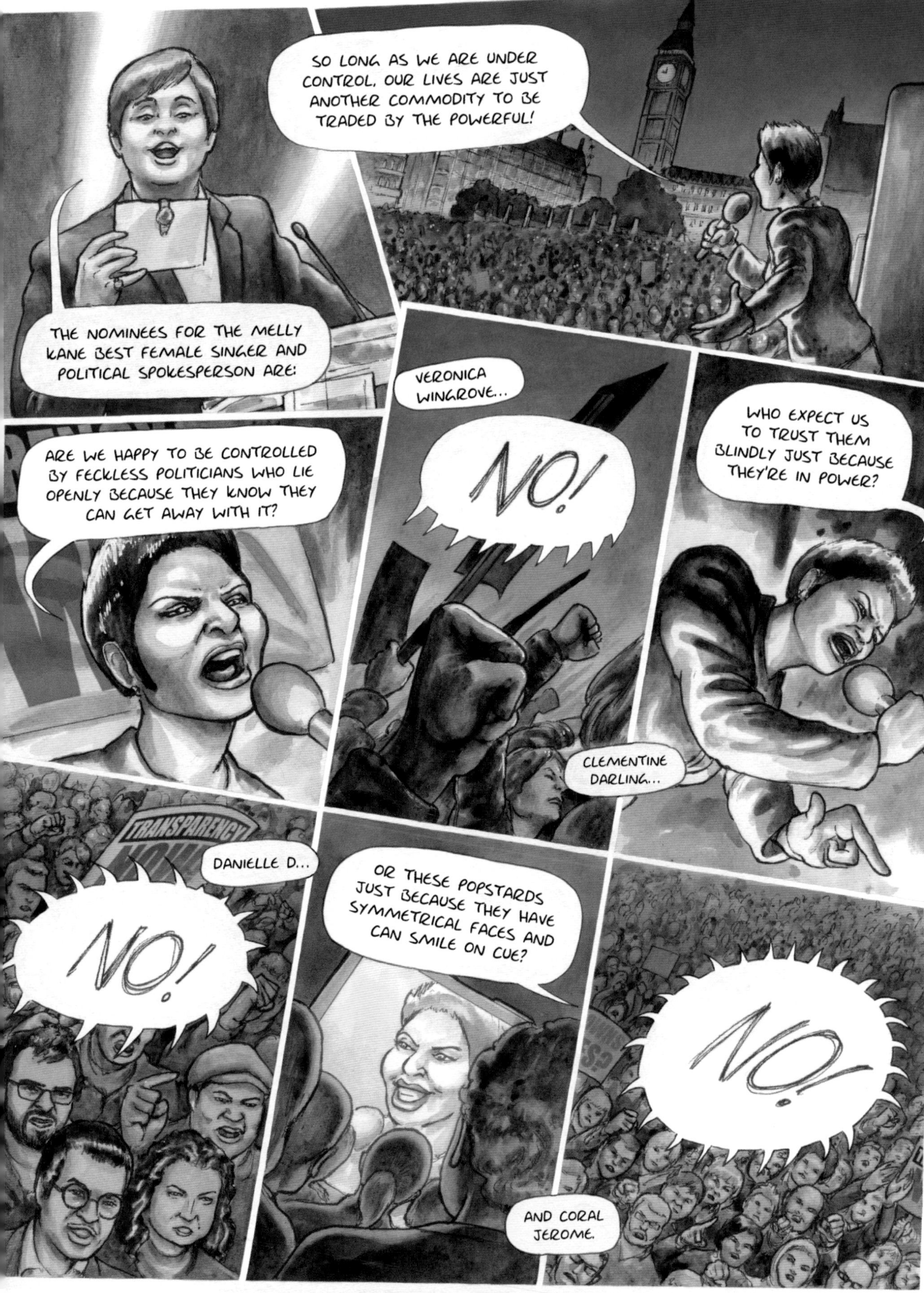
SO LONG AS WE ARE UNDER CONTROL, OUR LIVES ARE JUST ANOTHER COMMODITY TO BE TRADED BY THE POWERFUL!
THE NOMINEES FOR THE MELLY KANE BEST FEMALE SINGER AND POLITICAL SPOKESPERSON ARE:
VERONICA WINGROVE...
ARE WE HAPPY TO BE CONTROLLED BY FECKLESS POLITICIANS WHO LIE OPENLY BECAUSE THEY KNOW THEY CAN GET AWAY WITH IT?
NO!
WHO EXPECT US TO TRUST THEM BLINDLY JUST BECAUSE THEY'RE IN POWER?
CLEMENTINE DARLING...
TRANSPARENCY
DANIELLE D...
NO!
OR THESE POPSTARDS JUST BECAUSE THEY HAVE SYMMETRICAL FACES AND CAN SMILE ON CUE?
NO!
AND CORAL JEROME.

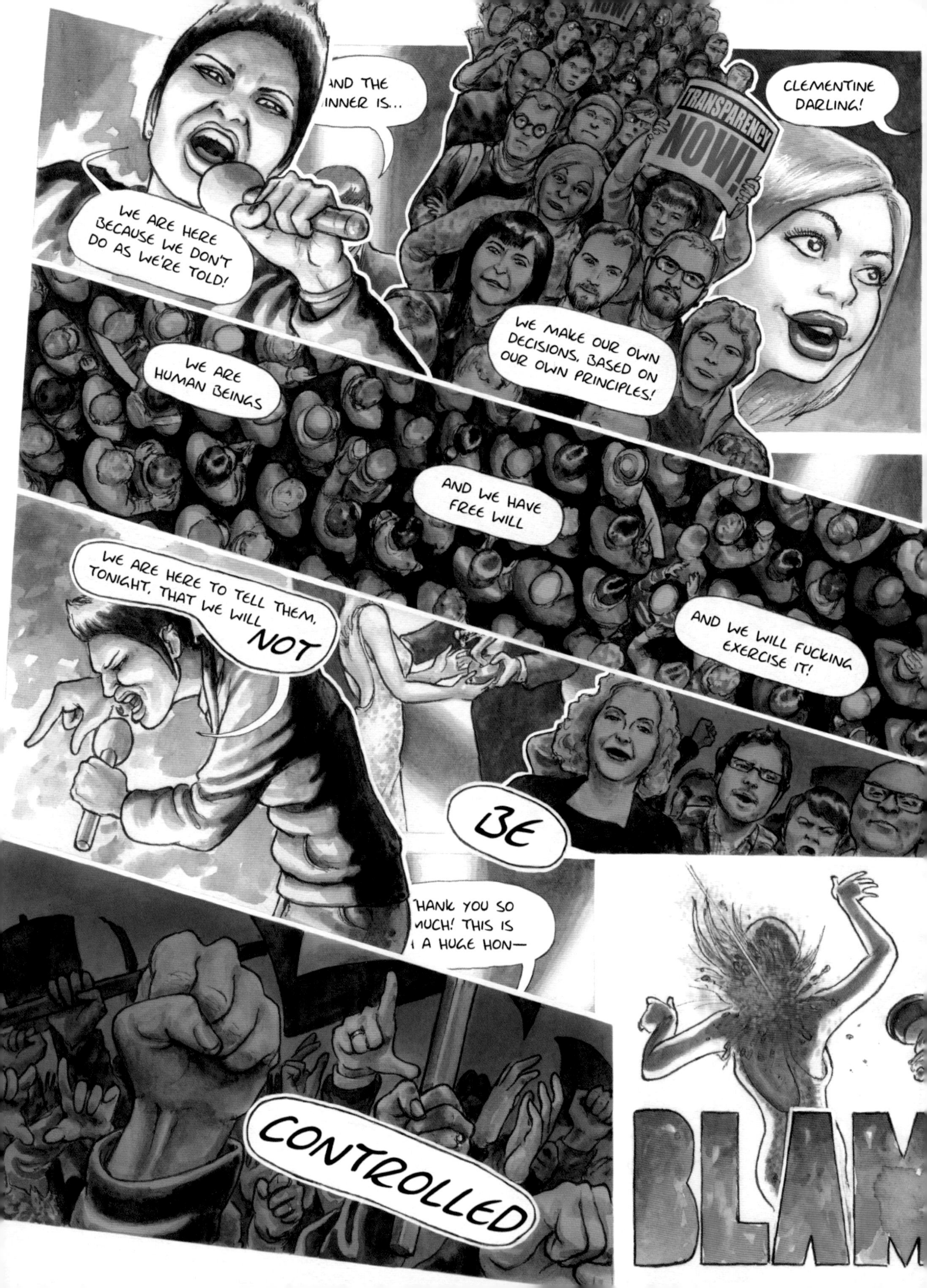

AND THE
WINNER IS...
CLEMENTINE DARLING!
WE ARE HERE BECAUSE WE DON'T DO AS WE'RE TOLD!
WE MAKE OUR OWN DECISIONS, BASED ON OUR OWN PRINCIPLES!
WE ARE HUMAN BEINGS
AND WE HAVE FREE WILL
AND WE WILL FUCKING EXERCISE IT!
WE ARE HERE TO TELL THEM, TONIGHT, THAT WE WILL NOT
BE
CONTROLLED
THANK YOU SO MUCH! THIS IS A HUGE HON—
BLAM

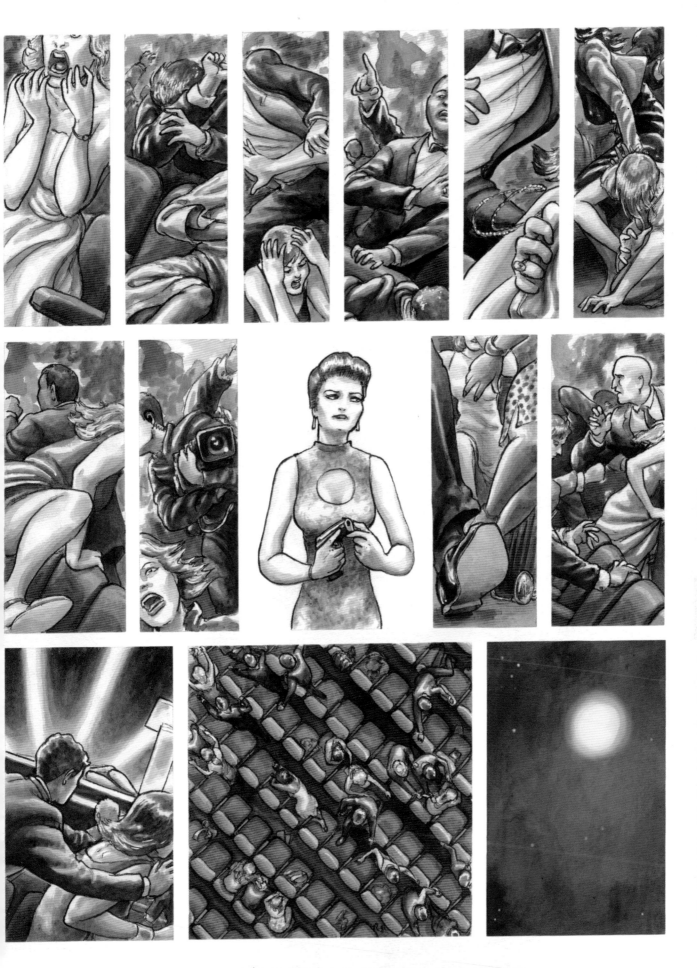

WHAT'S TRENDING

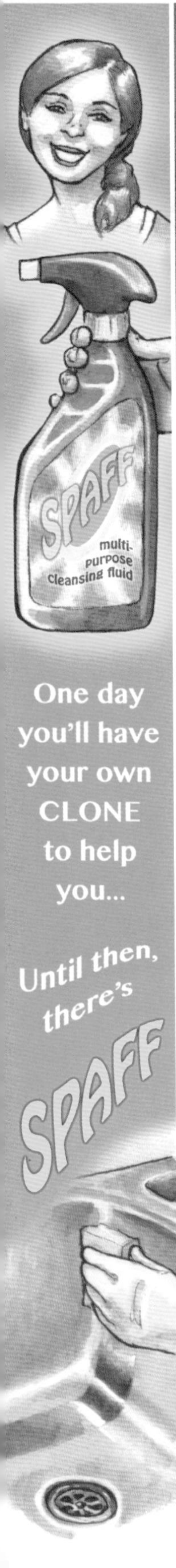

SPAFF
multi-purpose cleansing fluid
One day you'll have your own CLONE to help you...
Until then, there's
SPAFF

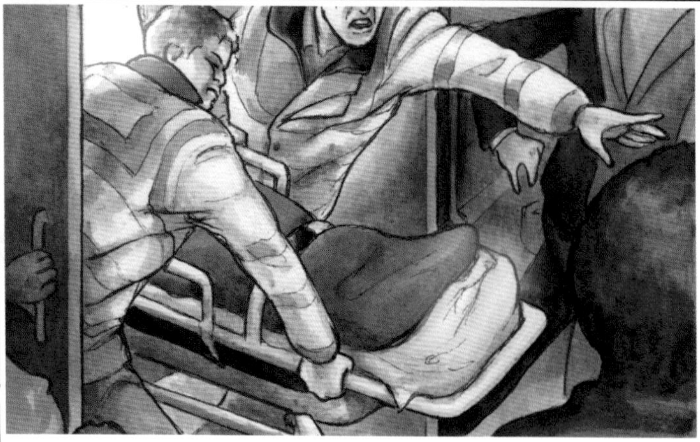

CLEMENTINE FIGHTING FOR LIFE

The young star is clinging to life following the shocking assault that took place as she received her award for Best Female Singer and Political Spokesperson at the Twammies

1154 comments

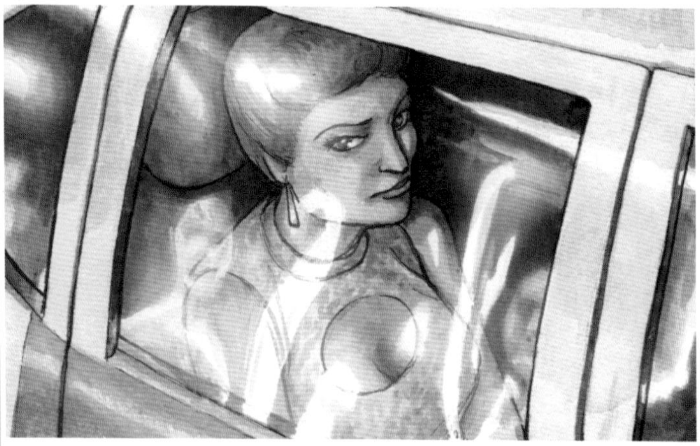

VICIOUS CORAL UNREPENTANT

Onlookers talk of chilling 'cold, dead stare' as police arrested the 20-year-old for the attempted murder of Clementine Darling and firearm offences

960 comments

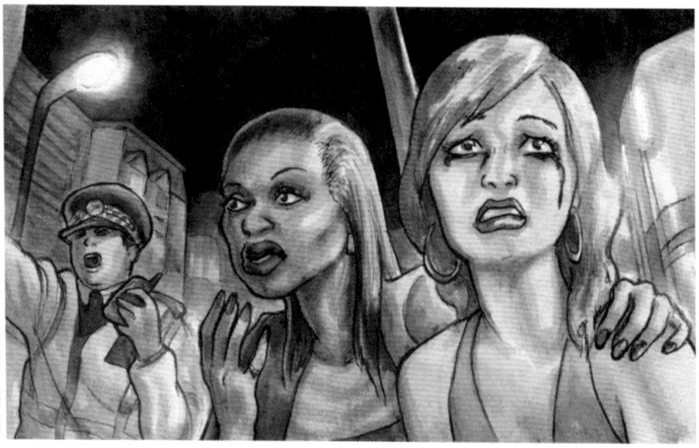

TRAGIC TWAMMY AFTERMATH

Disturbing eyewitness accounts of the scene that unfolded last

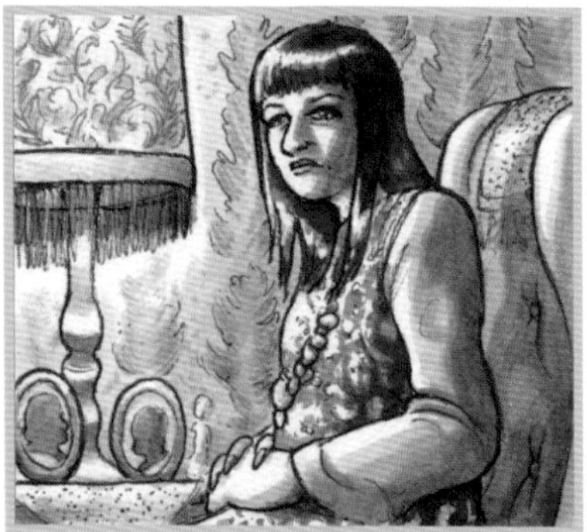

'I COULD HAVE SAVED CLEMENTINE': TV's Psychic Su learned of imminent attack from 'angels', but police dismissed her calls as 'rubbish'

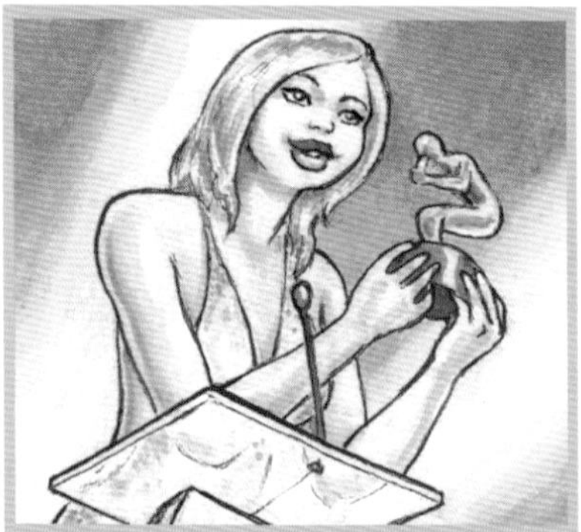

VIDEO: amateur footage of the shooting (WARNING GRAPHIC CONTENT)

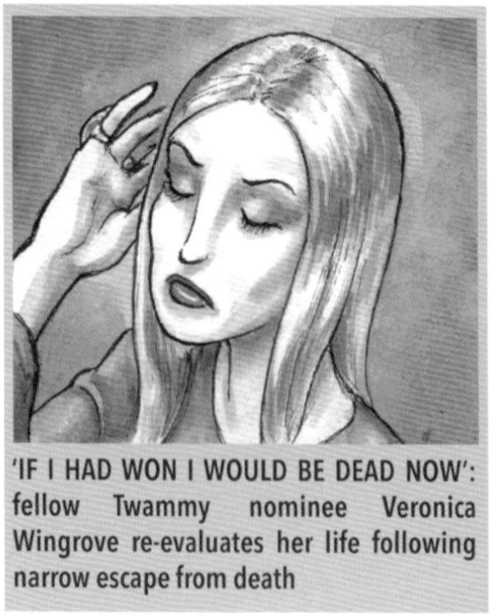

'IF I HAD WON I WOULD BE DEAD NOW': fellow Twammy nominee Veronica Wingrove re-evaluates her life following narrow escape from death

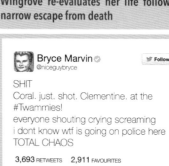

Bryce Marvin
@niceguybryce
Follow

SHIT
Coral. just. shot. Clementine. at the #Twammies!
everyone shouting crying screaming
i dont know wtf is going on police here
TOTAL CHAOS

3,693 RETWEETS 2,911 FAVOURITES

AS IT HAPPENED: what the stars said on social media during that terrible night -

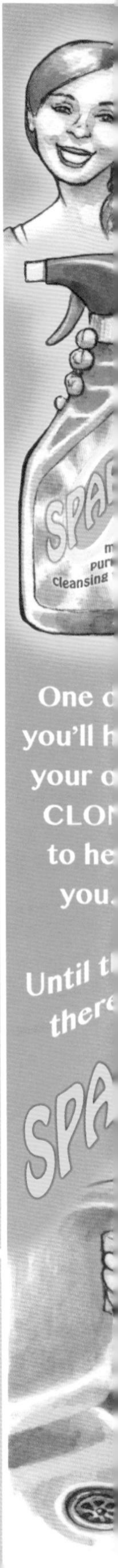

WHAT'S TRENDING

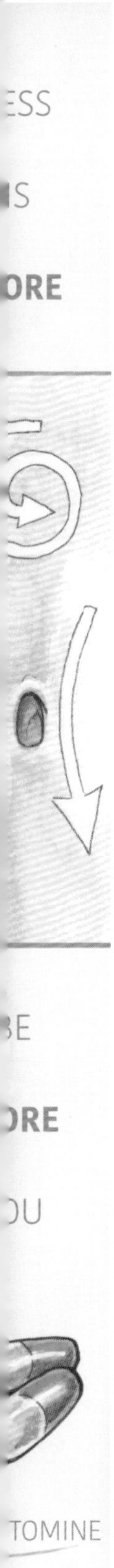

ESS
IS
ORE
BE
ORE
OU
TOMINE

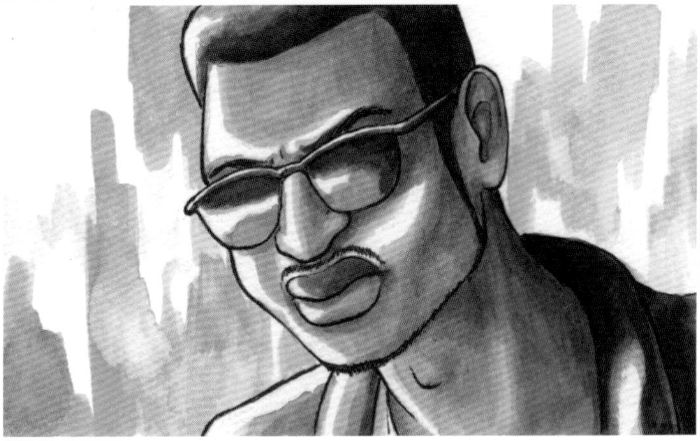

AYRE'S ANGUISH

Devon describes 'the worst kind of agony' waiting to hear if girlfriend Clementine will survive surgery to repair gunshot wound inflicted by Coral at the Twammies

216 comments

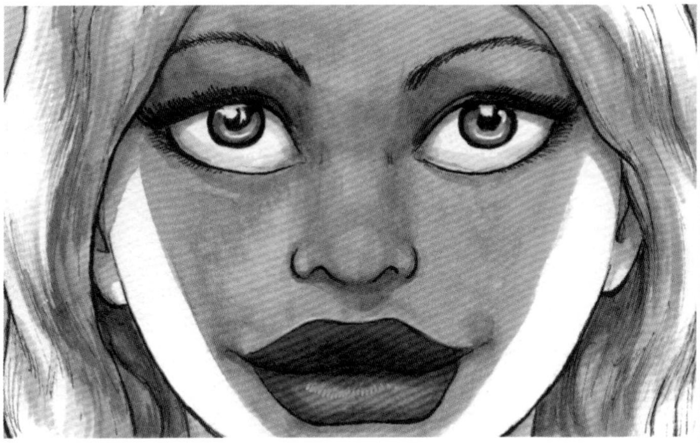

CLEMENTINE - A LIFE OF JOY AND LOVE

The top 10 moments in the life of Clementine Darling including the highs, the lows, and *that* incident with the beach ball...

363 comments

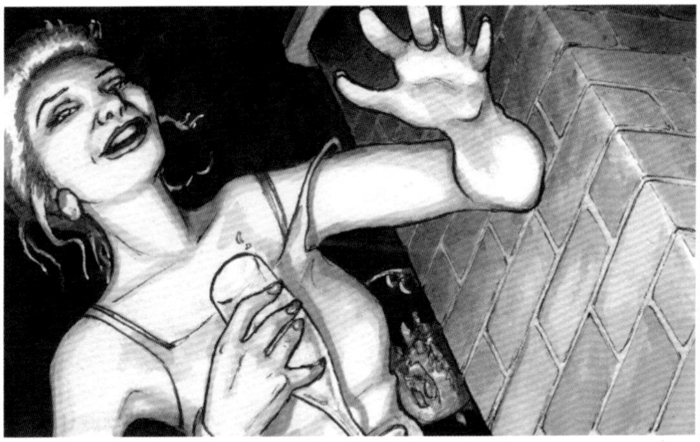

'IRREDEEMABLY FKED UP'**

Those closest to Coral Jerome reveal just how damaged the [illegible]alous singer really was with shameful stories of depravity

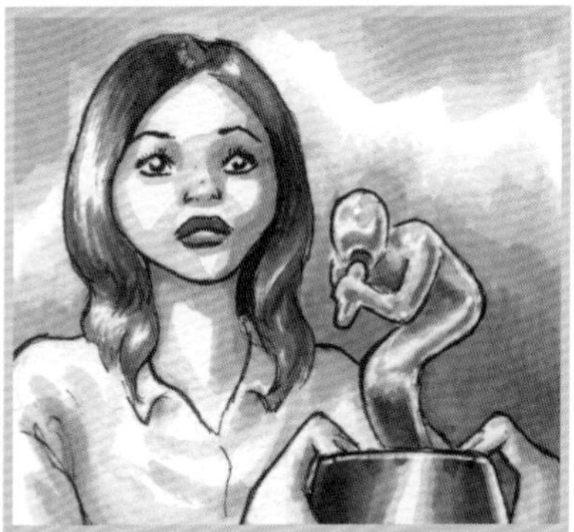

TAKE MY TWAMMY: Keeley Deen donates award to charity to prevent further attacks

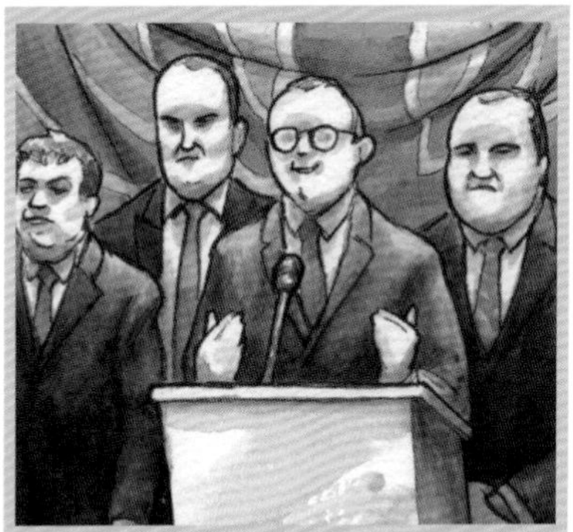

NEW HUMAN RIGHTS ACT: Parliament passes the new bill designed to offer greater protection to citizens

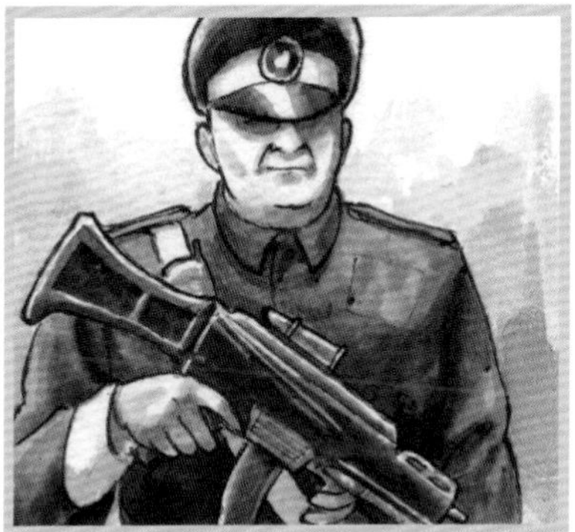

TWAMMY SECURITY UPGRADE: awards ceremony to employ SAIF Guards next year to reassure guests, promote order and prevent repeat of this year's assault

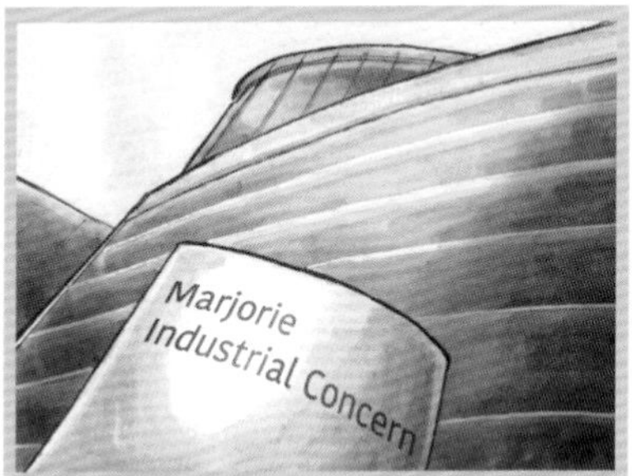

Marjorie
Industrial Concern

INQUEST DROPPED: public inquiry into corporation's activities concerning human cloning put on hold

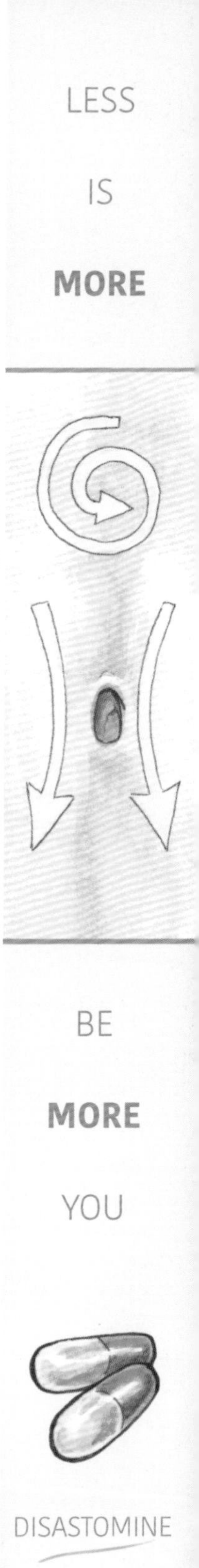

LESS
IS
MORE
BE
MORE
YOU
DISASTOMINE

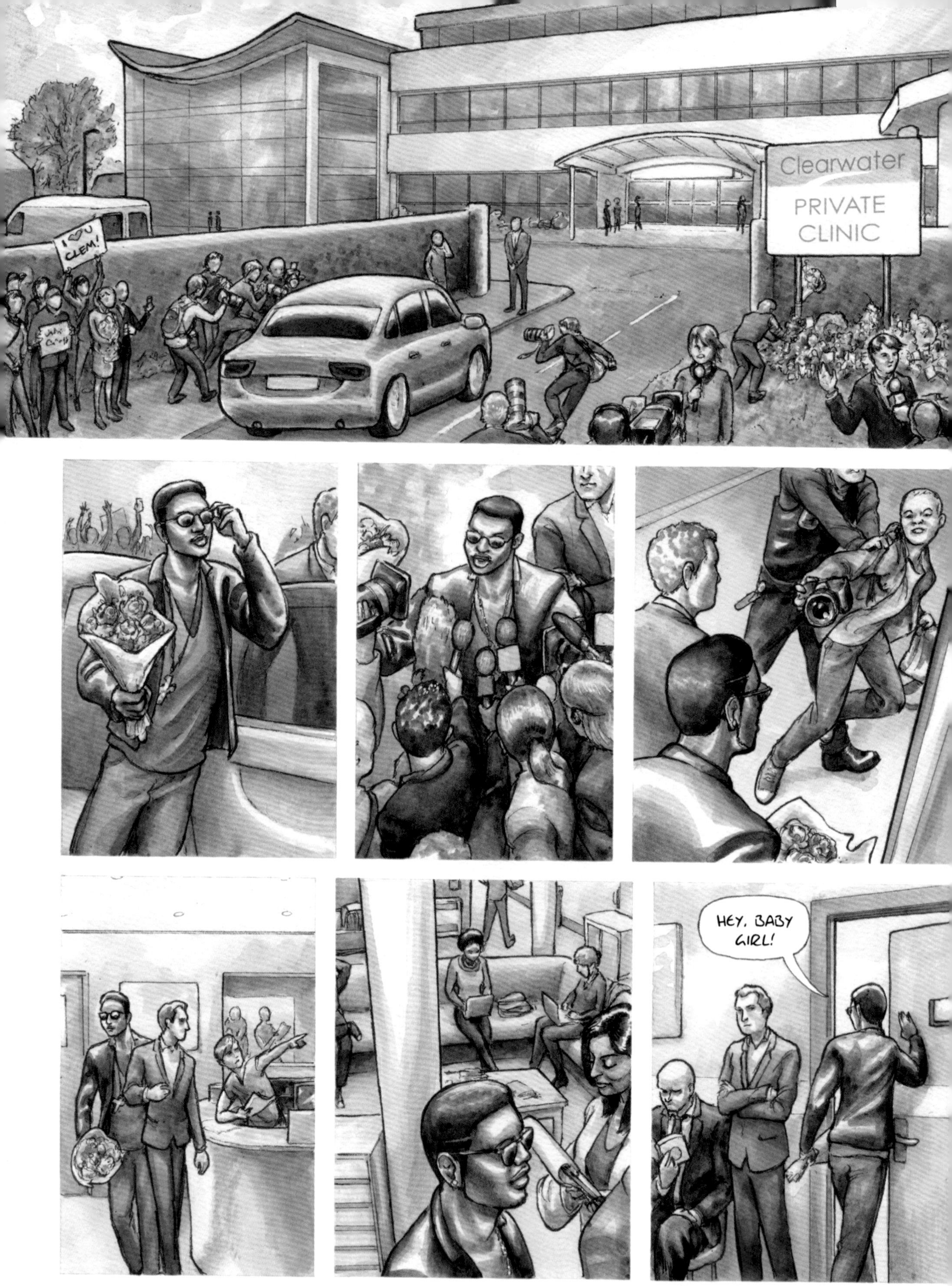
Clearwater
PRIVATE CLINIC
I ♡ U CLEM!
HEY, BABY GIRL!

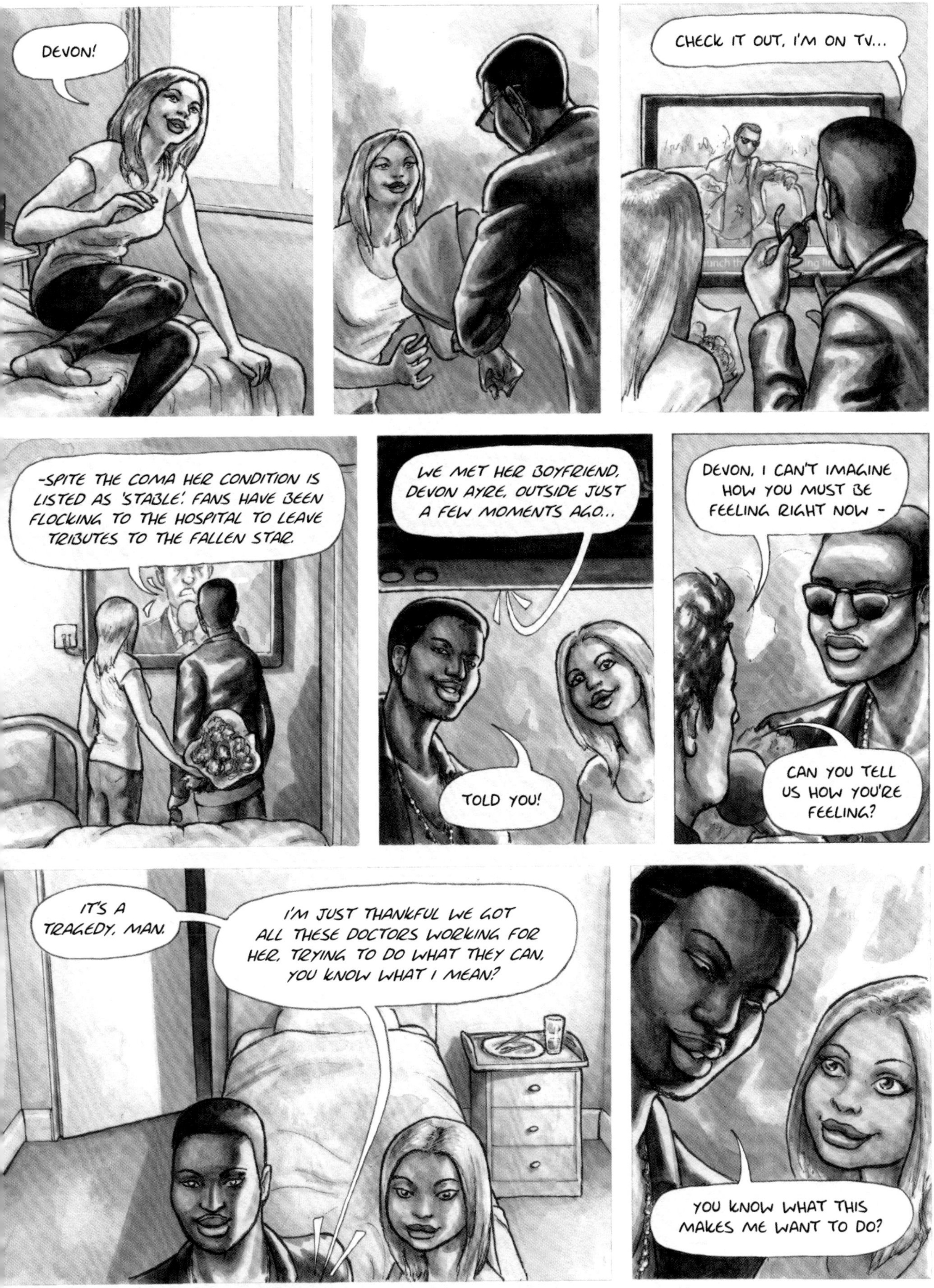
DEVON!
CHECK IT OUT, I'M ON TV...
-SPITE THE COMA HER CONDITION IS LISTED AS 'STABLE'. FANS HAVE BEEN FLOCKING TO THE HOSPITAL TO LEAVE TRIBUTES TO THE FALLEN STAR.
WE MET HER BOYFRIEND, DEVON AYRE, OUTSIDE JUST A FEW MOMENTS AGO...
TOLD YOU!
DEVON, I CAN'T IMAGINE HOW YOU MUST BE FEELING RIGHT NOW -
CAN YOU TELL US HOW YOU'RE FEELING?
IT'S A TRAGEDY, MAN.
I'M JUST THANKFUL WE GOT ALL THESE DOCTORS WORKING FOR HER, TRYING TO DO WHAT THEY CAN, YOU KNOW WHAT I MEAN?
YOU KNOW WHAT THIS MAKES ME WANT TO DO?

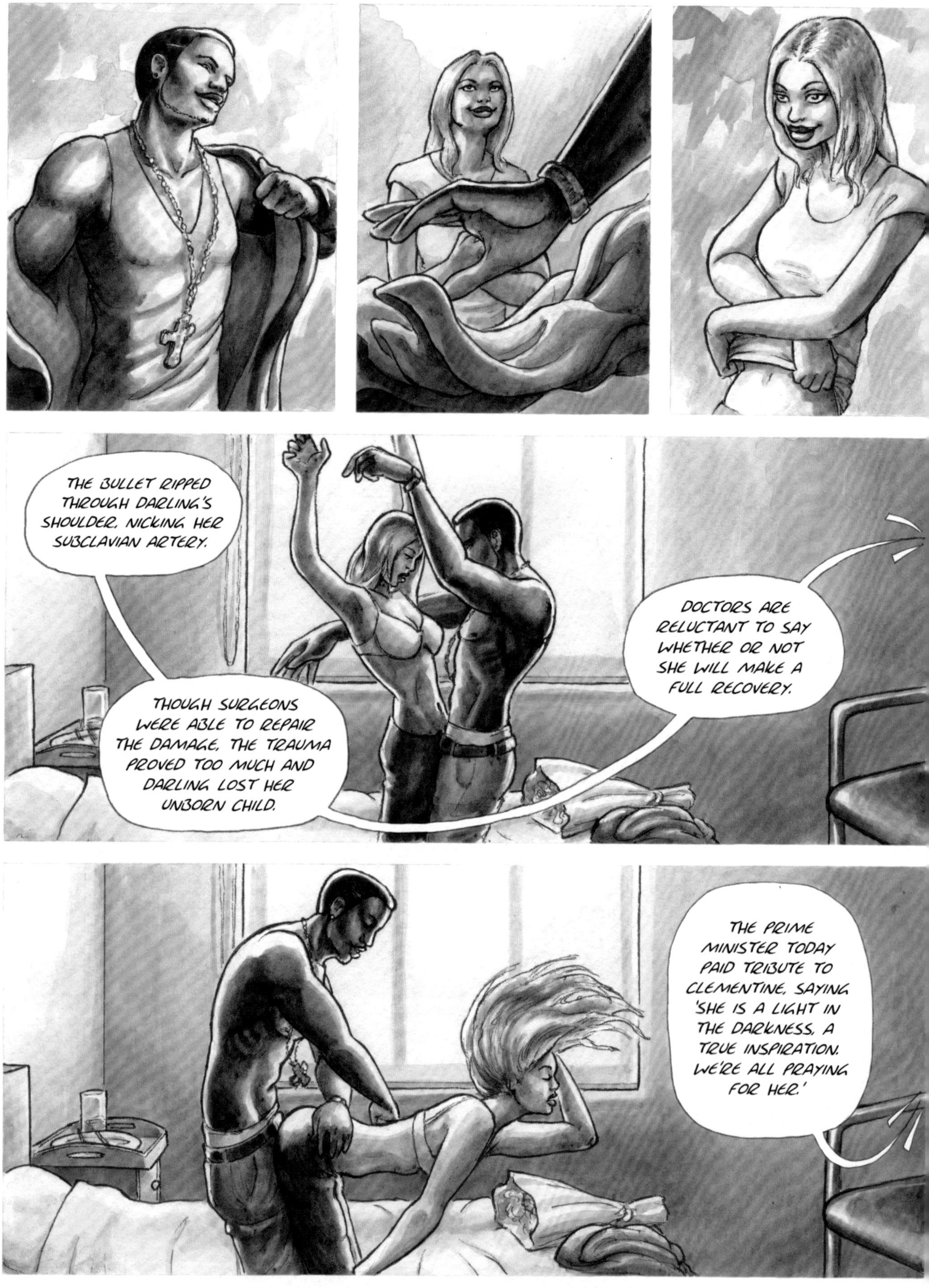
THE BULLET RIPPED THROUGH DARLING'S SHOULDER, NICKING HER SUBCLAVIAN ARTERY.
THOUGH SURGEONS WERE ABLE TO REPAIR THE DAMAGE, THE TRAUMA PROVED TOO MUCH AND DARLING LOST HER UNBORN CHILD.
DOCTORS ARE RELUCTANT TO SAY WHETHER OR NOT SHE WILL MAKE A FULL RECOVERY.
THE PRIME MINISTER TODAY PAID TRIBUTE TO CLEMENTINE, SAYING 'SHE IS A LIGHT IN THE DARKNESS, A TRUE INSPIRATION. WE'RE ALL PRAYING FOR HER.'

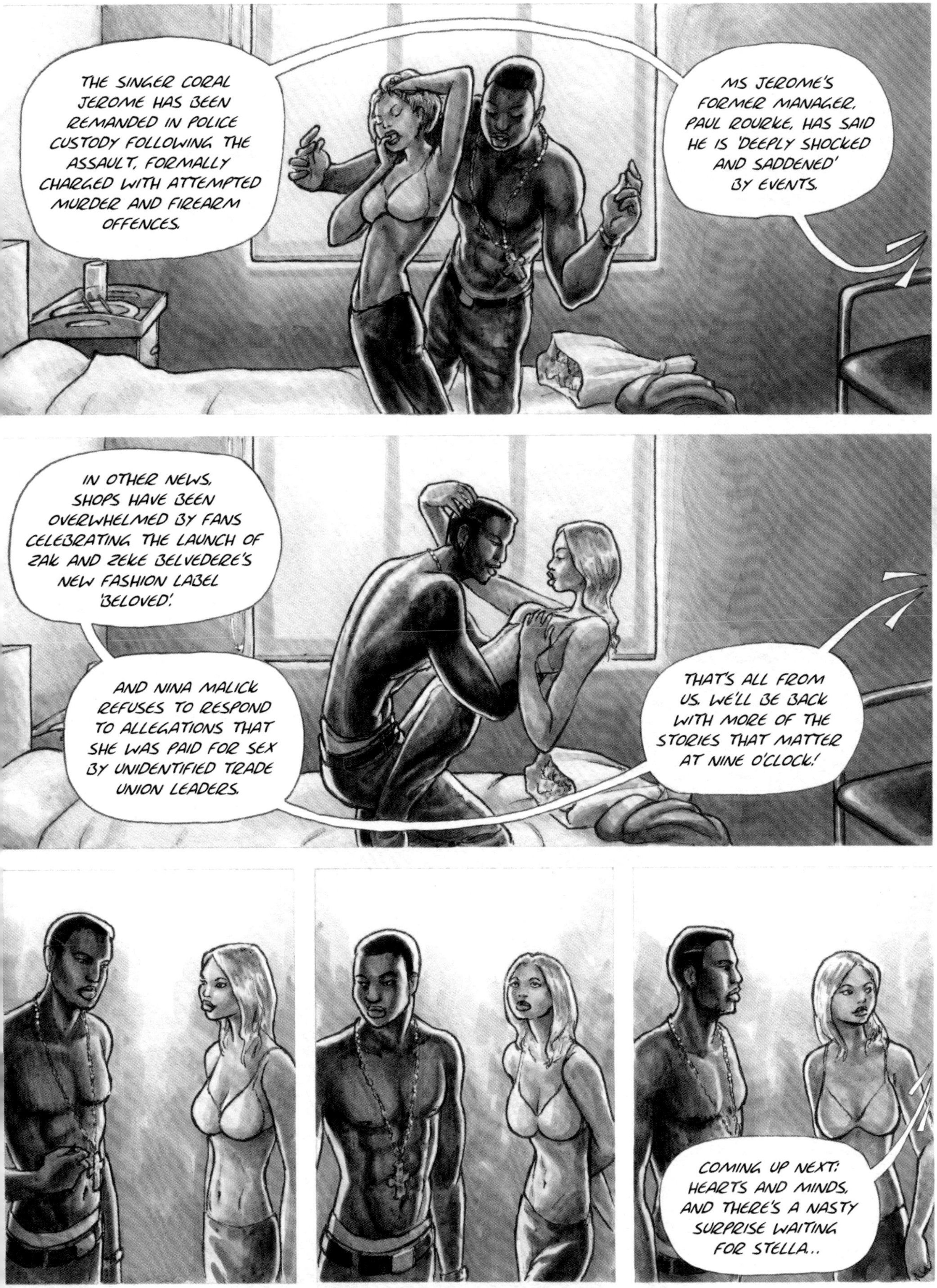
THE SINGER CORAL JEROME HAS BEEN REMANDED IN POLICE CUSTODY FOLLOWING THE ASSAULT, FORMALLY CHARGED WITH ATTEMPTED MURDER AND FIREARM OFFENCES.
MS JEROME'S FORMER MANAGER, PAUL ROURKE, HAS SAID HE IS 'DEEPLY SHOCKED AND SADDENED' BY EVENTS.
IN OTHER NEWS, SHOPS HAVE BEEN OVERWHELMED BY FANS CELEBRATING THE LAUNCH OF ZAK AND ZEKE BELVEDERE'S NEW FASHION LABEL 'BELOVED'.
AND NINA MALICK REFUSES TO RESPOND TO ALLEGATIONS THAT SHE WAS PAID FOR SEX BY UNIDENTIFIED TRADE UNION LEADERS.
THAT'S ALL FROM US. WE'LL BE BACK WITH MORE OF THE STORIES THAT MATTER AT NINE O'CLOCK!
COMING UP NEXT: HEARTS AND MINDS, AND THERE'S A NASTY SURPRISE WAITING FOR STELLA...

OH MORGAN, HOW I'VE MISSED BEING IN YOUR ARMS...

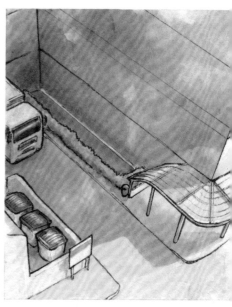

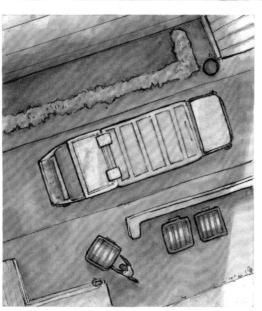